"This story will leave you with the uplifting message of hope and forgiveness. Thanks, Ruth, for your brave characters who face hard circumstances—full of faith and filled with God's grace. I love that this book nails both modern parenting and also God's eternal love. Read it!"

Christina Hergenrader,
author of *Last Summer at Eden*

Ruth has done it again! *Faith Alone* is the compelling sequel to *Grace Alone*. It is rare to find a book that combines a beautiful story with faith so clearly. The book is filled with so many conversations that could take place at your dining room table or mine. *Faith Alone* is a story you won't want to put down, filled with twists and turns - just like our own lives. Through it all, faith and grace are woven in clearly and gently, even in the most difficult moments. I truly appreciate how Ruth tackles some difficult issues for families and the church as a whole without preaching. *Faith Alone* will draw you in from the first page, and yet, you won't want to see it end. This is a thought-provoking, must-read book for Christians of all ages.

Kristen Whirrett,
Lutheran Blogger at Joyfully Thriving

I0742486

To the dear saints of FAITH Lutheran Church in Bridgeport, Michigan, whom I will always consider my family.

FAITH ALONE

A NOVEL BY RUTH E. MEYER

THE SOLA SERIES

TruthNotes Press

To Jesus we for refuge flee,
Who from the curse has set us free,
And humbly worship at His throne,
Saved by His grace through faith alone.
—Matthias Loy, 1828-1915

CHAPTER

1

"Kids! We're home!"

Faith's eyes widened at the sound of her mother's voice. What were they doing here already? They weren't due back for another two hours! Already she could hear her younger sister, Katie, squealing and running to greet her mother and new stepfather at the front door. That would distract them for a few minutes, but she didn't have much time.

"Spencer!" she hissed urgently, pushing herself to a sitting position on her bed. "You've got to get out of here!"

The blond-haired, blue-eyed young man remained where he was, a muscular arm tucked behind his head. His eyes held an amused look, and he clearly didn't understand the seriousness of the situation. Her mom would kill her if she found a boy in her room, even if they hadn't been doing anything but checking social media on their phones. Grace would never believe such an innocent claim.

"I thought you wanted to introduce me to your mom," he commented. "Let's go do it now." His voice seemed to thunder through her room, and her eyes darted nervously to the door.

She had the irrational fear that her mother would hear him and come charging in.

"Yeah, right! She'd forbid me from dating until I'm twenty-one if she finds out you're in here. I mean it! You'll have to go out the window!" Thankfully, her window faced the back of the house, not visible from the street or driveway. This fact had made it possible for Spencer to sneak in a handful of times already, and she wasn't about to get caught now.

Faith leaned over him to slide the window open, but he grabbed her around the waist and pulled her down on top of him, giving her a long kiss. Faith felt the familiar rush of adrenaline that accompanied a kiss from Spencer Young, and she wished she had time to enjoy this one, but she was running out of time. Grace and David had advanced into the living room, and Faith could hear excited conversation between her younger siblings and her aunt, who had stayed with them during Grace and David's honeymoon. Soon they would realize she wasn't out there, and someone would come to find her.

Impatiently, she pulled away from Spencer. "We don't have time for this!" she scolded.

"But doesn't the threat of being caught make it all the more thrilling?" he asked in a low, seductive voice. Normally, that voice would have sent a chill up and down Faith's spine, but now fear overrode every other emotion.

"You need to leave *now!*" she insisted. Heaving herself into a kneeling position, she resumed her mission to open the window, but she was too late.

"Faith?" It was her mother, knocking on the bedroom door. "Are you in there?"

Her heart nearly stopped. Now what? Her mom had just returned from her honeymoon, a ten-day trip. Faith couldn't get away with calling her greetings through the door. She knew she had to open it and hug her mom and act excited to hear all about the honeymoon. Desperately, she pointed at the closet door, and Spencer complied. He slid off the bed and grabbed her around the waist for one last quick kiss before he slipped into the dark closet and hid behind the hanging clothes.

Faith willed her heart to stop pounding as she opened the door. "Mom!" she exclaimed, forcing enthusiasm into her voice as she gave her mother a hug. "I wasn't expecting you yet! I was taking a nap."

"Oh, I didn't mean to interrupt you, hon," Grace said, taking a quick look at Faith's bed, which was still rumpled. At least that added credibility to the lie. "We decided not to stop at David's parents' on the way home after all. We were too eager to get back here and see you guys! Surprise!"

"It sure is a surprise!" Faith tried to laugh, but wasn't sure she quite pulled it off. Maybe it was her imagination, but she thought she could hear Spencer breathing in the closet. What if he sneezed or something? A surge of panic coursed through her. She had to get her mother out of there. Impulsively, she gave her mom another quick hug and said, "Oh, it's so good to see you! I missed you! Let's go out with the others. I want to hear about the trip!"

Before her mom could say another word, Faith linked arms with her and stepped out into the hallway, pulling the bedroom door shut behind her. She steered Grace toward the living room where the rest of the family was gathered. Her heart thudded so loudly she was sure Grace could hear it.

"Daddy's home!" Katie chirped happily, bouncing up and down on David's knee as Faith and Grace entered the living room.

"I see that, Katie," Faith said. "Welcome back, David." She forced a smile at him as she sat down cross-legged on the floor.

Despite the title, Katie wasn't David's biological child. But at the tender age of five, she had never known her birth father, and willingly accepted David as "Daddy" even before he and Grace had been engaged. Faith, on the other hand, still felt awkward around her new stepfather. She liked him well enough, but it was weird to think he would actually be *living* with them now.

David returned her smile and said, "Thanks, Faith! It's good to be back." She noted he hadn't used the word *home* yet, and realized for the first time that maybe this was strange for him as well.

Olivia, Grace's older sister, had a gift for making awkwardness disappear. "So, Gracie, Boston?" she prompted. "I want to hear all about it! I've never been out east before."

"It was fascinating!" said Grace, nudging Jackson's legs aside so she could sit next to him on the couch. "David picked a charming bed and breakfast, and we spent our days sightseeing. Boston is a neat city."

"But we didn't *just* see Boston," David pointed out.

"This is true," Grace said. Turning to Olivia, she explained, "One of his goals was to expand my travel repertoire for our honeymoon. We drove all over New England for day trips. We went to, what, David, seven new states?"

"Yep. Massachusetts, of course, New Hampshire, Vermont, Maine, Rhode Island, Connecticut, and from there we took the train to New York City for a day."

"Wow! Impressive!" Olivia responded. "And how was the Fourth?"

"Amazing," sighed Grace. "David arranged for us to watch the Boston Fireworks display on the Charles River. The Boston Pops performed too. Most incredible fireworks display I'll ever see."

"David, it appears you did a fine job planning the trip," Olivia said.

David beamed with pride as Grace smiled at him. "He certainly did," she seconded. "Best vacation ever."

Faith had only been half listening to the conversation up to this point, but she fully tuned out now as the adults prattled on. She was on high alert, her senses heightened as she strained to listen for any sounds coming from her room, any telltale thump that would give away Spencer's presence. Was that just his phone beeping, alerting him to a new text message? Did she hear the window squeak as he opened it, or was she just paranoid? And good grief, did he *have* to use such strong body wash? Some of the scent had rubbed off on her. Didn't anyone else notice she smelled like a walking Old Spice ad?

"Faith?"

She startled at her mother's voice, realizing Grace had asked her a question. "What did you say? I'm sorry, Mom."

Her mom gave her a strange look, but patiently repeated herself. "I thought you'd be at the daycare center right now."

"Oh, I switched days with Stacey so she can take a weekend trip," she said. "But tell us more about your honeymoon. Did you get fresh seafood while you were out there?"

"The food was great," admitted Grace with a groan. "*Too* good, in fact. I gained back everything I lost before the wedding." She had a stubborn twenty pounds she was always vowing to lose, and she'd managed to lose six pounds in the months preceding her wedding.

"Which just proves you're exactly the weight you're supposed to be," insisted David.

Faith resisted an eye roll. Was this the kind of sappy talk she had to look forward to? Her aunt, on the other hand, took the comment in stride. "Right answer, David!" Olivia laughed.

"Andy would be proud." Her husband, Andy McNeal, often joked that he needed to give David a crash course in understanding and dealing with women.

"Will you and Andy be staying for dinner tonight?" David asked.

"Oh, no," dismissed Olivia with a wave of her hand. "We've been eating dinner here all week. We'll let you guys have a nice family dinner without us hovering around."

"We don't mind," insisted Grace. "Besides, I can smell that you've already got something cooking. If you went to the trouble to make dinner for us, you might as well stay to enjoy it."

"Seriously, Gracie, I didn't go to any trouble at all. I threw a pork roast and a jar of banana peppers into the slow cooker. It took me all of two minutes. It'll take longer to shred the meat for pulled pork sandwiches, and I'll let Faith do that." Olivia winked at her niece. "Besides, Andy said he'd take me out to eat once he's done with work. I've been craving Chinese all week long."

Faith suspected her aunt and uncle also craved some peace and quiet. Their own three children were all college-aged, and it had been a while since they'd dealt with the chaos and drama of younger children.

"If you change your mind, you're certainly welcome to stay," said Grace. "It would be nice to catch up with Andy too."

"We'll stop by over the weekend," Olivia offered. "Deal?"

"Perfect. Now, David, we should get our suitcases out of the car. We got souvenirs for each of you kids. Jackson, come help us, will you?" asked Grace.

Jackson groaned in protest, but Katie jumped up excitedly. "I'll help too!" She tugged on David's hand to lead him toward the door. Freddie, likewise, clamored outside.

Faith took the opportunity to slip back to her room while everyone else was distracted. She opened the door and shut it quietly behind her. "Spencer?" she asked in a stage whisper. "Are you still here?" She opened the closet and swept aside the hanging clothes, finding no one there. Just to be sure, she peeked under both her bed and Katie's bed. No sign of Spencer. He must have snuck back out the window and shut it behind him. Faith breathed a sigh of relief.

That had been way too close for comfort.

CHAPTER

2

"He's *how* old?"

"Mother! I've already told you all this! He's gonna be a senior this year." Faith had waited until her siblings were finished with breakfast before telling her mom and stepdad about Spencer. She knew Grace expected to be introduced to any boy before Faith was allowed to date him. But clearly, she should have waited at least until Grace had drunk her second cup of coffee before broaching the subject.

"And you're a junior," Grace reminded her. "A fairly young one, at that. You just turned sixteen a couple months ago. But Spencer is one of the older ones in his class, right?"

Faith sighed melodramatically. "*Yes*, Mother. So what? He'll be eighteen in a few weeks."

Grace and David frowned at each other over Faith's head. They were standing in the kitchen while she sat at the table.

"Is he a Christian?" asked David.

"Oh, for crying out loud. What is this? The Inquisition?"

"Faith Elizabeth! You will *not* speak to us that way," Grace reprimanded. "Answer the question politely. Be grateful that we care enough about you to ask these things."

She glared at her mother before answering. "Fine. No, he's not a Christian." Then, seeing the look on both of their faces, she hastened on. "And neither were you, Mom, when you met David."

"True," conceded David. "But I didn't officially ask your mom to date me until she *was*."

"Look, I'm not asking to marry the guy," Faith protested. "Just let me go out with him a few times and see where that takes us. We'll cross the whole religion thing when we come to it." She could tell by the way her mom crossed her arms over her chest that the answer had not appeased her. Faith tried another tactic. "Mom, please. At least let me go out with him. Spencer is the cutest boy in the entire school. Every girl dreams of having him ask her out. How lame would it be if I told him my mom won't let me go out with him because he's not a Christian? Who knows? Maybe in time he can start coming to church with me. It worked for you two!"

She hadn't the slightest inclination to invite Spencer to church, but she wasn't above a little white lie if it made her mother feel better about the situation.

"Yes, but this is different," insisted Grace. "Your best reason for going out with him is that he's cute? *That's* why you want to date him? What about his character? Who is he under his good looks? Will he treat you with respect? Or are you just another pretty face to him?"

"Oh, *Mother*! Seriously!" Her mom drove her absolutely crazy at times. "He's super nice. Really sweet. I like him a whole lot, and all I'm asking is that you let me go out with him. Give him a chance. Let's have him over for dinner so you can get to know him. You'll see for yourself how nice he is. Please?" She was unabashedly begging.

Grace looked at David to gauge his reaction, who shrugged and gave an almost imperceptible nod. "Okay, Faith. Let's have him over for dinner. I'd like to meet this young man who has stolen your affections."

Faith jumped up in excitement to hug her mother. "Thanks, Mom! You'll just love him! I know you will. I'll invite him over tonight."

"No, you won't," Grace said. "David and I just got back from our honeymoon. We all need a chance to adjust and get used to each other before you invite Spencer over."

"Mom! We've already been waiting for you guys to get back!" That wasn't entirely true, of course, but Grace didn't need to know that. "I don't want him to think you don't want to meet him!"

"He'll understand," she said. "It's not asking too much to wait until the weekend. Why don't you invite him over for dinner on Friday? We'll have more time to plan a menu by then. Maybe David will even be willing to grill his famous ribs."

Faith considered this. A few extra days wasn't unreasonable, and David's ribs *were* good. Spencer would love them. "Okay," she conceded. "I'll see if he can come on Friday. Thanks, Mom!"

She made her escape before either adult could further question her about Spencer, already pulling her phone out of her pocket to text the invite to him.

Back in the kitchen, Grace turned to David with a slight frown. "I can't quite place a finger on it, but I don't have a good feeling about this," she admitted.

David sighed as he ran his hand over his short hair, graying around the temples. It was a nervous habit, and he joked that it was the reason for his receding hairline. "I know," he said as he walked over to hug her. "We're venturing into unknown territory. It's kind of intimidating."

She accepted her husband's embrace and rested her head against his chest. She was thinking the very same thing. It was scary to watch her kids grow up.

CHAPTER

3

When the appointed evening came for dinner with Spencer, Faith was practically beside herself with excitement, carrying on about how much her mother was going to love him. Grace, for her part, was beginning to regret the whole thing. She was sick and tired of hearing about how perfect Spencer Young was.

Spencer arrived right on time, and Faith squealed and ran to the door when she heard the doorbell ring, Grace following behind her.

"Mom, this is Spencer Young," Faith said, looking at him with obvious adoration in her eyes as she giggled and flipped her long brown hair over her shoulder.

Spencer was strikingly good looking with dark blond hair styled with gel, a deep tan, perfectly straight white teeth, sparkling blue eyes, and noticeable muscles bulging underneath his shirt. He could have been an actor straight from a California surfer movie. Definitely cute according to high school standards. *Very* cute. Grace felt a surge of panic.

Confidently, Spencer stepped forward to shake Grace's

hand. "Nice to meet you, Mrs. Neunaber," he said. "Congratulations on your wedding. Faith told me it was beautiful. And thanks for having me over tonight. I appreciate the offer. I could smell the ribs as soon as I got out of my car."

"You're in for a treat!" Grace assured him. "Faith, why don't you take Spencer out back and introduce him to David? I think the ribs are just about ready. I'll bring stuff out from the kitchen. It's nice enough to eat outside this evening."

Faith ushered Spencer into the backyard and introduced him to David while Grace recruited Freddie to help her bring out plates and silverware and napkins. After exchanging greetings with David, Spencer turned and saw Jackson tossing a football toward an old soccer net, trying to perfect his aim.

Spencer's eyes lit up as he saw what Jackson was doing. "Hey, man, wanna play some football?" he asked. "I'm a tight end on Varsity this year, but I've played QB too. I can give you some pointers."

Jackson's face brightened considerably at this. No one else in his house was any good at football, and Grace knew he despaired of ever making the middle school team because of it. Secretly and selfishly, Grace sort of hoped he wouldn't make the team. Faith would be on the Varsity volleyball team, and it was hard enough having to work around one practice and game schedule. Two sport schedules just might put her over the edge. Still, she knew Jackson loved sports and had a lot of natural talent as an athlete. He had such a competitive spirit that he wanted to be the absolute best player at every sport he tried.

Spencer spent a few minutes working with Jackson on his throw while Faith hovered nearby, swooning about how thoughtful Spencer was. Katie, Grace's little socialite who knew no strangers, bounced up to Spencer and tugged on his hand.

"Can I play too?" she asked sweetly.

"No way!" Jackson answered hotly. "Girls don't play football! You wouldn't even know what to do anyhow. You're too little!"

Katie pouted, and Spencer came to her rescue. "How about we have a game? Girls against boys?" He winked at Jackson, who grinned back. Sure, he'd play a game he was certain to win.

"I'm in," he said.

"How about it, Faith?" Spencer teased. "Are you brave enough to take us on?"

"Oh, yeah," she boasted in an overly confident voice. "Game on!"

"I hate to burst your bubble," David called, "but the ribs are ready. How about you play your game after we eat?"

Jackson grumbled about this but reluctantly followed the others to the picnic table. Katie tagged along with Spencer and begged to sit next to him, already enamored with him nearly as much as was Faith. Jackson sat across from him, peppering him with questions about football even as Katie chattered incessantly next to him. Freddie seemed unusually reserved, but carefully observed Spencer and Faith throughout the meal. Grace wondered what he was thinking.

When Grace decided they'd heard enough about football, she seized upon a lull in the conversation to say, "So, Spencer, tell us about your family."

He nodded and swallowed a mouthful of ribs before answering. "My dad is the VP for Stamport Enterprises. Their main office is in Grand Rapids, and their latest thing is expanding their venue in Europe. They already do business in England, but now they're trying to branch out into other countries. My dad is their main liaison in Europe, so he's over there a lot.

"My mom doesn't work, but she does organize a lot of charity stuff. You know, fundraisers and benefits and stuff like that. She's a good organizer, especially when it comes to ritzy parties. That's totally her niche.

"And then I have two older brothers. Parker is eight years older than I am, and he's trying to make it as a stockbroker in New York City. Callan's six years older, in his second year of law school in California. I don't really see either of them much anymore."

Grace wondered about the dynamic of Spencer's family, with a father out of town so often and two brothers on opposite sides of the country. Her entire family was in the same town, and she couldn't imagine it any other way.

"Are either of your brothers married?" asked David.

"Not anymore. Parker was married for two years but got divorced. His wife didn't like taking second place to his career."

"So what do you hope to do with your life?" Grace asked.

"I'd like to be a doctor. I'm hoping to go to U of M next year for pre-med."

David nodded in approval. "Excellent choice." He was a staunch University of Michigan fan himself.

"What kind of doctor do you hope to be?" she asked.

"I'm leaning toward cardiology. I want to do open heart surgery someday."

Grace shuddered. "I couldn't do that. I get queasy at the sight of blood."

"So does my mom," he laughed. "I just think it's amazing how the body works. Advanced Bio was my favorite subject last year when we studied anatomy. It's incredible."

"That's very true," David agreed. "The human body is an

amazing creation."

Faith, apparently eager to be part of the conversation, swooped in. "In the meantime, Spencer's working for his dad over the summer, aren't you?" She batted her eyes at him.

"Oh, um, yeah. I am. I'm sort of his intern, as weird as that sounds. Parker and Callan both had to do it before their senior year too. I think Dad hoped one of us would follow his lead and go into business."

"Well, it's better than my summer job," lamented Faith. "Mine is only minimum wage, and I have to deal with whiny kids all day."

Spencer laughed, and then turned to David. "You must like being the principal. I've always thought teachers have it made because they get the whole summer off."

David tensed a bit at the comment, and Grace spoke up quickly. "*I'm* the one who gets the summer off. I work at the school cafeteria, so I only work when school is in session. But teachers actually work all summer. They have to set up their rooms and plan their curriculums for the next school year. It's a lot of work getting a classroom ready. David was a teacher for twenty years before moving to Michigan. Now that he's principal, he's even busier. I assure you, he doesn't have the summer off. Other than our honeymoon, he's been busy at the office almost every day."

Her husband shot her a grateful look as Spencer seized upon the change of subject. "Oh, yeah, hey, your honeymoon! Faith said you went out east. How was that?"

Grace was only too happy to relive the memories of their trip, so she and David spent the next few minutes talking about the places they'd gone on their honeymoon.

"It sounds like you guys did some great sightseeing while you were out there," said Spencer.

"Yeah, and we've never even been out of Michigan," Jackson complained.

"Well, other than Chicago, I'd never been out of state before either!" Grace reminded him.

"So you're saying I have to wait until I'm *that* old?" Jackson asked in despair. "We don't even take real vacations. We just go to Houghton Lake to Aunt Livy and Uncle Andy's cottage."

"Hey, that counts, man," insisted Spencer. "Houghton Lake is awesome."

"Yeah, but I bet *you've* gone on better vacations than that," argued Jackson. "Where do you guys go?"

"Well, we usually go to Hawaii for spring break each year," Spencer admitted. "And we've been to Florida and California too. Once we went skiing in Colorado, and one year Mom wanted to do an Alaskan cruise. We've also been to Cancun and the Caribbean."

"See?" Jackson whined.

"I like Michigan," inserted Katie firmly. "But are we ever gonna have dessert?"

Everyone laughed, and Grace went into the house to grab the pan of brownies she'd made. She was pleased that dinner had gone so well. Spencer seemed like a nice enough kid. He was polite in answering their questions, and he interacted easily with Jackson, which was no small feat. And while he was clearly interested in Faith, he didn't seem to be the type of guy who needed to be constantly holding her hand or keeping his arm around her. Grace was thankful for that. It would have been very awkward to have the two of them hanging on each other like some high school couples she'd seen. Maybe this dating thing wouldn't be so bad.

Once the brownies were polished off, Jackson reminded Spencer of the football match between boys and girls. The teams split up to confer with one another before starting their game. It was a pitiful affair. Katie, of course, had no clue what she was doing, but mostly stood in the midst of the commotion squealing and jumping up and down. Faith made her sister the honorary quarterback, which meant Katie simply held the ball and handed it to Faith to run it down the "field." Jackson and Spencer easily caught her before she made it anywhere near the designated end zone. The boys, on the other hand, made touchdown after touchdown. It was basically two against one, but everyone seemed to be having fun.

Grace kept track of the game through the kitchen window as she rinsed plates to put in the dishwasher. For a guy who didn't have younger siblings of his own, Spencer seemed fairly comfortable interacting with Jackson and Katie. Grace realized with a start that Freddie was nowhere to be seen, so she went to find him.

"Freddie?" she asked when she found him in his room. "Don't you want to go outside? They're playing a football game out there. I'm sure they'd let you play."

"Nah, that's okay, Mom. I don't really like football."

"Do you at least want to come out and watch?" she prompted.

"I'm okay."

Grace frowned slightly. Something was going on with Freddie. He was naturally a quiet kid anyhow, easily dwarfed by his vociferous and more opinionated older brother, but this was unusual even for him. He'd barely said two words at dinner.

"Freddie, talk to me. I can tell something's bothering you. What is it?"

He remained silent, but Grace waited him out. At length he sighed and spoke. "I'm tired of everyone telling me what to do and what to think."

Grace's eyes widened in surprise. The kid had a point, but he'd never stood up for himself much before. He wasn't one to voice his opinion on many things.

Freddie continued, his voice raised. "Jackthon always tells me what to do, and he picks the games and tells me my ideas are dumb! And no one even athked me if I wanted to play batheball this year. I don't. No one cares what I think."

The reappearance of his lisp proved that he really was upset. He'd been working with a speech therapist for two years now, and when he thought about it, he could control his lisp.

Grace took a deep breath. Freddie wasn't wrong. Jackson was bossy and opinionated, basically viewing his younger brother as a subject to rule. And truly, Grace hadn't asked Freddie about Little League. She'd thought it would be good for him to have the experience and be part of a team, but she hadn't talked to him about it first.

"Sweetie, I'm sorry you feel like everyone bosses you around. I'm sorry that we don't ask your opinion on things. You're right. We should be more sensitive to what you want. What, specifically, are you upset about now?"

Freddie quietly said, "My birthday." He spoke slowly to form his words properly. "I told Jackth—Jackson what I wanted, and he told me it was a th—ssstupid idea."

"And what do you want?"

"A telescope."

Grace's eyebrows shot up. She never would have guessed that. "Oh, really?"

He nodded. "We had a unit in science about the solar system last year, and I really liked it. I want to be able to see the stars and planets. I want to learn more about the constellations. It's really cool."

She took a moment to digest this. Honestly, she thought it was a great idea. It wasn't one more toy to clutter the house, and if Freddie learned something from it, all the better. She remembered that his class had taken a field trip to the Planetarium the previous school year, but she hadn't realized it made such a big impression on her son.

"Honey, I'm glad you told me. I wouldn't have thought of that on my own. I'll consider it as a birthday idea. As for baseball, I'm sorry I made you join. If you don't want to do it next year, that's perfectly fine. Just tell me. I'll respect your wishes. And as for Jackson, yes, he can be bossy. He also says things without really thinking first sometimes. If he puts you down or tells you your ideas are dumb, don't let him get to you. Remember when you got Buzz Lightyear two years ago for your birthday? Remember how Jackson teased you that it was such a babyish toy? Well, guess what? When you were brushing your teeth later that night, I found him in your room playing with Buzz himself!"

Freddie laughed at this information. "I didn't know that," he said.

"And who was the one who stood up to his older brother about Jesus a few years ago? Remember how Jackson tried to tell you the Bible stories were a bunch of fairy tales? You didn't let him get away with that, and you stood your ground when you told him the stories were true. That was a key moment for me too, Freddie. Seeing how insistent and brave you were to stand up to him made me stop to consider it as well. You believed in Jesus before I did, and your witness helped convince *me* that Jesus is real!"

Freddie looked inordinately pleased with this bit of news. "I didn't know that, either," he confessed.

Grace hugged her son. "I'm very proud of you, Freddie, and

I want you to feel comfortable telling me what's on your mind. If you ever feel like we aren't listening to you or that we're bossing you around, speak up. Okay?

"I will. Thanks, Mom."

"You're quite welcome," she responded with a kiss on the top of his head. "Dad and I love you very much. You know that, right?"

"Yeah. I know."

"Good. You sure you don't want to go outside and watch them play football?"

"No, thanks."

"Wanna help me clean up in the kitchen?"

"I'm good."

Grace laughed and gave him one more quick hug before exiting the room to continue the cleanup process.

As she took up her post in the kitchen once again, she glanced out at the football game in time to see Spencer tackle Faith from behind and pull her down in a hug, tickling her as they went down together.

"Watch those hands, young man," she warned under her breath, breathing a sigh of relief when he stood up and offered Faith his hand. Faith giggled as he pulled her up, then ran back to her position by Katie. Grace took a deep breath. Dating was a whole new ball game.

CHAPTER

4

"Hmm. This can't be right," David muttered as he frowned at his laptop.

School was to start in a couple weeks, and Grace assumed he was getting things ready for the upcoming school year—his third as principal of St. John Lutheran School. He'd been working on last-minute things all week, both at his office and at home.

Grace flipped a page in her magazine and asked without much interest, "What can't be right?" Faith was due home from an evening with Spencer and his parents by ten o'clock, and the fast-approaching hour occupied her mind.

"Oh, this bill. I'm going over our credit card statement to make sure all the charges are legit."

That surprised Grace. She'd always set her credit card statements to be paid automatically, and saw no need to go over the charges first. "So what doesn't look right?" she prompted.

"Take a look at this," he said, turning the computer toward her so she could see the screen. He pointed at the offending charge. "Here, for Kroger."

Grace looked at it and shrugged. "What about it? I bought that. It's legit."

He raised his eyebrows. "What was the occasion?"

"What are you talking about? It's called grocery shopping!"

"You spent *this* much on food? Was it for Freddie's birthday party?"

"David!" Grace looked at him in astonishment. "I *always* spend that much on food!"

"Seriously?"

"There are six of us in this house, you know," she reminded him.

"Yes, I'm aware of that. But some of them are children who eat considerably less than adults. I knew our grocery bill would be higher than my own was, but I budgeted three times more. I figured that was safe. This is over four times as much!"

"Whoa, whoa, whoa. You made a *budget* for us? And you didn't even discuss it with me?"

"Every household needs a budget. Of course I made one."

"Okay, Mr. Math Minor. Look, I've never had a budget, and somehow I've always managed to stay out of debt. I know about how much I'll need for food, clothes, gas, and medical stuff, and I'm frugal. I always use digital coupons and shop sales. Years of living as a single mom taught me how to cut out extra expenses."

"Fine, but have you been setting anything aside for college for the kids? Retirement for you?"

"Heavens, no! There's no extra money for all that!"

"With a budget there would be," insisted David. "That's why I keep one. Is there any way we can cut down the food bill a bit?"

"Oh, sure, David." Now her voice was sarcastic. "Let's have

a lottery each week. Which kid doesn't get to eat this time? Unless you want to cut out meat or live on mac and cheese, the food bill is what it is. I buy generic brands, but I also try to get lots of fruits and veggies, which add up. We go through a gallon of milk every other day, and I try to get good snacks for the kids like cheese sticks, which are considerably more expensive than chips. Eating well is more expensive than eating junk food."

David sighed. "I'm going to have to redo the budget, then."

"Oh, my goodness! Who cares about the stupid budget?" Grace tossed aside the magazine impatiently. "You never even told me about it in the first place! I don't want to be reporting to you every cent I spend. I've been managing money on my own quite responsibly for the last number of years, thank you very much, and I don't need to start asking your permission for every little thing now!"

"I'm not asking you to do that," he returned testily. "I'd just like to have a plan and a general ballpark figure for stuff like groceries."

"I can assure you that having kids is not inexpensive."

"I see that."

"All things considered, we could be spending a whole lot more. Freddie and Katie get free tuition at St. John with you on staff, and Jackson and Faith go to the public school. We're paying nothing for education. You get health insurance through your job, which is another big expense taken care of. Most of the kids' clothes are hand-me-downs from Olivia, and I do most of my own shopping at Goodwill. If groceries are more expensive than you thought they would be, so be it! Be glad I'm buying good food for us!"

"I know, but—"

"No! No 'buts,' David! Besides, I still have my job at the

cafeteria. Why don't you do a budget for your own salary and let mine go toward groceries? That way we don't have to fight about it anymore!"

There was a moment of silence until David said, "You know, that's actually not a bad idea."

"Gee, thanks. Every now and then I have a moment of brilliance," she retorted dryly.

"No, I'm serious. I was lumping everything together, but this might work out better the way you suggest. We haven't had the chance to combine our bank accounts yet anyhow. Let's just keep them separate, and I'll get a credit card with a higher cash back percentage for grocery stores. We can link it to your account and use it exclusively for food. I'll budget out my own salary for everything else. I can allot more of it toward college funds this way. It's genius!"

David looked almost excited about the idea, and Grace shook her head. She had no idea her husband was so fastidious about money. She was glad she wasn't a fashion prima donna like her sister. Olivia would need a special category in the budget for her own clothes.

"Out of curiosity, are you budgeting any extra money?" she asked. "I mean, like, for dates? Or is that a thing of the past now that we're married?"

He looked surprised and slightly hurt by the question. "Of course I have that budgeted! We at least get free babysitting with your family so close, so we can afford to splurge now and then for a real date."

"Well, that's a relief. But if we didn't get free babysitting, we wouldn't go on dates?"

"Nope." He grinned to let her know he was teasing.

Despite herself, Grace laughed. "Then I'm glad we live so close to my family. We're due for a date. We haven't been alone since our honeymoon. Slot me into the budget in the next couple of weeks, will ya?"

"I'll see what I can do," he told her smugly.

Just then, the door opened, and Faith entered with Spencer. "Sorry to barge in on you, Mr. and Mrs. Neunaber," he said, "but I wanted to see Faith in safely. We had a lovely dinner tonight with my parents. Have a good evening."

He kissed Faith on the cheek and let himself out. She came into the living room and sighed blissfully as she sank down on the couch. "Oh, you should see his house," she swooned. "It's like a mini mansion. They have a personal gym on their third floor and a game center in their basement with a Wii, Xbox, ping pong table, pool table, and a huge TV with surround sound. They even have an enclosed swimming pool. It's perfect," she concluded dreamily before standing and tossing a kiss in their general direction. "Night, night," she sang as she floated back to her room on cloud nine.

Suddenly, Grace felt absurd about the discussion she and David had been having. She was willing to bet her hat that Mr. and Mrs. Young had never once had an argument about budgeting.

CHAPTER

5

Grace looked up in alarm as the front door burst open. Faith excitedly ran in and grabbed her hand, dragging her back toward the still-open door. "Mom, you've gotta see his birthday present!" she exclaimed. "It's amazing! Is David here? He has to see this too!"

Faith had been at Spencer's house for a pool party to celebrate his eighteenth birthday, along with the entire popular crowd from school. Grace had been slightly uneasy about it because she didn't like the idea of Spencer gawking at Faith in a bathing suit, but she'd consoled herself with the fact that at least Faith didn't have a bikini.

Jackson had already run outside by now, and Grace heard him yell, "No way! Cool!"

As she and Faith exited the house, she caught glimpse of a brand-new Mustang convertible sitting in their driveway with the top down. "He got a *car* for his birthday?" she exclaimed in disbelief.

"Isn't it amazing? He gave me the first ride too!" giggled Faith. "Everyone else was totally jealous."

"Can you take me for a ride? Please?" Jackson begged.

"Me too!" Katie chimed in, tugging on Spencer's hand. She had followed Grace outside.

David and Freddie had come out as well. "You've gotta be kidding me," David muttered under his breath to Grace. "Who gives their kid a Mustang for his birthday?"

Grace wondered the same thing, although she suspected he was also jealous. David loved Mustangs.

Spencer was grinning away. "Sure, I'll take you for a ride. Hop in! That is," he hastened, "if your mom will let you."

"Please, Mom!" Jackson and Katie pleaded together.

Grace had no idea what kind of driver Spencer was, although he had always gotten Faith home safely. She didn't like sending her kids off with a teenager who was still giddy from the excitement of a new car, but she was also somewhat cornered now. She didn't want to be the killjoy.

"Well, okay," she said reluctantly. "But, Spencer, no showing off. Jackson, don't tempt him to speed to show how fast it can go. Drive out past town to Johnson's Farms. You can get up to fifty-five on that road, and that's plenty fast, especially with the top down. And everyone has to wear a seatbelt. Katie, grab your booster."

Everyone clamored to get in the car, and Spencer turned to Freddie. "You wanna come, bud?"

"Nah, that's okay. Thanks."

Spencer shrugged and went back to the car as Faith made sure Katie's seat was fastened properly. Then they were off, Spencer honking as they left. Grace turned to her son. "Why didn't you want to go, Freddie?"

"Oh, I dunno," he said. "I'm not really sure what I think of Spencer. Faith acts all weird whenever he's around."

Grace hid a smile. "Yeah, that's what girls and boys do

when they're dating," she said with a wink at her husband. "Was I like that when I first started dating Dad?"

"Not like Faith," he insisted. "You were happy, yeah, but Faith is… I don't know… like, almost a different person around him. I don't like it."

David ruffled his hair. "Someday you'll have a girl doing that around you," he said, "and then you'll like it."

Freddie scoffed. "I hope not," he said. "If I ever have a girlfriend, I hope she just acts normal. I like plain old Faith better than Faith with Spencer. She shouldn't have to try to impress him. She's good enough the way she is."

Grace and David exchanged a glance. For an eight-year-old, Freddie was incredibly astute. Grace hadn't realized he was so protective of his older sister, nor had she realized how much he was taking this dating thing to heart. "Well, honey, if they keep dating, eventually she'll stop acting like this around him," she soothed. "Faith's just really excited about it now. And I think once school starts, things will calm down a bit. She and Spencer won't have as much time to spend together because she'll have to fit homework in around volleyball."

"Maybe." Freddie seemed unconvinced. "I just don't trust him."

Grace furrowed her brow. "You don't trust him? Why not?" It was an odd statement for a kid his age to make.

Freddie merely shrugged and looked away. Now Grace was becoming concerned. "Freddie, why don't you trust him? What makes you say that?"

He looked at the ground a long moment before responding. "I saw him sneak into Faith's room once."

Grace sucked in a sharp breath and felt the blood drain from her face. She looked wide-eyed at David and saw that he had a similar expression of shock on his face.

"You saw him sneak into Faith's room?" she repeated. At Freddie's nod, she asked, "When was this? How did he get in?"

"It was when you guys were on your trip," Freddie replied.

"Our honeymoon?"

"Yeah. I was in my room reading, and I heard a noise in the backyard, so I peeked through my blinds and saw him climbing in Faith's bedroom window."

Grace felt anger and panic rising inside her, and she fought to keep her voice even. "Did you see him leave later?"

"Mm-hmm."

"And how long do you think he was there?"

"About an hour."

Now Grace was furious. *She knows better than that!* she thought. *What were they doing in her room, anyway? I am going to ground that girl for life. Maybe longer. Why, of all the sneaky, irresponsible—*

"Where was everyone else?" David's voice interrupted her thoughts, and she marvelled at how calm he sounded when she knew he must be upset too.

"Aunt Livy took Katie to the library for story hour. Jackson was playing Nintendo."

That made sense. Without Katie to barge into the room, Faith would have been a lot more free to entertain visitors. So this hadn't been a casual drop-in by Spencer. He and Faith had deliberately planned this out in advance. That made Grace even more mad.

"Mom, don't tell her I told you, okay?" Freddie looked into her face worriedly. "I don't want her to be mad at me."

"I think she'll figure it out one way or the other. You and Jackson are the only ones who could possibly have seen Spencer. But even if she gets mad at you, remember that you did the right thing telling us, Freddie. That's definitely something I need to know so I can discuss it with her. She knows that's not allowed, and she'll have to face the consequences for it now."

Her answer appeared to do little to assuage Freddie's fears, so she gave him a hug and said, "Thanks for telling me, hon. I know this has been weighing on your mind, because you've had to keep this a secret for a month. But I'm glad you told me. Thank you."

He nodded, then asked, "Can I go back into the house now?"

At her affirmative answer, Freddie walked back inside, and Grace turned to David. "I'm so mad right now I can hardly think straight."

"Same here."

"What was she thinking? David! They could have been doing *anything* in there!"

"I know. But speculation won't help us right now. We need to talk to her and see what she has to say for herself."

Grace pressed her fingertips to her temples. "Didn't she learn anything from that episode of sneaking out last year? I thought we were over this! Is *this* what we have to look forward to for the next few years? This time she let an older boy sneak *in!*"

David didn't have time to answer. Just then, Spencer returned with everyone, and the kids piled out of the car, enthusiastically thanking him for the ride. Faith leaned over to kiss him before slipping out of the car, and he backed out of the driveway with a wave and a beep of the horn. Grace was glad he was gone. She just might have chewed him out too had he stayed.

"Faith Elizabeth!" she barked. "In my room, now!" All three kids looked at her in alarm. Clearly, they hadn't anticipated such an abrupt outburst.

"Deep breaths," David whispered. "Don't let your emotions get the better of you."

Grace knew he was right, but it irritated her that he felt the need to try to calm her down. "I'll be fine," she said shortly, turning on her heel and stalking into the house as Faith followed.

Once inside the safety of the master bedroom, Grace wheeled around and said, "Were you ever going to tell me?"

Faith looked confused. "Tell you what?"

"What you were really doing while we were on our honeymoon?"

Grace thought she saw Faith's eyes flash a spark of panic, but the expression passed so quickly she might have imagined it. "I don't know what you're talking about, Mom. Honestly." Now her eyes were wide with innocence. By golly, where did her children learn to be such good liars?

"Hmm. Is that so? Well, let me refresh your memory. Spencer sneaking into your room while Aunt Livy and Katie were gone. Does this ring a bell?"

She definitely didn't imagine the panic in Faith's eyes this time. Grace could almost hear the internal struggle in Faith's mind between sinner and saint as she debated how to respond. "Where did you get such a ridiculous idea?" she finally demanded. "I know better than that, Mom!" Clearly, the sinner had won that round.

"That's what I thought too. But *knowing* and *doing* are two very different things. Just because you know better doesn't mean you'll always do the right thing. Faith, this is serious! What am I supposed to think you were doing all alone in your room with a boy?"

"Mom, I don't know where this is coming from, but you can

trust me! I wouldn't let Spencer sneak in my window!"

"Even if you weren't doing anything physical—" Grace cut herself off abruptly as Faith's words registered in her mind. "You just admitted your own guilt! I never said he snuck in your window."

"I—Yes, you did!"

"No, I didn't. I said he snuck into your room, but I didn't mention the window. How else would you know that detail unless it really happened?"

"Mom, it's the only logical thing—"

"Enough! Faith, stop denying it, and have the character to accept responsibility for your actions!"

"But I—" Faith stopped and paused for a long moment. Her shoulders sagged as she responded quietly, "Okay, you're right. He snuck in. Three times."

"*Three* times?!" Grace balled her hands into fists and clenched her jaw so tightly it hurt. She closed her eyes and took several long breaths before she was able to respond. "And what were you doing with him all that time?" Her teeth were still clenched, and her voice was almost a growl.

"Nothing, Mom. I swear. We just wanted to hang out."

"You expect me to believe that you snuck him in three times just to hang out? No kissing or touching or… more?" She couldn't even bring herself to voice her biggest fear.

Faith's cheeks flamed red. "No, Mom. Nothing like that! Most of the time we were on our phones. We just wanted to be together. That's it."

"*Most* of the time. What about the rest of the time?"

"I mean, yeah, we kissed a little, but that's as far as it went, Mom. I promise you that. Nothing else happened." She stared earnestly at Grace, and despite Faith's recent track record with lying, Grace was inclined to believe her this time. Faith did have the look of one telling the truth, and she was initiating eye contact, which further supported her sincerity. Or maybe it was the fact that Grace desperately wanted to believe that kissing was the only physical activity in which they had engaged.

"Faith, I *really* need to be able to trust you with boys. But this is the second time I find out you've been sneaking around behind my back. And this time it's going on right in our own house!"

"Mom—"

"No! Let me talk. I know the temptations that face teenagers, Faith. Believe me, those same temptations face adults too. Even kissing can easily lead to more, and you need to be able to safeguard yourself against that. Being alone with a boy—in your *bedroom* of all places—is putting yourself in a very risky situation. You may not mean for anything more than kissing to happen, but in the heat of the moment, when your heart is doing the thinking instead of your head, yeah, anything is possible."

Faith looked down. "I know," she whispered.

"From now on, whenever you're with a boy, whether Spencer or anyone else, make sure you have an 'escape route.' Make it your personal policy not to be alone with a boy. There's just way too much freedom with no one else around to see or hear anything. And if you have him over, or go to his house, make sure your room door is always open enough that other people can look in. That will cut back on temptations too, if you know your mom can pass by and peek in at any moment. And if Spencer ever tries to go further than you're comfortable, push him away and get out of the room. Call for help if you have to. Controlling one's desires is not always easy."

"I know. I *get* it, Mom." Faith was still beet red, clearly uncomfortable to be having this discussion. Grace didn't enjoy talking about such personal matters either, but her daughter needed to hear this.

"Now, there's still this pesky issue of punishment for disobeying my rules." Faith grimaced as Grace went on. "You will have three consequences for the three times you broke the rules. One, you are grounded until school starts."

"But, Mom! That's two weeks! And what about volleyball and work?"

"David or I will take you to volleyball and work. And be glad I'm only making it two weeks. I can make it longer if you wish." Faith made a face but remained silent, and Grace continued. "Two, you will take the bus to school for the first two weeks."

"Mom! Seriously?" wailed Faith. "That's so not fair!" Spencer had already offered to pick her up for school, and especially now that he had a Mustang, Grace knew Faith would be the envy of the entire female population at Mapleport High. Grace was well aware that this would be a particularly difficult burden for her daughter to bear.

"Then maybe you'll think twice before making such a rash decision next time, hmm? And three, you have to copy the Sixth Commandment and its meaning and all the Bible verses that go along with it in the Catechism. Three times for all of it. By tonight." She was stretching it with that one, but she'd run out of other ideas for consequences. It would do.

Faith groaned. "Mom, please. I'll copy the Catechism stuff, even more than three times if you want me to, and you can ground me longer, but please at least let Spencer take me to school. We've already agreed. It would look lame if I told him I have to take the bus."

"You could explain to him *why* you have to take the bus,"

suggested Grace. "Or if you prefer, I can explain it to him. Or David. Maybe he needs a good man-to-man talk about chastity."

Faith blanched. "That's mortifying, Mother. Don't you dare mention any of this to Spencer. The last thing I need is my mom or *stepfather* talking with him about any of this. He'll think you guys came straight from the eighteenth century when courting was still a thing."

"The consequences stand, young lady. I suggest you stop complaining. Be glad I love you enough to do this."

Faith snorted, but didn't argue any further. "Are we done, then?" she asked.

Grace ignored the snide tone. She knew Faith was smarting from being discovered and figured she could let one rude comment slide for now. "Yes, we're done. Go to your room and start on the Sixth Commandment."

Her daughter tossed her hair defiantly over her shoulder as she stalked out of the room, and Grace sank onto the bed. She always second-guessed herself when it came to doling out punishments, wondering if she'd handled the situation well enough. But her second-guessing wasn't the only reason for the sinking feeling in the pit of her stomach. She was concerned about Faith. Had she learned her lesson? Or was it only a matter of time before something like this happened again?

CHAPTER

6

Dinner was halfway over when the front door opened and David walked in.

"Nice of you to join us," Grace said icily.

"I know, I know. I'm sorry, guys," he said. "I completely lost track of time at the office. I had to finish up some stuff, and I didn't realize it was getting so late."

"You didn't even answer my texts."

"Yeah, I know. My battery died."

"You *do* have a landline in your office. You could have called."

"I'm *sorry*, okay? By the time I realized how late it was, it was just as fast to walk over as it would have been to call. You could have called my office phone too, you know." David's voice had turned accusatory as well.

Grace glared at him and promptly started giving her husband the silent treatment as she jabbed a spear of broccoli with considerably more force than was necessary. The kids exchanged uncertain glances, and Faith tried to smooth over the situation.

"So! I had my first World Geography test today, and I think I aced it! I studied really hard, and I was one of the first ones to finish. I think I may have gotten them all right!"

"That's great, Faith!" David tried to feign enthusiasm, but his voice was strained at best. He was sitting down by now, eating his lukewarm plate of food. He knew it would just make Grace more upset if he got up to microwave it, so he forced himself to eat it as it was.

"Who cares about geography?" complained Jackson. "I mean, why do we even have to learn it in the first place? That's totally what GPS is for. I don't need to know where all those countries are on the other side of the world, and besides, they're changing all the time anyhow."

"It never hurts to be knowledgeable about the world in which we live," David answered. "And speaking of tests, didn't you have a math test today?"

"Yeah," Jackson sighed. "I don't think I did very good on it."

"Very *well*," corrected Faith.

"That either. I don't know. I mean, I think I get the stuff, but then when I take the tests it seems like I make all these dumb mistakes."

"That's why you should double check the answers," Faith said. "You always try to race through, but then you make easy mistakes like adding wrong."

"If I checked my answers, I'd have to do the whole problem over again. It would be like taking the test twice. Who wants to do that?"

"People who want to get an A," put in Freddie.

David had to smile at that. "Good call, Freddie. So no games or practices tonight, huh, guys?"

Grace broke her silence to insert pointedly, "No, this was the *one night* this week we could all eat dinner together, remember?"

David bit back a snarky reply. Maybe if she wasn't stonewalling him, they could actually enjoy that one dinner together. Or part of it, anyhow.

By now the kids were done eating, and Grace excused them to clear their plates, take showers, and finish homework. David sat alone at the table, listening to his wife slam plates into the dishwasher just in case he didn't realize she was still mad at him. He was starting to wish he'd stayed at school.

The tension between the two was evident the rest of the evening, and once the kids were in bed, David confronted Grace in the living room. "Look, I'm *sorry*, Grace. I don't know what else to say. You don't have to ruin this evening by giving me the silent treatment and holding a grudge."

"David, this was the one night you were even going to be around! Last night you had a budget meeting. You had to miss Faith's game. She did great in it, by the way. Tomorrow night you have choir, so you'll miss another volleyball game. Thursday you have a voter's meeting, so you'll miss Jackson's game, which is really a bummer since he's been doing so well lately. And on Friday you have an all-day meeting in Grand Rapids, and you'll probably be going out to eat afterward. So is it really so much to ask you to be on time for one meal?"

"Grace! Stop! I know this week is crazy. Most weeks are with the sports schedules. And, yeah, I have more meetings than usual too. But because of that I also have more work to catch up on during the day. Today I had a parent drop in unexpectedly to discuss stuff with me, and it really set me back. I was trying to finish earlier. But I was also a bachelor for twenty years, and I'm not used to having someone waiting for me at home. If I didn't leave the office until nine thirty, no one would have cared."

"Oh, well, I'm sorry we're such a burden to you now," she snapped.

David rolled his eyes and gritted his teeth. "That is not what I meant, and you know it! Don't try to put words in my mouth or make me the bad guy here! Why won't you let this go? It's not that big of a deal!"

"It *is* a big deal, David! At least, it is to me! Having your office half a block away is convenient, but it's also dangerous. You can pop in there whenever you want, just to do one 'quick' thing, and then before you know it, you've been there two hours. I don't want to wonder if you'll be home for dinner or not!"

"*O-kay!* Grace, I am sorry." He over-enunciated each syllable, exasperated. "This is the first time all year this has happened. You know I'm not in the habit of missing dinner."

"Yes, but it's only the middle of September."

"What's that supposed to mean? You think now that the school year is in full swing, I'll do this more often? If *this* is what I can expect when I get home, then maybe I will just stay at the office!"

With that, he stalked out of the living room and shut himself in their bedroom at the end of the hallway. Grace stayed in the living room, stewing about the whole exchange. She crossed her arms and pouted. It was barely after nine o'clock, and she knew Jackson and Faith were still awake reading in their rooms. They'd probably heard the whole stupid thing. And now she had no idea what to do. She honestly just wanted to go to bed, but David was in their room, and the last thing she wanted was to encounter him again so soon after their fight. She leaned her head back against the couch, fighting tears. She'd blown the thing out of proportion, but it was too fresh for her to go make amends yet. They both needed space to cool off and calm down.

"Mom?" It was Faith, tiptoeing cautiously into the living room, looking around as if scared she would meet David lurking in a corner.

"Yes, Faith," she replied wearily. "What is it?"

Faith crept over to the couch and sat down next to her mother, pulling her legs up underneath her. "Is everything alright?" she asked in a low voice.

"Oh, just peachy," she said with a trace of bitterness.

"I heard you fighting."

"I know."

There was a moment of awkward silence until Faith asked in a tiny voice, "Are you guys gonna be okay?"

Grace looked at her, startled. "We'll work it out eventually, yes. Why wouldn't we be okay?"

Faith looked embarrassed. "Oh, I don't know. I just don't want you guys to start fighting all the time like you and Dad did at the end."

She winced at the comparison. "Sweetie, I don't want that, either. But don't worry—David and I aren't on the brink of divorce over this little tiff. Am I mad at him right now? Yes. Is he mad at me? Yes. But I still love him, and I know he loves me. I mean, I'm not feeling particularly amorous toward him at this exact moment, but love is deeper than that. It's more than romance."

Deciding this was as good a time as any for a teaching moment, and figuring she could use the reminder herself, Grace sat up straighter and shifted so she was facing Faith. "Women in particular crave romance. We like to watch 'chick flicks' so we can swoon and dream of 'happily ever after.' Dating is all about romance. Everything is new and exciting, and both you and your significant other are putting your best foot forward, trying to impress each other.

"Marriage, on the other hand…" She paused, searching for the right words. How on earth was she to describe marriage to a teenager who was still in the puppy love phase of dating? "Marriage isn't romantic. Sure, sometimes it is, but when you settle into a comfortable routine, neither of you put as much effort into it anymore. You see your spouse before he's taken a shower in the morning or before he's brushed his teeth and still has morning breath. You notice irritating things you didn't notice while you were dating. Marriage isn't a romantic, sweep-you-off-your-feet journey. It's work. And it requires forgiveness and a willingness to compromise with each other— two lessons that are much more difficult than they seem. But David and I are both in this for the long haul. We'll apologize to each other and make up and keep going. And we'll do the same thing the next time we disagree, and the time after that, and so on."

Faith nodded. "Okay, good. I just don't like to hear you guys argue. Spencer and I never fight."

Grace bit back a snide comment. The last thing she needed was her lovestruck teenage daughter giving her advice on relationships. Or insinuating that her relationship with David was inferior to that of Faith's with Spencer. They'd been dating a whopping two and a half months, and apparently the whole discussion they'd just had about dating and romance had been lost on Faith.

"Well, Faith, for your sake I'm glad," she managed. "But eventually you two *will* argue about something. The people you spend the most time with are also those who tend to get on your nerves more. You're around each other so much you can't help but disagree at some point. But just because you disagree or fight doesn't mean the relationship is over. Think about our family. Think about *us*—you and me. Remember when I found out about Spencer sneaking into your room?" Faith shifted uncomfortably as Grace continued. "I was furious with you, and you were mad at me when I punished you, but we worked through it and kept loving each other, right?"

"Yeah, I guess that makes sense."

"Good. Now get to bed. Spencer will be here early tomorrow."

Faith giggled and gave her mom a kiss on the cheek. "That's true," she said. "And besides, you probably wanna go talk to David before he goes to bed."

"Also true," Grace affirmed. "Good night, honey. Thanks for coming out." She was surprised to find she meant her last comment. Their discussion had put her in a much better frame of mind.

After Faith went back to bed, Grace locked up the house, brushed her teeth, and walked back to her own room. She entered only to find David already asleep. Her shoulders sagged with defeat, and tears filled her eyes. This wasn't the way she wanted either of them to go to bed, still mad at each other with unresolved issues hanging over them. But neither did she want to risk waking him and making him even more upset with her, so she silently changed into her pajamas and slid into bed next to her sleeping husband.

"Good night," she whispered, leaning over to graze his cheek with her lips. Then she turned onto her side, her back to him, but sleep did not come easily.

"Hey, are you awake?" David's voice was barely a whisper in the grey light of the early morning. Their alarm hadn't gone off yet, but both were awake.

"Yeah, I'm up," she said.

He reached for her hand under the covers. "Honey, I'm sorry about last night. I should have been more considerate about dinner. I don't want to give the impression that work is more important to me than you are. I'll try my best not to let it happen again."

"I'm sorry too," she confessed. "I completely overreacted. It was such a stupid thing to fight about. By the end, I was just arguing because I didn't want to admit I was wrong. You were right—I ruined what could have been a nice evening together."

David pulled her into a hug. "Well, hey—let's try again tonight. I'm gone too much this week as it is. I'll skip choir this evening so we can all go to Faith's game and grab a bite to eat on the way. Deal?"

"Sounds good to me, as long as you're okay with skipping choir. I don't want to get Dorothy on our bad side."

The two chuckled together. Dorothy Wilcox was the most even-keeled soul they knew. "I'll take the risk," said David. "I'd rather be with you guys tonight anyhow. I want to see Faith play."

Grace smiled. "You know, she and I had a lovely little mother-daughter chat last night after you came back here. She tried to dole out some advice by pointing out that she and Spencer *never* fight."

"Oh, brother," muttered David. "How can we ever measure up to such a perfect relationship?" They laughed again, and Grace turned so she could give him a kiss.

"I'm glad we aren't fighting anymore," he whispered when she pulled away.

"Me too," she said. "The only good thing about a fight is making up afterward."

"Agreed. And that being said, I owe you at least one more kiss. We have to make up for lost time last night."

Willingly, she complied, thinking to herself that making up almost made that fight last night worth it. She wouldn't mind if they started every morning like this.

CHAPTER

7

"Okay, I'm ready. Let's go!" Jackson urged. "Practice starts in fifteen minutes!"

"Let me see your math homework first," said David firmly.

Jackson stared at him, his mouth wide open. "Are you *kidding* me?" he exploded. "We have to go!"

"Did you or did you not do your math?" David persisted.

"Not all of it, no, but I'll do it when I get back. Come on!" Jackson looked panicked now.

"Exactly how much did you do?" pressed David.

"Some," Jackson mumbled. "But I promise I'll finish first thing when I get back!"

"Nope. Sorry. I told you when you got home that you had to finish your homework before I'd take you."

"Okay, look. I don't get it at all. It's stupid the way they teach this stuff. It doesn't even make sense. And those story problems are ridiculous. I don't even understand what they're asking. Math is pointless anyway. We have calculators for a reason. Please, let's just go! I tried, okay? Come *on*!"

"If you didn't understand, you could have asked me. I do

know a thing or two about math. You had plenty of time. We've been home an hour and a half. What were you doing in there all this time?"

"Other stuff," Jackson said. "It's none of your business."

"Actually, it is. At least, it is when your ride to practice hinges upon you finishing your homework. You know you don't have time to do it after late practices like this. By the time you get home and take a shower and eat a late dinner, you're exhausted. Math is now or never."

Jackson stared at him incredulously. "You seriously aren't gonna take me? I have to be at practice! Mom would take me if she was here!"

"Well, she's at the store with Katie, so you get to deal with me. I'm sorry, Jackson. Schoolwork comes before sports."

"If I miss practice they won't let me play!"

"You have another practice tomorrow."

"That's not how it works!"

"Jackson, if you aren't getting at least a C, you'll be ineligible anyway. I saw your last math test. You got fifty-eight percent. Tests count for half of your grade. Your homework hasn't been anything great either. You need to keep your grade up or you'll be off the team for real."

Jackson glared at him. "This is what I get for Mom falling in love with a *teacher*," he spat. "You think grades are so important. So I'm not a great student. Live with it! I always get B's and C's. I'm sorry I'm not good enough for you. I bet my *real* dad would take me to practice. You aren't my dad, and you know what? You never will be!"

He stomped to his room and slammed the door so hard a picture fell off the wall. David closed his eyes and took a deep breath. Jackson seemed to forget that his birth father had walked out on them six years ago and hadn't had any contact with the kids since.

Freddie spoke up from his spot at the table where he'd been reading a book. "Mom's not gonna be happy about this," he said uneasily.

"I know," said David dryly, already anticipating another unpleasant encounter when his wife arrived home. He didn't doubt that Grace would have taken Jackson to practice, and she was sure to be mad at him for refusing. To keep his mind off this fact, he decided to start dinner. Maybe he could score minimal brownie points that way.

Jackson was waiting at the front door when Grace and Katie walked in twenty minutes later, each with three plastic bags of groceries. "Jackson! What are you doing here? You're supposed to be at practice!" Grace said in alarm.

"Ask *David*," Jackson replied mockingly. "He won't take me!"

Grace bustled into the kitchen and looked at her husband in disbelief. "What is going on here?" she asked. "Why is he not at practice? He's going to get in trouble!"

Jackson stood behind his mother, glaring at David with a triumphant gleam in his eye. He'd obviously counted on his mother taking his side.

"Grace, I can explain, but not in front of everyone. Come on," said David, steering her back to their room. "Jackson, Freddie, finish unloading the groceries and help put the stuff away," he instructed over his shoulder.

Once they were in their room, David shut the door and turned to find Grace glaring at him, her arms folded across her chest. "I know, Grace. Just hear me out. As soon as he got home, I told him he had to finish math before he left for practice. He barely even touched it, so I told him I wouldn't take him."

"Seriously?" She sounded just like Jackson had earlier. "David! That is not your call to make! You can't just make him skip practice because of a few math problems. That's ridiculous!"

"It is my call if I'm the one here with him. He was well aware of the conditions. He needs to know I mean what I say. If I back down on the first major altercation, he'll learn he can walk all over me when I ask him to do something."

"Oh, I see. So this is a power play? Show him who's boss?"

"Of course not! But at the same time, he does need to know I actually have some authority in this house, and you drilling me like this isn't helping the cause!"

"So now *I'm* the bad guy?"

"If you side with him and take him to practice anyhow, then yes, because you would be completely undermining any authority I have over him." Grace scoffed, and he continued. "We talked about this in pre-marital counseling and agreed to back each other when it comes to parenting. The kids need to know we're a team, and they need to know they have to listen to me, just like they have to listen to you. We both knew Jackson would be the biggest challenge, the one to push the envelope. This is one area that may actually get through to him. Losing football practice is a serious consequence for him. It'll leave an impression. I have to stick with it now."

"Over *math*? Really?"

"Over schoolwork, yes. Unless I'm mistaken, learning is the reason he goes to school. Not sports."

"Fine, then take away video games for the weekend or something! Not an entire practice!"

"That wouldn't have nearly as much impact, and you know it. Jackson is as smart as a whip. If he applied himself, he could be making A's in math, no problem. But he's content to just slide by. He got a D on his last test, and his homework grades have been hovering in the low seventies. At this rate, he's going to kick himself off the team if he can't pull up his grade! I'm doing him a favor!"

Grace sighed and pinched the bridge of her nose. "I do *not* like this at all," she said. "In the future, I would really appreciate it if you didn't dole out such a consequence without discussing it with me first. At least we could brainstorm ideas and decide together. But yes, fine. I'll back you on this, because I don't want Jackson to have the satisfaction of pitting us against each other. But as I said, I still don't like it."

"Noted. And for the record, I don't like it either. But I'll bet in the future we won't have any trouble with him doing his homework on practice nights."

"There is that," she said cynically.

"So you're with me?"

"Yes," she said reluctantly. "But let's not make a habit of this."

"Trust me, I wouldn't dream of it," he assured her.

When they emerged from their room, Jackson practically pounced on his mother to ask, "So you'll take me? I promise I'll finish my homework when I get back. I can still make half of the practice at least!"

"Sorry, Jackson. David told you what you had to accomplish first, and you failed to do so. I don't like you missing practice either, but in this case, you chose that for yourself. Next time maybe you'll make a better decision."

"Mom! Are you kidding me?" Jackson's eyes turned hard. "Yeah, I see how it is. He moves in and now you can't make any decisions for yourself anymore. Whatever *he* says goes. I for one wish you guys had never even met in the first place. We were doing just fine on our own without *him* coming in and telling us what to do!"

Again, he stormed to his room and slammed the door, knocking another picture off the wall. David and Grace held each other's gaze for a long moment until they heard Faith clear her throat pointedly from the entryway. Grace's eyes widened in alarm. Spencer was supposed to take her home from practice, and he usually walked her into the house. There was a good chance both he and Faith had just heard that entire exchange. With great trepidation, Grace turned and walked the remainder of the hallway until she rounded the corner to find the two high schoolers standing there trying to look innocent.

"Hi, Mom!" Faith said in an overly cheery voice. "What in the world is going on here?"

She was giving Grace the *look*—the one Grace gave her children when they were acting out in public and she didn't want to yell at them with everyone watching. They dubbed it the "evil smile." Faith's eyes were wide open and shooting daggers as she smiled and spoke through clenched teeth.

"Oh, don't mind us!" she exclaimed acerbically. "Just having an open and honest family discussion."

Faith was clearly humiliated that Spencer had witnessed such a moment. Grace could almost hear her thoughts. *Spencer's family* never *argues. Why can't we be more like them?*

Grace also noted that David was nowhere to be seen. He must have slunk back into their room to avoid Spencer and Faith. *Thanks, honey,* she thought sarcastically. *Leave me out here alone to deal with them.*

"Hey, I need to get back anyway," Spencer told them hastily. "Um, Faith, we're good for the morning? I have to get there early again."

"I know. I'll be ready," she assured him. "Thanks for the ride. We aren't always like this at home, you know."

Grace shut her eyes. But she didn't have time to respond to her daughter's last comment because suddenly the smoke alarm started blaring. *You have got to be kidding me!* she thought. *We look like a bunch of bumbling idiots!*

David came racing past them down the hall, through the living room, and into the kitchen. "Sorry!" he yelled as he passed them. "Totally forgot about that. It's been one of those days…" He yanked out a pan of burned drop biscuits, and the putrid smell met their nostrils the moment the oven door opened. Faith looked at her mother, her expression pained. Grace could only grimace in return, as embarrassed as her daughter.

A minute later, after David had turned on the stove vent and fanned the alarm to make it stop beeping, he walked meekly back to the entryway where Grace stood with Spencer and Faith. Spencer stared at David with wide eyes, a fake smile pasted on his face, while Faith looked like she was on the verge of tears.

"Anyone want a biscuit?" he asked, holding out the pan of blackened lumps that looked more like charcoal. That did it. Grace broke down and started laughing at the sheer absurdity of the situation. Soon she had tears streaming down her cheeks as she gasped for air. David had joined in by now, the two of them helplessly convulsed in fits of laughter. At this point Grace didn't even care what Spencer thought anymore. He probably thought they were certifiably insane, but so be it.

As their laughter died down, Grace wiped the tears off her face and turned to find Spencer grinning away. "I love coming over here," he said. "You guys are always so… alive, I guess. It's never boring. Kinda makes me wish I had younger siblings too. Or that my dad was home more often. It's fun with this many people in the house."

"I wouldn't exactly label it as *fun*," Faith said. "More like out of control."

"Well, *I* think it's fun," he insisted with a chuckle. "I'll leave you to your dinner. I'll bet those biscuits are nice and flaky on the inside! See you tomorrow, Faith." He kissed her cheek and let himself out, still smiling broadly.

Faith turned to her mother, a dark red blotch on each cheek. "Well! You certainly are doing your best to humiliate me in front of him! What do you suppose he thinks of us? First we walk in to hear Jackson screaming at David, and then the whole smoke alarm thing happened, and then you both ended up laughing like hyenas! What is wrong with you people, anyhow?"

"Oh, Faith, lighten up," said Grace. "It could be worse. At least David wasn't wearing his red sweatpants!" She winked at her husband as they both burst out laughing again. Grace had insisted he toss the offending pants before they'd even gotten married, replacing them with a much more suitable pair of pajamas.

Faith was not amused and continued to stare at them both in disdain. Grace went on, trying to placate her daughter. "Honey, Spencer's been here before. He knows we aren't always like this. Besides, he thinks we're 'fun.' You heard him yourself!"

Faith rolled her eyes and stalked back to her own room, clearly mortified to have such a pathetic excuse for a family.

David said, "I'll see what I can salvage from the rest of dinner. I have chicken and rice simmering in the electric skillet. With my luck today, the water is completely absorbed by now, and the rice is burnt to the pan."

"I'll go with you," offered Grace. They passed Freddie and Katie in the living room, who were staring at their mother and stepfather, as if unsure what to make of the last few minutes. Grace grinned at them and said, "It's alright. Some days are just like this." Then she joined David in the kitchen to help throw supper together.

Their evening meal was anything but ordinary. Faith sat haughtily in her chair, her back ramrod straight, giving everyone the silent treatment. Jackson scowled at David the entire time, eating in stony silence himself. He was only at the table because his mother told him he wouldn't eat otherwise. Had it been left to him, he would have stayed in his room to avoid everyone and come out later for leftovers.

The chicken was overcooked and dry, and the rice was clumpy. Even the frozen peas weren't quite right because they'd been left on the counter too long and thawed before they were cooked. The salad Grace made was the only decent part of the meal. The burned biscuits sat untouched on the kitchen counter, but whenever Grace caught sight of them, she couldn't help but giggle.

CHAPTER

8

The following morning, as Jackson sullenly ate his cereal in the kitchen, David walked in and said, "Good morning!"

Rather than answer, Jackson picked up his bowl and marched past him into the dining room to eat there. David exchanged a look with Grace as he poured coffee into his travel mug and debated whether or not to respond to Jackson. Before he could decide, Faith sashayed in.

"Spencer is dropping me off after school," she said in a superior voice as she swooped her long hair up into a ponytail. "We should be here by four o'clock, so can we all please attempt to be normal today? Yesterday was mortifying."

"Mommy! Can you fix my hair?" Katie rushed in before anyone could answer Faith, and Grace set to work on the laborious task of combing through Katie's thick curls. The poor child had inherited Grace's unruly hair. Fixing it each morning took the better part of ten minutes.

"Is Freddie up yet?" asked David, still not answering Faith. "I haven't seen him."

"Oh, goodness! Probably not!" Grace said in panic. "I

already gave him two wake-up calls, but you know how he is. He's a bear to get up." She abandoned Katie's hair for the moment and raced to Freddie's room to shake him awake.

A horn sounded from outside, and Faith jumped. "Gotta go!" she hastened, grabbing a granola bar and her backpack as she rushed out the door. "Remember, be good this afternoon!"

Jackson snorted and muttered something under his breath from his spot at the table, and David carried his own bowl over to sit across from him. "What was that?" he asked, thinking that he didn't like Spencer honking rather than coming to the door.

"Nothing," mumbled Jackson, averting his eyes.

"No, no, I insist. What did you just say?" David looked at him sternly over the top of his glasses.

Glaring at him, Jackson replied, "I said maybe we *would* be good if you'd actually take me to practice tonight!"

"That's entirely up to you, now, isn't it?" he returned levelly, matching Jackson's gaze.

"I'm probably not gonna play on Thursday, and it's all your fault!" Jackson hissed. "Do you even care about that? Do you know how much football means to me? You're totally ruining my season. I hope you're happy." With that, he grabbed his own backpack and stormed to the front door. "I'll wait out here for the bus. Not that anyone cares anyhow!"

He slammed the door behind him, and David sighed. The boy had an iron will, and David knew it would be awhile before he could merit Jackson's good graces again. He knew what Grace meant when she'd said it felt like she was taming a wild mustang in raising Jackson.

Freddie came out dressed and rubbing his eyes, one section of his light brown hair sticking straight up as usual. Grace poured him a bowl of cereal and ran her hands under water to slick down his hair before returning to Katie's mess of curls. Then she grabbed her purse to leave for her shift at the cafeteria. Quickly, she bent to give David a kiss. "Have a good day," she told him. "Don't worry about Jackson. He'll come around eventually. Maybe school will get his mind off last night."

But the exact opposite held to be true. When Jackson burst through the door that afternoon, he was like a tornado, seeking to destroy everything in his path.

"Well!" he yelled, hurling his backpack down. "Coach Conway is really mad at me because yesterday was an unexcused absence for practice. Everyone was asking me where I was. What was I supposed to tell them? That my *stepfather* wouldn't take me because I didn't do all my homework? I don't think so! I look like an idiot!" He stormed off to his room, muttering under his breath.

David was certain Jackson had told all his friends that his stepfather wouldn't take him and left it at that. No mention of the homework bit. So now he was the bad guy to the entire football team and probably the coach as well. He looked at Grace with a question in his eyes, but she shook her head. Confronting Jackson now would only make matters worse. He needed time to cool down. Besides, Faith was due home any moment with Spencer, and heaven forbid they have another episode like the one yesterday in front of him.

As if on cue, the front door opened, and Faith called deliberately, "We're here! Is everyone presentable this time?"

David narrowly avoided snorting out loud. Grace rolled her eyes at him as she answered. "Yes, Faith, you're safe. Mr. Hyde is locked away. Only Dr. Jekyll is here."

The door opened all the way, and Faith led Spencer in. "I hope you don't mind, but Spencer's gonna help me study for

Advanced Bio. We'll be in my room." She pulled him down the hallway quickly, as if to avoid him catching a glimpse of anyone else in her crazy family.

"As long as you keep your door partly open, that's fine," Grace called after her.

Freddie was doing a worksheet at the dining room table, and David pulled out his laptop and joined him there to finish a few things he needed to get done. Grace sat on the couch with Katie to work through her beginner reader with her. For a few moments, the house was relatively peaceful with everyone going about their own business, until David got the feeling he was being watched. He turned to see Jackson standing in the doorway behind him, scowling mightily.

"Ah! Jackson! Didn't realize you were there," he said. "What's up?"

"Okay, look," Jackson said reluctantly and defiantly. "I need your help. But I'm only asking you 'cause you're the only one who gets this stuff. I'm still mad at you, so don't think this is gonna be bonding time or anything dumb like that. But I *am* going to practice today, so if you can help me, we can get this out of the way and be done with it. Deal?"

David bit back a smile. If nothing else, Jackson was brutally honest. "Deal. I'm glad you're making a wise decision today. Let's see what you've got."

Jackson handed him his paper, and David scanned it quickly. He had to suppress a chuckle when he saw the "Take It Home" section, questions intended to make students think through the math processes and verbalize their answers. One question asked, "How could you make sure your answer to the previous question is reasonable?" Underneath, Jackson had written, "You could do exactly what I did in that problem!" David knew it would be marked wrong, but he didn't have the heart to make him change the answer. *Ask a stupid question...* he mused.

"I have good news for you, buddy," he said, flipping to the front side of the worksheet. "You're making this way harder than it has to be. You've been adding an extra step. When you multiply a fraction, you don't need to worry about a common denominator. Just multiply the top first, and then the bottom, like this." He jotted down a few examples to show Jackson, who looked at him incredulously.

"That's it?" he asked in amazement. "That's not even hard!"

"I know! This is one of the easiest things to do in math. When you divide a fraction, though, you have to remember to flip the second one before multiplying it like we just did. Here, like this..." Again, he worked through a few problems until Jackson nodded.

"I think I get it," he said. "It's just so hard to remember all these different rules. Fractions are dumb. I'm never gonna need to know this stuff, so I didn't pay attention when she was trying to teach it. And then when they throw in negative fractions it gets even more confusing."

"Just pay attention to the equation. When there's only one negative, the answer will be negative. When there are two negatives, the answer will actually be positive."

"That doesn't make any sense at all."

"Sure it does. It's the same with English. If I say, 'I'm not taking you to practice today,' that means I won't. It's a negative answer. But if I use two negatives, they cancel each other out and it's a positive meaning. 'I'm not *not* taking you to practice,' means I am. See what I mean?"

"I guess that sorta makes sense. Let me try a few to see if I get it, and then you can check them?"

"Absolutely."

A few minutes later, Jackson handed David his homework sheet, completely finished.

"You did all of it?" he asked. "Wow, I'm impressed. I knew you'd catch on quickly. You're a sharp student." He checked over the paper and noted one correction regarding the negative sign. "Jackson, that's great! You've got it! I think your teacher will be pleasantly surprised."

Jackson smiled smugly then caught himself. "Well," he sniffed, "now that that's done, will you actually take me to practice today?"

"You betcha! And I'll talk to your coach to let him know why you weren't there yesterday."

Jackson scoffed. "Little good it's gonna do me. He'll still make me sit out at least the first half of the game on Thursday, if not the whole thing."

"Then I guess you'll be sure to do your homework from now on, won't you?"

Jackson didn't grant him the courtesy of a reply. Instead he grunted something and stalked back to his room, not exactly slamming the door, but closing it loudly enough to indicate his displeasure over his stepfather's rigid rules.

David shook his head. He felt like with Jackson it was always one step forward, two steps back. He wondered if his stepson would ever fully accept him as part of the family.

CHAPTER

9

By the time Homecoming arrived in mid-October, Grace was sick of hearing about it. Faith talked about it constantly and labored over what to wear. Spencer, naturally, had been picked for Homecoming Court and was almost certain to win the title of Homecoming King. Faith had to be appropriately dressed to accompany him. She begged her mother to buy her a new dress, but Grace adamantly refused. The lavender dress she had worn for Grace and David's wedding would be just fine.

The Varsity football team won their game on Friday evening, and Spencer was indeed voted Homecoming King. Faith was giddy from the excitement of it all, and come Saturday, she could talk of nothing else as she got ready for the dance. She fussed over her hair and makeup all afternoon, and when Spencer came to pick her up at five for dinner beforehand, the entire household was relieved to see her go.

Grace acknowledged with a bit of alarm that her daughter looked much older than sixteen. Her dress was modest but flattering, and Faith had curled her hair and piled it on top of her head. She could have been nineteen, and the look in Spencer's eyes when he saw her indicated that he was well aware of that as well. They made a stunning couple.

But Grace couldn't dwell on that fact for long, because she was getting ready for Jackson's birthday party the following afternoon. She spent Saturday evening baking and frosting his cake, prepping food, and getting the house ready for her family to arrive the next day. She was exhausted by the time Faith got home at eleven thirty, and had fallen asleep on the couch, her head in David's lap as he read a book.

"How'd it go?" asked David as Faith entered, startling Grace awake.

"It was great," Faith said.

Grace frowned. *It was great? That's it?* She'd expected a bit more enthusiasm, given Faith's incessant swooning about it beforehand.

"I'm really tired, though," she continued. "It's been a long day. I'll tell you more about it tomorrow."

"Okay, honey, that's fine," assured Grace. "We're glad you're home safely. Sleep well."

Faith waved a response as she walked to the room she shared with Katie. Grace looked at David and shrugged. Teenagers were hard to understand.

The following morning as everyone was getting ready for the Sunday School and Bible class hour, Faith stayed in her room longer than usual. Finally, Grace went in to check on her only to find her daughter still sleeping.

"Faith! What are you doing? Bible class starts in ten minutes! Why are you still in bed?"

"I know, Mom, but I have a terrible headache," groaned Faith. "I'm sorry. Can I skip Bible class just this once? I'll come over for church later."

Grace arched an eyebrow. "You weren't drinking last night, were you?" she asked with a hint of trepidation.

"Mother! Good grief, no! It's just that the music was really loud and the lights were low, and they had a smoke machine. It totally messed with my eyes and ears. My head still feels like I can hear the rhythm pounding. I just need to sleep it off. I'll be fine."

"Well, okay," she said reluctantly. "Maybe it'll do you some good to stay in a quiet house for another hour. Set your alarm so you don't miss church, though."

"I will," Faith mumbled, already trying to fall back asleep.

Grace shut the door quietly and joined the rest of the family, scowling slightly. She whispered an explanation to David on the way over, though the kids were oblivious. But after Bible class, Faith was still nowhere to be seen. Grace dashed back home to check on her and found her sound asleep. She debated waking her, but realized seven minutes wasn't nearly enough time for her daughter to get ready anyhow. Sighing, she made her way back to church and slipped into the pew next to David, hastily explaining the situation. Both were unhappy about it, and Grace found it difficult to concentrate on the service that morning.

When they arrived home, however, they found Faith showered and dressed and making waffles for everyone, seemingly feeling much better.

"Hi! There you are!" she exclaimed in a perky voice. "I'm really sorry about church. I had my volume turned down low, and I completely slept through my alarm. I promise I'll go to the Monday service tomorrow night. But I feel a lot better. I guess I needed the sleep. Maybe we shouldn't have stayed so long last night. The gym was crazy loud."

"I'll bet," inserted Jackson snidely. "Or maybe you were too busy making out with Spencer to even notice."

"Shut up!" Faith returned hotly, her face turning red.

"I heard you talking about it with Chelsea," he taunted. "He's a *fabulous* kisser, isn't he?"

"Jackson, shut *up!*" shrieked Faith. "Do you ever know when to be quiet? You're the stupidest, most annoying brother in the universe!" With that, she shoved past him and stormed to her room, slamming the door.

Before Grace or David could say anything, Freddie spoke up. "You shouldn't make fun of her, Jackthon," he insisted reproachfully. "Why do you always have to be a jerk?"

Jackson glared at his younger brother. "My name is *Jackson*, not *Jackthon*," he mimicked. "And I'm just teasing. She doesn't have to take it personally. No one in this house can take a joke! Everyone always yells at me for everything I do!"

Now it was Jackson's turn to stomp away to his room, leaving Freddie red-faced and blinking back tears from Jackson's insult. Katie stood nearby whimpering and fighting tears herself. She hated it when anyone got mad.

Grace and David simply stared at each other in astonishment, still trying to process what had just happened. Within the span of two minutes, the mood of the entire household had drastically shifted.

"Let's give them each a few minutes to calm down, shall we?" Grace asked brightly. "I'll go talk to them in a bit. But first, you two wash up so we can eat these yummy waffles Faith made. They're best when they're still warm."

They ate the meal in relative silence, even Katie quieter than usual. Afterward, Grace excused herself to talk to Jackson and Faith each in turn, and negotiated an uneasy truce between the two of them, complete with insincere apologies to all parties involved. *Good enough*, she thought. Jackson's party was quickly approaching, and she didn't have time to fully deal with the drama before her family would arrive. She banned the topic of Homecoming for the rest of the day and sent each of the kids to separate rooms in the hope of avoiding any more hard feelings.

When Olivia and Andy arrived, their cheerfulness and enthusiasm were infectious. Before long, everyone was in a better mood. Andy invited Jackson to the backyard for some football, even convincing David and Freddie to play. Olivia stayed in the house with Grace, listening patiently as Katie chattered away.

"Psst! Is Jackson outside?" It was Faith, peeking in the doorway, whispering her question.

"Yes, he is," Grace whispered back, resisting an eye roll. Sometimes even her teenager acted like a preschooler. Faith's shoulders relaxed, and she entered the room.

"Hey, girl!" exclaimed Olivia. "How was the dance last night?"

Faith blushed and looked at her mom. Grace shrugged. "You can talk about it with Liv. Just not with Jackson." She glanced at her sister and muttered, "Don't ask. Sore subject."

"It was really nice," Faith said to her aunt. "We went out to eat first, and—"

"Where did you go?" Olivia interrupted.

"Um, well… Actually, we went to Le Poisson," admitted Faith, coloring deeper.

Grace's eyes widened. She didn't know that. Le Poisson was an upscale seafood restaurant in Forest Springs that required reservations a month in advance. "I thought you guys were going to Olive Garden with the rest of the Homecoming Court!" she exclaimed.

"Yeah, well, we were going to," Faith said uncomfortably,

"but he wanted to surprise me and take me out alone."

"I see," replied Grace, not really sure she was okay with the idea. Le Poisson wasn't the type of restaurant high schoolers frequented. She and David considered it "their" restaurant. It was for special occasions, and most high schoolers couldn't afford even an appetizer. Then again, Spencer wasn't just any high schooler. He probably could have bought dinner for the entire Homecoming Court there.

"It was really good," continued Faith, "and then we met the rest of the Court at Olive Garden for dessert before we went to the dance."

"Spencer was Homecoming King, wasn't he?" Olivia asked.

"Mm-hmm." Faith nodded.

"Girl, I'm telling you, that boy is *cute!*" sighed Olivia dreamily. "He was on the football team with the twins last year, so I'm well aware of his charm. All the girls in the crowd swooned when he took off his helmet. Even with his hair all sweaty he looked *good.*" Faith giggled, and Olivia went on. "Did you take pictures from last night? You're a beauty yourself. I'll bet you two looked great together."

"They did," admitted Grace, pulling out her phone to show her sister the pictures.

"Ooh, girl, look at you!" Olivia squealed. "You look like you're eighteen! Love what you did with your hair! You could be a model. So… what's with Jackson about Homecoming?" she ventured cautiously.

"Oh, *that,*" Grace sighed. "You know how he can be. He was taunting Faith about it. Making snide remarks about what a great kisser Spencer must be."

"Sounds about right," Olivia said, then lowered her voice conspiratorially. "But just between us girls, I bet he *is* a great kisser." She winked at Faith, who turned deep red. "Aha!"

crowed Olivia. "I knew it!"

"Alright, that's enough of that," Grace scolded. "Otherwise I'll ban the subject for you too!"

They laughed and ventured into other topics until Grace's parents, Carol and Walt Anderson, arrived with Gramps in tow. Grace noted sadly that her grandfather shuffled quite a bit more than usual. He was slowing down, and Grace wondered how much longer either of her grandparents would be around. Gram was already in a nursing home for her losing battle with Alzheimer's.

Welcoming her parents and grandfather with warm hugs all around, Grace invited them in to make themselves comfortable. The autumn air had a chill in it despite the sun, and the football players didn't stay out long. Soon enough, everyone crowded into the kitchen and living room, munching on chips Grace set out and the cheese and cracker tray Andy and Olivia contributed.

"Hey, Jackson, great game on Thursday," Olivia congratulated her nephew.

She and Andy made a point to come to a volleyball or football game at least once a week. Now that their three children were all off to college, they claimed they needed something to occupy their evenings.

"Yeah, bud, you were awesome out there!" Andy chimed in. "Two touchdowns! Way to go! You're a natural."

Jackson visibly swelled with pride. The boy was as competitive as anything and equally vain. Grace knew it greatly boosted his ego to have others take note of his athletic abilities.

"I remember when Justin and Jason started out back in middle school," continued Andy. "Those were fun games."

"Oh, my goodness—hysterical!" Olivia said. "Some of the kids had never been on a team before and had a hard time remembering the rules. They'd line up wrong or have too many players on the field. Drove the coaches crazy."

"One of their first games they were tied with the visiting team. Whopping score of six to six," Andy started.

"Oh, yes! I remember that game!" Olivia interrupted excitedly. "The clock had one second left. It was the last play of the game for Mapleport—"

"I'm telling it!" insisted Andy. "So they line up. Hike the ball. QB sees his mark. He throws a Hail Mary pass—"

"Which gets picked off by the other team. They run it back—"

"Seventy yards for a touchdown to win it!" Andy cackled. "Seventy yards! The team was devastated, but honestly, I couldn't stop laughing. It was just too funny."

The rest of the family was laughing as well. Grace loved the way the two interrupted each other while telling stories. They could make even a mundane story funny by their presentation.

"So is the pizza ready?" Jackson asked. "I'm starving!" Grace chuckled. Jackson couldn't fool her. His real motive had nothing to do with hunger. He just wanted to get to his birthday presents.

After a dinner of homemade sausage pizza, the family sang "Happy Birthday" and devoured almost all of the chocolate cake before Jackson ripped into his presents. The first gift was a University of Michigan sweatshirt and hat from Andy and Olivia.

"Awesome!" he enthused as he pulled it out of the box. He was only in the seventh grade, but Jackson already envisioned himself playing football for U of M one day.

"The hat is actually from your cousins," Olivia informed him. "We figured you needed some appropriate college wear."

"Definitely!" grinned Jackson, adjusting the hat on his head. "I'll wear these to school tomorrow. Thanks!" He was glad his aunt and uncle weren't as cheap as his mom was. The only U of M shirt he currently owned was a hand-me-down from his older cousins. This was the first brand-new Michigan stuff he'd ever owned.

Next, Jackson opened an envelope from Freddie with three packs of gum inside. Jackson wondered if Freddie had used his own money to buy it. He was pretty sure his brother still had a little bit left from his own birthday.

Katie presented her older brother with a card she'd made just for him, complete with the words "I LuV Yu, jaxN." For a kindergartner, it wasn't bad, and everyone oohed and aahed at Katie's writing as she proudly grinned away.

Faith handed Jackson a small package, and he opened it to find a set of math flashcards—addition, subtraction, multiplication, and division. "Seriously?" he asked, looking at her in disbelief.

"Don't say I don't care about your grades," she said with a smug grin. "Now you won't have to double check your answers and take your math tests twice."

David and Grace chuckled as Jackson scowled at his sister. "Yeah, great. Thanks for thinking of me. It's my *favorite* gift."

"Hey, *I* like it!" objected David. "I think it's a great idea! I'll go over them with you!"

"My math teacher told me I was average when I was in junior high," Walt spoke up. "I told her she was mean."

David burst out laughing. "That's a good one," he said. "I'll have to remember that."

The other adults groaned, but Jackson looked at his grandpa in confusion. David explained, "In math the word 'mean' means average. So to tell his teacher she was *mean* is telling her she's average too. It's a double meaning."

Jackson shrugged at Faith, still not finding it terribly humorous. Instead, he picked up the gift Gramps had brought. He was incredibly disappointed that it came in a gift bag rather than an envelope, because that meant it wasn't money. He lifted a handwriting workbook out of the bag and stared at his great-grandfather in dismay.

Gramps smiled. "This is part one of your gift," he told Jackson. "You need to know how to write in cursive. So when you've worked through this book, you write me a letter in cursive. A real letter with paragraphs. At least one full side of notebook paper. Mail it to me. When you've done that, I'll mail you back another letter in cursive, and I'll include your monetary gift at that point." He smiled, clearly pleased with his own cleverness.

Jackson was at a loss as to how to respond. He personally thought it was the stupidest idea he'd ever heard, but he could hardly say so out loud. So instead he mumbled, "I'll see what I can do." He was afraid Gramps may not be alive long enough to make good on that promise, but he was scarcely in a position to voice that concern. Disappointed, he tossed the handwriting book next to the flashcards, two non-gifts in his mind.

David handed him one last envelope, which he eyed with considerable wariness. For all he knew, his family had gotten him tutoring sessions or something.

"This is from Grandma and Grandpa as well as your Mom and me," said David.

When Jackson reached into the envelope, he pulled out four U of M football tickets. "No way!" He looked at his mother and stepfather, hardly daring to believe they'd gotten him tickets to an actual game. Maybe they weren't as cheap as he thought. "I get to go to a game?"

"You sure do!" David said. "With me and Uncle Andy and Grandpa. We'll go out to eat first and make a day of it. It'll be a guys' day out. We get to go to the Big House!" He sounded almost as excited as Jackson was.

"And I'll take you guys on a tour of the campus and show you the best place to eat in Ann Arbor. U of M is my alma mater, you know," inserted Andy proudly, catching the excitement.

Consulting the tickets, Jackson said, "It's not till November, huh?"

"Yeah, I know November is still a ways off, but late-season games like this are more challenging and competitive since more and more hinges on each game. I thought it would be good to see a game that's more exciting and could make or break their chance for a top Bowl game after the season. I think it'll be worth the wait."

"Totally!" agreed Jackson. "Thanks, guys! This is great!" He was so excited he gave his mother an unprompted hug and a high five to David. "This is the best birthday present ever!"

He thought about his birthday gifts as he put the tickets carefully back into the envelope. The flashcards and the cursive book were totally lame, but the sweatshirt, hat, and tickets were cool. Maybe his family wasn't completely hopeless after all.

CHAPTER

10

When the Michigan game rolled around three weeks later, both David and Jackson were beside themselves with excitement. They were almost as bad as Faith had been at Homecoming. And with both of them in the same house, they fed off each other's enthusiasm. Grace was very glad to see them leave bright and early in the morning. The game started at noon, and it was a three-hour drive. They wanted to get to Ann Arbor early enough to walk around the city and grab an early lunch before the game. Andy offered to drive, since he was most familiar with the area, so promptly at seven he picked David and Jackson up, Walt already in the car. The four of them made a boisterous departure, decked out in their maize and blue, munching on the breakfast burritos Walt bought at McDonald's.

Shaking her head as she closed the door, Grace revelled in the silence of the house as she made her way to the kitchen for a cup of coffee. Amazingly, the other three kids were still sleeping, and Grace enjoyed fifteen minutes of quiet as she sipped her coffee and read her devotion for the day. When

Katie emerged at seven fifteen, rubbing the sleep from her eyes, Grace decided it was time to start mixing the ingredients for pancakes. Freddie joined them a few minutes before eight, and they sat at the table eating breakfast together companionably.

By mid-morning, the breakfast dishes long since cleaned up, she'd gotten a text from David assuring her the guys had made it to Ann Arbor, and Grace was ready to take Freddie and Katie to the library. Faith was still in her room, which both concerned and irritated Grace. She marched into the room Faith and Katie shared and shook her teenager's shoulder.

"Faith, it's already quarter to eleven! Get up! Katie and Freddie and I are going to the library. I don't suppose you want to come?"

Groaning, Faith turned away. "No, Mom, I don't want to go to the library. Why do you care if I'm up or not? You won't even be here anyhow. Just let me sleep."

Grace frowned. Faith had been unusually subdued as of late, and Grace wasn't sure what to make of that. And while Faith slept in on Saturdays whenever she could, she was normally up by nine or ten.

"We left you some pancakes in the microwave when you get up. We'll be gone about an hour. Are you okay?"

"I'm *fine*, Mother."

"Alright. We'll see you around lunchtime then."

Grace left with Freddie and Katie, her bag full of the books they'd checked out last time. Mapleport had a nice library for the size of the town, and the recently remodeled children's section was a huge draw for her kids. They had a reading nook with pillows and bean bag chairs, and even though Katie couldn't read well yet, she sat in there with Freddie and looked through books.

When the three got back home, Faith was up and about,

but still in her pajamas and slippers as she heated up two cans of tomato soup.

"Hi, sweetie!" Grace greeted her. "Thanks for starting lunch! Want me to make some grilled cheese sandwiches?"

Faith shrugged, but Katie and Freddie were enthusiastic, so she heated up the skillet and started buttering the bread. Freddie retreated to his room to pore over the new book he had checked out about planets, and Katie went to the couch and pulled out the half dozen books she had picked. Grace could hardly believe how quiet it was without Jackson there. The entire dynamic of the house was altered. It was... *nice*. Grace felt guilty even admitting that to herself, but it was true.

Yet at the same time, the relative peace in the house also served to highlight Faith's despondent mood. Without Jackson around to take the attention, Grace was acutely aware that her daughter wasn't her normal self. So after lunch, she let Katie and Freddie pick a movie before venturing into Faith's room for a chat. She knocked lightly on the door and let herself in. Faith had been texting, and when she saw Grace at the door, she quickly slid her phone under her pillow and looked up, almost guiltily.

"What's going on?" asked Grace.

"What do you mean?" Faith asked innocently. "I was just texting, and I don't want you reading my messages to my friends. What's wrong with that?"

"No, I mean that all day you've been reserved and moody. Even during the week you were quieter than usual. What's wrong?"

Faith's eyes filled with tears, and she looked away.

"Sweetheart, I'm your mother. Talk to me. Please, tell me what's wrong."

Faith stared at the ground and said in a small voice,

"Spencer and I had a fight."

It took all of Grace's willpower not to say anything snide to ruin the moment. Apparently all was not perfect in paradise after all. But Faith was genuinely upset, and Grace knew she needed sympathy rather than sarcasm. Instead, she walked to Faith's bed to sit next to her as she replied, "Oh, hon, I'm sorry to hear that. About what?"

Faith's cheeks flushed, and she glared at her mother. "It's none of your business! I don't want to talk about it!"

"Okay, okay, I'm sorry," Grace quickly amended. "I'm just worried for your sake, and if you do want to talk, I'd be happy to listen."

Faith sighed dramatically and said, "Let's just say that I'm seeing a different side of Spencer now. He's not charming all the time after all."

That served only to heighten Grace's curiosity, and she said gently, "I suppose all of us have a 'different side,' honey. No one can be charming and sweet all the time. He can't live up to that expectation. It's not fair to expect him to."

"Whose side are you on, anyhow?" accused Faith. "His or mine?"

Grace's eyes widened. "I didn't think I was picking a side! I didn't realize it was serious enough for that. Honey, I don't know what your fight was about, but I do know that no relationship is perfect or immune from problems. You know that too—you've heard David and me fight, and we're still in what they call the 'newlywed phase.' So even in good times, couples will disagree. And that isn't necessarily a bad thing. It's a chance to discuss each other's thoughts and opinions."

"I guess," mumbled Faith.

"Honey, you and Spencer are only in high school. You're dating. You aren't in a long-term commitment. Maybe you'll eventually make that kind of commitment, but then again, maybe you won't. If you two aren't right for each other, I'd rather have you realize that now than later."

Faith merely shrugged.

"Did you have an argument over religion?" she asked cautiously. She couldn't help herself.

"Yes and no," Faith answered vaguely.

"Okay. Not really an answer…"

"I mean, that wasn't the main subject, but it was sort of a factor in the grand scheme of things. We don't believe the same thing, and that is a concern."

"Yes, it really is. I only asked because that was one of the sticking points between David and me, as you well recall. Remember when he 'broke up' with me?" She grinned wryly. Even though they hadn't been dating, they were definitely interested in each other, but David had told Grace he couldn't date her if she wasn't Christian. To this day, she still teased him that he had broken up with her.

"That made me mad," she continued, "but it also showed me how serious he was about his faith. He didn't want to date someone who didn't share his beliefs. And now I completely agree with that stance. If Spencer has no interest in Christianity, quite frankly, I don't want the two of you getting too serious."

Faith was crying now. "Why does everything have to be so complicated?" she wailed. "I'm not thinking about marriage or anything crazy like that. I just want to go out with him and be happy."

"I know, sweetie, but that's not how it works. At first, sure, things are great. But as you get to know one another more, inevitably differences will come up. If you can live with those differences, you'll keep dating each other, but if not, you'll break up and eventually find someone else. Dating is much more complicated than it seems."

"Got that right," Faith said dejectedly.

"Oh, honey, come here," soothed Grace, pulling her into a hug. "I'm sorry about your fight, and I hope you work it out. But I also hope that you'll be strong enough to end the relationship if it comes to that. I don't want you to stay in a bad relationship out of guilt or to prove something. And I hope that whatever happens, you feel comfortable talking to me."

"I do. Thanks, Mom."

"You're welcome." Grace kissed the top of Faith's head and changed the subject. "Now, my phone has been vibrating away this entire time. I have a feeling the guys are sending pictures of the game. Wanna see?"

She pulled out the phone to look at the pictures David had texted. There was one of David and Jackson in front of Michigan Stadium, another of Jackson with the football field behind him, and yet another with all four guys standing together grinning away like a bunch of schoolboys. They were obviously having a blast, and it warmed Grace's heart to see David spend time with Jackson. The game had been David's idea. To a casual observer, he and Jackson were father and son.

After sending back a "Go Blue!" text, Grace abruptly said, "Let's get some fresh air. Wanna go for a walk? Freddie and Katie will be okay here for a few minutes. They're only halfway done with their movie anyhow."

"Sure, why not?" Faith replied.

Soon the two were zipping their jackets and heading out into the brisk November breeze for a walk around the block. They didn't say much on the way, but they didn't need to. Their earlier conversation had bridged a gap, and Grace felt like they'd forged a stronger mother-daughter connection as a result. It was amazing what could happen with less people in the house. Maybe she should schedule partial family outings more often.

CHAPTER

11

With the passing of November came the end of the volleyball season for Faith. Now that Spencer was done with football as well, the two could have spent a lot more time together, but that wasn't the case. In fact, Faith almost appeared to be avoiding Spencer lately, which greatly piqued Grace's curiosity.

The Saturday before Thanksgiving, Jackson and David were watching college football in the living room while Grace read *Charlotte's Web* to Katie and Freddie. Faith came into the house and slammed the front door, tears streaming down her cheeks. Startled, Grace's head snapped up. "Faith! What happened?"

"*Nothing!*" she yelled, and stomped to her room to slam that door as well.

Grace exchanged a look with her husband. Faith had taken David's car to Spencer's house, and hadn't been there that long. Given her current disposition, it was a good bet they'd broken up.

"Well, *that's* over," sighed Jackson. Apparently he'd come to the same conclusion. "I guess he won't be helping me with football anymore."

"Oh, Jackson," scolded Grace. "Think about how Faith feels. She's far more upset than you are right now." He shrugged indifferently, and Grace rolled her eyes and walked back to Faith's room. She could hear her daughter crying before she reached the door. Walking in without being invited, she sat down next to Faith on her bed and stroked her hair.

"He broke up with me," Faith cried into her pillow.

Despite her daughter's obvious distress, Grace was secretly pleased by the news. But this was hardly the time to point that out, so she simply said, "I'm sorry, sweetie."

Faith sat up and grabbed a tissue to blow her nose. "He's a jerk!" she said vehemently. "A real jerk. I should never have started dating him in the first place."

Now Grace was surprised. Faith had been madly in love with Spencer from what she could tell. Spencer must have said or done something incredibly stupid. And Grace was dying of curiosity to know why they had broken up, but she didn't dare pry.

"Now I'm going to have to start riding with Chelsea or take the bus again," Faith continued. "Forget him and his stupid Mustang. He's totally arrogant and stuck on himself anyway. He thinks he's all that. Well, he's *not!*"

Grace tried her best to sound sympathetic as she put her arm around Faith. "Honey, I'm sorry you're going through this right now. No matter the circumstances, breaking up is hard. It'll be weird at school too. I wish there was something I could do to help."

"It's my own fault for falling for him in the first place. I know you and David weren't thrilled about it even from the start. You didn't like the fact that he wasn't Christian. I should have listened to you. I would have been better off." Now she sounded bitter.

"Some lessons can only be learned through experience," she said gently.

"I guess you can say 'told you so' now, huh?"

"Oh, sweetheart, I'm not going to do that! I know you really liked him, and I'm sure you're mad, confused, and heartbroken all at once right now. It'll take time to get over a breakup. You guys were dating over four months. It'll be an adjustment for sure. Give yourself time."

Faith's phone rang then, and she glanced down. "It's Chelsea."

"Go ahead and talk to her," Grace said. "I'm sure you need to hear her voice." She gave Faith a quick kiss and let herself out of the room, closing the door quietly behind her.

David looked at her curiously as she reentered the living room, his eyes asking the question on his mind. She simply nodded, and he breathed a sigh of relief. Even though it would be hard on Faith, they were both glad the whole thing was done.

Only it wasn't. Over the course of the next few days, Faith moped around and was liable to burst into tears for no apparent reason. She snapped at her siblings over little things and spent most of her time in her room when she wasn't in school. Grace doubted she was even doing her homework.

When Thanksgiving arrived, they attended church together in the morning before loading up to go to Carol and Walt's house for Thanksgiving dinner. Grace hoped being around the rest of the family would cheer Faith up again.

Olivia and Andy were already there when the Neunabers arrived. Olivia was helping Carol in the kitchen while the guys set up camp in the den, preparing for the Detroit Lions football game that was a Thanksgiving tradition. Carol had sandwich fixings set out for people to help themselves to lunch and snacks during the game, with the main turkey dinner to be served after the game. Claire was back from college to celebrate with the family, but Grace noted that the twins hadn't made it home. She guessed an eight-hour drive wasn't worth it for such a short weekend.

As everyone assembled in the kitchen, Grace turned to Olivia. "So did Justin and Jason have to stay at school or did a friend invite them over for Thanksgiving?"

"Excellent question!" Olivia grinned away like the Cheshire cat. "Who wants to guess where the twins are?"

Andy jumped in. "I want to tell them!"

"No! Grace asked me!"

"I could tell everyone," said Faith with a sly grin, surprising Grace. She hadn't realized Faith kept in contact with the twins.

"Don't you dare! You promised!" warned Olivia.

"They must not have stayed on campus, or you wouldn't be this excited," Grace said, trying to get the conversation back on track. Sometimes her sister drove her crazy getting to the point of a story.

"Nope. Not on campus," Andy said. "And they're not in Michigan, either."

"Andrew McNeal!" shouted Olivia. "Stop it!"

"Then they have to be in Wisconsin," David interrupted. "It's not that far from Houghton, relatively speaking."

"Yep. They're in Wisconsin. Not too far away from Green Bay, in fact," Andy said hastily as his wife darted over to him and slapped her hand over his mouth.

"They're staying with the Barlowes!" she blurted out triumphantly before her husband could say anything else.

"Sally and Trevor?" David asked incredulously. "I had no idea! Guess I should talk to my own sister more often…"

"I made her promise not to tell you, either," Olivia informed him. "I wanted to be the one to break the news. Now, ask me why they're there. Go ahead, ask." Her smile stretched from ear to ear.

"Okay, why are they there?" Grace asked obediently, wondering why everything had to be so dramatic with Olivia.

"Amber." Andy beat his wife to the punchline, wiggling his eyebrows as he said her name.

Grace gasped. "No way! Jason?"

"Justin!" Olivia and Andy exclaimed in unison.

"*Real*-ly!" Grace was astonished. Jason was the more outgoing of the two, the one who'd had regular girlfriends in high school. Justin, on the other hand, was more reserved. Grace had never seen him with a girl before. Maybe Olivia did have a valid reason to be excited this time.

"So they obviously met at our wedding?" asked David.

"Oh, yes. They hit it off," Olivia said.

"I had no idea!" Grace exclaimed. "I didn't even see them together!"

"Of course not, sis! You were a bit preoccupied that weekend." She elbowed Grace playfully.

"They met at the rehearsal, of course," inserted Andy. "Then the next day—the morning of the wedding—Jason decides to trick Amber and Victoria. You know him. He likes to pull stuff like that. They've switched places before."

It was true. He and Justin had even been known to switch places for a class on occasion so Justin could take a test for Jason and get a better grade.

"So Jason greets Amber that morning," Olivia continued, "and asks, 'Do you know which one I am?' She says, 'You're Jason,' and he says, 'No, I'm Justin.' Amber walks over to the real Justin and looks at his eyes and says, 'No, *you're* Justin. I can see it in your eyes.'"

The boys had hazel eyes, but Justin had a very subtle dark fleck in his right eye.

"He was smitten from that moment," Andy said. "*Smitten.* You know Justin. Liv and I never even heard him *talk* about girls in high school. But he talks about Amber. A lot." He grinned broadly.

"So are they dating?" asked Grace.

"Not officially," Faith offered. She was good friends with both Amber and Victoria. Now it made sense why she knew where the McNeal twins were. "But if Justin asked, she'd go out with him. She really likes him too."

"Hmm, I'll pass that bit of info on just so he won't get cold feet…" Andy mused.

"Well, that's great!" said David, then turned to his wife. "Just think, my dearest, we can claim responsibility if they end up together. Had it not been for our wedding, they never would have met!"

Everyone laughed, and Walt pointed out, "Hey, it's almost kickoff time! Let's go!" The guys hustled into the den, hoping to see the Lions pull out a victory.

The Lions were winning at halftime, but fell apart in the second half and lost the game. It was not pretty, and the males amongst them were not happy. It was with a fair bit of despondency that the table was set for dinner. *Even Faith might be in a better mood than the guys,* Grace thought. *This could be an interesting family meal.*

After the family had taken their places at the table, David was asked to offer a prayer, and then came the flurry of activity as everyone passed dishes around and loaded their plates. The good food buoyed spirits and helped ease the pain of the loss. Once everyone was eating contentedly, Erwin spoke up.

"Okay, folks. As the patriarch here, I guess I should say something wise or profound. Problem is, I can't think of anything that would fit those criteria." He grinned as everyone chuckled. "But instead, I'd like to do something we used to do when the kids were growing up, remember, Carol?" He smiled fondly at his daughter. "We always went around the table and took turns saying things we were thankful for. So I'll start, since it's my idea. I'm thankful that I get to visit my beautiful wife tonight. Even after all these years, she's still my blushing bride, and I'm thankful God blessed us with so many years together."

Carol squeezed her father's hand as tears shone in her eyes. "That's sweet, Dad," she told him, then addressed the group at large. "I'm thankful that my little girl is happy again." She looked at Grace with a small smile on her lips.

"Ditto that," said Walt. "And for family in general. We have a good bunch here."

"I'm thankful for God. And Jesus," Katie announced firmly. Grace was proud of her answer. Carol and Walt were not churchgoers, and Grace prayed that her parents would come to know the Lord. Katie's genuine answer was just the kind of witness they needed to hear.

"Duh!" Jackson cut in. "Jesus *is* God!"

"I know!" insisted Katie. "But don't interrupt me. I'm not done!" Grace hid a smile at her daughter's response as Katie continued. "And I'm glad that I can do my letters. And that I can almost read. And for my new daddy." She batted her eyelashes bashfully as everyone chorused in unison, "Ohhh."

Grace hugged Katie and said, "I second that. I'm thankful for the wonderful husband God blessed me with, and for the fact that we're all adjusting to the new dynamic in the house."

David smiled at her as his turn arrived. "At the risk of

sounding repetitive, I'm thankful for my new bride, of course, and for such great kids who are willing to put up with me barging in on their routines in their house. All things considered, it's been a fairly decent transition, and I'm glad we're all working together to make that happen."

"I'm happy I can talk right," Freddie said next. "Most of the time I remember to say my S's, and I'm glad."

Jackson looked uncomfortable as everyone turned to him. "I guess for football and basketball. It's fun to be on a team, and I'm awesome at both of those sports."

Andy laughed and ruffled his nephew's hair. "Yeah, you are, bud. And I'm thankful—"

"For our silver anniversary!" cut in Olivia before he could finish. Andy stared at his wife in astonishment. "What?" she asked innocently.

"Did you seriously think I wouldn't mention that? You had to provide the response for me?"

"I didn't want you to steal my answer," she responded with a haughty sniff.

"Unbelievable," he muttered in disgust. "See what I have to put up with?"

"Really, Andy, after all these years, does this still surprise you?" Grace asked before her sister and brother-in-law could get into a fight in front of everyone.

"Not a bit," he answered darkly.

"And you're still madly in love with me," insisted Olivia, leaning over to kiss his cheek.

Andy broke into a reluctant grin. "Yeah, I am. I hope we have at least twenty-five more years together." Not to be outdone, he pulled Olivia close for a real kiss.

Claire shook her head at her parents' antics. "I'm thankful that I finally figured out I want to major in social work!" she exclaimed with relief.

Faith was the last of the family members to speak, and Grace was apprehensive about what her daughter was going to say. She'd been so moody lately that she didn't know if Faith would think of anything for which to be thankful since her breakup with Spencer less than a week ago. But Faith surprised her with a fairly deep answer for a high schooler.

"I'm thankful for forgiveness and new beginnings."

"Excellent!" Erwin beamed as she finished. "We sure do have a lot to be thankful for, don't we?"

Gramps was obviously quite pleased with himself for instigating the discussion and sat with a smile on his lips the rest of the meal. As everyone dished up food for seconds, Grace's thoughts returned to Faith's answer. *Forgiveness and new beginnings.*

She had no idea how much they were going to need both of those things in the weeks to come.

CHAPTER

12

Grace pulled her coat a bit tighter around herself as she hurried up the driveway with the mail. There was a wicked north wind blowing in, and the mid-December air was downright frigid. She breathed a sigh of relief as she entered the warmth of the house.

Flipping through the mail, she saw two Christmas cards, their electric bill, a magazine, some junk mail, and an envelope addressed to "Mr. Jackson Williams." Inspecting it, Grace realized it was from Gramps. Her eyes widened. Did that mean Jackson had actually written him in cursive, as stipulated in his birthday gift? She knew Jackson thought it was a dumb idea, but then again, Jackson would do just about anything for money. Maybe learning cursive had been worth it for him to get cash from his great-grandfather.

Setting aside Jackson's letter, Grace glanced at the clock. She had at least an hour before everyone else came home, and there was nothing on tonight's schedule for once. It was time to pull out the Christmas tree to decorate.

David arrived home with Freddie and Katie first, the three

of them bustling into the house quickly to get out of the wind. David's glasses fogged up in the warm air of the house, and he removed them to wipe them off.

"Hey, look!" he exclaimed when he saw Grace in the living room surrounded by boxes of Christmas ornaments, the artificial tree set up in the corner. "Time to decorate, huh?"

"I left the lights for you," she grinned. "That's my least favorite part. Hanging lights can be your job."

"Gee, thanks," he grumbled good-naturedly. "It's *my* least favorite part too." Nevertheless, he picked up a strand of lights and plugged it in to make sure they all worked before attempting to hang them on the tree. Grace went into the kitchen to make hot chocolate for everyone, pausing on the way to pop in a Christmas CD to help set the mood.

By the time Jackson and Faith arrived home on the bus, David was on his third attempt at the lights as Katie and Freddie sat at the table sipping hot chocolate. Grace was setting out other Christmas decorations around the living room when David finally heaved a sigh.

"There! Good enough! Why do we even bother to hang lights on a Christmas tree anyhow?"

"Because it looks pretty," Grace said. "You did a wonderful job, sweetie. Thanks for doing that. I appreciate it." She gave him a hug around the waist, which he grudgingly accepted. Grace knew his pride was wounded that he hadn't succeeded until the third try.

"Oh, Jackson! You got a letter today!" she exclaimed, changing the subject. She retrieved the envelope and handed it to him. "I didn't realize you had been working on your cursive all this time."

Jackson looked embarrassed. "I only did it to get the money," he confessed, ripping into the envelope.

Grace smiled broadly. Everyone knew that, and it was clever of Gramps to have picked the one thing that would motivate Jackson to learn cursive.

Stuffing the money into his pocket with a grin, Jackson read the letter Gramps had written him. When he finished, he said, "You know, it's kinda fun getting a real letter in the mail. Maybe I'll write him back. It wasn't as bad as I thought."

Grace raised her eyebrows at David. She certainly hadn't anticipated that. Maybe Jackson was starting to grow up a bit.

By now, Grace had sorted ornaments into piles for the kids to hang on the tree. Each of them had a few personalized ones, and Katie always got the non-breakables to hang up. For the next fifteen minutes, things were hectic as everyone jockeyed for position at the tree trying to hang their ornaments. Predictably, the bottom half had considerably more ornaments than the top of the tree, sometimes even three or four clumped onto one branch. Grace just grinned and shrugged at David. Such was Christmas decorating with kids.

"Faith, you're tall," she said. "Why don't you put some ornaments at the top to balance out this tree?" When her daughter didn't answer, Grace looked around to realize Faith wasn't even in the room. "Where's Faith?" she asked.

"She hasn't been out here at all," Jackson informed her from the couch. He had long since tired of trimming the tree and wandered over to lounge and watch everyone else work.

Frowning slightly, Grace walked to Faith's room and let herself in with a knock. "Faith? Why aren't you out there with the rest of us? Your ornaments are all in a pile waiting for you."

"Oh, Mother, please! That was fun when I was, like, six. I'm way past that now."

"I see," Grace replied, trying not to show how hurt she was by her daughter's answer. "Well, won't you come out and join us anyhow? It would be so nice for all of us to be together."

Heaving a dramatic sigh, Faith rolled her eyes and stood. "Oh, *fine*," she groused. "Let's go have some family bonding time." With that, she stalked out of the room, leaving Grace wondering if perhaps she should have let her be after all.

Katie's eyes lit up when she saw her older sister enter the living room. "Faith! Can you help me hang the one you got me? You always help me with it." She held up a "Baby's First Christmas" ornament.

Faith's eyes softened at her little sister's question, and her voice lost the sarcastic edge she'd used with Grace. "Sure, Katie! Where do you want to put it?"

Decisively, Katie pointed to a bare spot near the top of the tree, and Faith lifted her up. "There!" exclaimed Katie when she was finished. "It looks good, doesn't it? You can see it better there than at the bottom."

"You're right. It's the perfect spot for it," agreed Faith.

"Here. These are yours," Katie ordered, handing Faith a few ornaments. "You have to hang them yourself. But don't put them too close to my ornament up there."

Faith grinned at her little sister and complied. Grace was shocked at the change in attitude. Apparently Katie was capable of charming even her moody teenage sister.

"So, Faith, did Mrs. Wilcox ask you about singing for Christmas Eve?" David inquired.

"Yes, she did," Faith admitted. "I told her I would."

"Wonderful! It's quite an honor that she asked. She said your voice was so pretty when you sang for our wedding that she started planning right then and there to recruit you to sing for church on occasion. I'm glad you agreed to it. You have a very mature voice."

Faith blushed slightly as she reached for another ornament.

Clearly she was uncertain how to handle compliments from David.

"What about the pickle?" asked Katie.

"The pickle?" David asked in confusion.

Grace laughed as Jackson answered. "It's a dumb tradition that Mom always does. She hides a pickle ornament on the tree when we're done decorating it and whoever finds it gets a piece of candy or something. It's babyish."

"It's supposed to teach you to appreciate all the ornaments on the tree," Grace protested. "You guys always used to scramble to find it."

Jackson scoffed, but Freddie spoke up. "He only thinks it's dumb because he didn't find it last year," he said with a grin.

David laughed as Jackson stuck out his tongue at his younger brother. "Ah, the truth comes out," he said. "Personally, I like your mom's tradition. It's a great idea."

"Good!" exclaimed Grace. "Because you get to do the honors this year. After these last few are hung, you can hide the coveted pickle ornament."

A few minutes later, the ornaments were all hung, and Grace handed each child an empty box to take back out to the garage so David could hide the final ornament. When they came back in, Katie and Freddie ran to the tree to start looking immediately, and despite his earlier protest, Jackson hastened over as well. Even Faith was curious enough to take part in the search, although not nearly as excitedly as the others.

"Aha!" Katie shouted happily. "I found it!"

David had hidden it on a branch with multiple ornaments already, tucked between a Nutcracker ornament, a green foam wreath, and a popsicle stick snowflake.

"See? I told you this was dumb," Jackson complained. Grace figured he was mad that he hadn't found it this year either.

The adults laughed, and David suggested, "Why don't we turn off all the lights except the ones on the tree? It always looks so pretty that way."

Katie ran to do his bidding. By now the sun had set, and the Christmas tree looked brilliant against the darkness, even if some branches had two strands of lights and others had none. The ornaments were still largely concentrated on the bottom half, and the front of the tree was loaded down while the back had virtually none. It looked rather unprofessional, truthfully. But when David put his arm around Grace to whisper, "It's the most beautiful Christmas tree I've ever seen," she had to agree. Uneven lights, pickle, and all.

CHAPTER

13

Faith stepped toward the front of the choir loft as Mrs. Wilcox began the introduction to her solo during the offering at the late Christmas Eve service. She cleared her throat quietly and began.

See amid the winter's snow,
Born for us on earth below,
See, the gentle Lamb appears,
Promised from eternal years.

She continued into the refrain, allowing herself to be immersed in the beautiful melody and familiar words.

Hail, O ever blessed morn!
Hail, redemption's happy dawn!
Sing through all Jerusalem:
"Christ is born in Bethlehem!"

The first verse had been nearly flawless, her pitch exactly on key, the high notes hit perfectly. People turned discreetly to glance at her. With no balcony at St. John, the choir loft was off to the right side, hidden slightly by the organ console. Faith saw her family watching her from their usual spot four pews from the front, proud smiles on the faces of Grace and David. Even her grandparents, who weren't churchgoers, had come to hear her. She smiled at her family and took a deep breath to begin the second verse.

Lo, within a stable lies
He who built the starry skies...

She was in trouble. She'd sung the words before, yet this time they hit her with a profound effect. This humble baby in a manger was the One by whom all things were created. How incredible! Her voice faltered slightly as tears filled her eyes, and Mrs. Wilcox glanced at her. She soldiered on, her voice strained.

He who, throned in height sublime,
Sits amid the cherubim...

Faith knew there was no way she was going to reach the high D to start off the refrain. But suddenly she felt a light touch on the small of her back as Aaron Sullivan stepped up next to her from his post by the bell at the back of the choir loft. Now his voice, strong and sure, rang out with hers.

Hail, O ever blessed morn...

His rich baritone surprised her. Aaron had a downright lovely voice. Faith had never heard him sing before. Really never thought much about him at all, honestly. She had a few classes with him at school and saw him nearly every Sunday in Youth Bible Class and church, but otherwise knew very little about this young man who had stepped forward to rescue her.

As the refrain continued, people were openly turning and craning their necks now, wondering who was singing and why he wasn't listed in the bulletin. Faith was bolstered by his presence and her voice grew stronger as the refrain neared the end. He motioned that he would take the next verse, and she listened as he sang the third verse alone.

> *Sacred Infant, all divine,*
> *What a tender love was Thine,*
> *Thus to come from highest bliss*
> *Down to such a world as this!*

Faith joined him in the refrain again, their voices blending in a beautiful swell. She caught his eye, and he nodded, a silent encouragement to continue into the last verse together.

> *Teach, O teach us, holy Child,*
> *By Thy face so meek and mild,*
> *Teach us to resemble Thee*
> *In Thy sweet humility.*

He surprised her by singing the bass line on the last verse and refrain. It sounded good. Really good. She could see people wiping their eyes, and the incredible power of music struck her.

As they finished the refrain together, the piano fell silent and their voices faded away. The entire sanctuary was hushed as if the congregation held its collective breath. The moment was simply sublime.

***

The service ended one minute after twelve, well-timed by Pastor Lixon, who always chose the closing hymn "It Came upon the Midnight Clear" for that very purpose. People stood to greet each other and wish one another Christmas blessings, and Faith was surrounded by members complimenting her on the solo that had become a duet.

Faith accepted the compliments, blushing at the praise, but keeping one eye on the lookout for Aaron. She needed to catch him before he left with his family. After the solo, she had smiled her thanks at him before slipping out the rear door to the loft so she could rejoin her family for the remainder of the service. But now she had to thank him properly.

As people started to thin out, Faith saw the Sullivans in the narthex getting coats on, Aaron surrounded by a small crowd himself. He shook the hand of Edgar Miller and started to walk away, following his parents out of the church. Abruptly, Faith cut short her conversation with Mrs. Thompson and hurried down the aisle after Aaron, only briefly shaking Pastor's hand. The Sullivans were already outside by now, and Faith broke into a jog to catch them in time.

She pushed open the doors to the parking lot and was met with a frigid wind in the December night air. The chill took her breath away, but she wrapped her arms around herself for warmth and located the Sullivans before calling out, "Aaron!"

He turned at the sound of her voice and smiled. His mom said something to him, and he nodded, heading back to meet Faith halfway as his parents got into the car to warm it up. She studied him as they approached one another. Aaron, like both of his parents, had a solid build—not truly overweight, just broad and sturdy. He wasn't lean or muscular, and he was only a couple inches taller than she. Like many other redheads,

Aaron had a freckled complexion, and Faith vaguely recalled that he'd only recently upgraded from thick glasses to contacts. He wasn't a guy to turn girls' heads, but he had a wonderful voice, a fact for which Faith was grateful.

"Hey," she began as they reached each other, "I just wanted to thank you for stepping in on that solo. I got choked up on the second verse, and I don't think I could have made it the rest of the way. You saved the day for me. I really appreciate it."

Aaron smiled. "You're welcome. I could tell you were struggling, and I figured you could use an extra voice to help out. I'm glad I was there. And I'm glad I didn't completely mess it up for you. I was terrified my voice would crack on the first note and ruin the whole thing."

"I'm glad that didn't happen!" she laughed. "But seriously, I thought it sounded really good. You have a nice voice. I didn't know you could sing so well."

Her compliment sent a rush of warmth through Aaron. He couldn't help but notice how pretty she looked standing there in the frosty air, her dark brown hair blowing gently around her face, framing it in the semi-darkness of the parking lot.

"I got a lot of compliments on our duet," she continued. "Maybe we could do another one sometime?"

Aaron could hardly believe she'd even made the suggestion. He never would have dreamed someone like Faith would ask him to sing a duet with her. That meant deliberately practicing together beforehand, a fact he wouldn't mind in the least.

Realizing he hadn't answered her, he quickly replied, "That would be great. I'd love to. Anytime." *Careful, Aaron, don't sound desperate,* he cautioned himself. *You don't want to scare her away already.*

Faith broke out in a smile that lit up her entire face, as if she truly was happy about his answer. He noticed a small dimple in her left cheek as she responded. "Wonderful! Maybe during Lent? There are some really pretty hymns in the hymnal."

"Sure," he responded, attempting to be casual. He was thrilled she was making specific plans, rather than a vague, *Okay, well, someday...*

A sudden gust of wind caught them off guard and made Faith gasp. He realized she wasn't wearing a coat, and her knee-length skirt left her legs exposed with only nylons to protect them from the cold. "You'd better get in," he told her. "It's freezing out here."

"Yeah, it is. Literally," she said, her teeth chattering. "Thanks again, Aaron. And Merry Christmas." She leaned over and gave him a quick hug before turning and running back into the warmth of the church.

He stared after her, oblivious to the cold, a huge smile on his face. Her response was the best gift he could have asked for.

CHAPTER

14

Grace smiled as she surveyed her surroundings. Olivia had outdone herself with Christmas decorations this year. Full evergreen wreaths with bright red bows hung outside the McNeals' house, garland looped around the porch rail, and a nativity set was displayed in their front yard. Their live Christmas tree in the living room was full and fragrant, decorated with elegant silver and gold ornaments, while their artificial tree stood in the family room, bedecked with the mismatched ornaments they had collected over the years. Every room had Christmas decorations of some type, and the dining room displayed a table runner stitched with holly leaves and berries. Soft Christmas carols played in the background, and the intoxicating smell of baked ham permeated the house.

Despite the idyllic setting, however, the mood in the house was anything but serene. With fourteen people there, the result was nothing short of bedlam. While the cousins amused themselves, the adults crowded into the kitchen, talking and laughing as multiple conversations took place at once. Grace and Carol helped Olivia get the last side dishes ready, while

David carved the ham and Andy opened the wine bottles.

Olivia and Andy had toted in two card tables for extra seating in the dining room, and everyone crowded around, accepting seating arrangements as Olivia directed. It was a tight fit, but they made it work. Andy extended his hands to Faith and Justin, who were sitting on either side of him, and everyone followed suit and joined hands. As the crowd hushed, he bowed his head to pray.

"Lord, we thank You for this gathering today. Thank You for the gift of family, but most importantly, we thank You for the gift of Your Son, our Savior Jesus, whose birth we celebrate this day. Bless this food to our health and Your glory. Amen."

A chorus of "amens" followed the prayer, and everyone reached for the dishes in front of them, spooning food onto their plates and passing to the left as Olivia requested. Once everyone had started eating, Andy said, "So, kids, great job on the Christmas program last night!" Although the McNeals went to Andy's home church in Forest Springs, they'd come to St. John for the children's Christmas Eve service. Even Carol and Walt had joined them.

Katie's eyes lit up as she asked proudly, "Didn't my class do a good job with our song? Want me to sing it again?" Her kindergarten class had sung the first verse of "O Little Town of Bethlehem."

"No, we do *not*," said Jackson. "We heard you sing that nonstop at home for the past month. I'm sick of it. I can sing it in my sleep!"

"Then why don't you quote *your* verse for us again?" Olivia asked with a twinkle in her eye. "We'll see if you still remember it."

Jackson scowled at his aunt but complied. "'But you, O Bethlehem Ephrathah, who are too little to be among the clans of Judah, from you shall come forth for me one who is to be ruler in Israel, whose coming forth is from of old, from ancient days.'"

"And the Bible reference…?" asked Andy.

"Micah 5:2," Jackson said in exasperation. Grace hid a smile. She was sure he wished he'd let Katie sing her verse after all.

"Want to hear mine again?" Freddie asked eagerly.

Grace didn't miss Jackson's weary sigh. Undoubtedly, this wasn't the topic of conversation he would have picked. But he remained silent as the adults nodded encouragingly at Freddie.

"Mine is Luke 2:16," Freddie said. "'And they went with haste and found Mary and Joseph, and the baby lying in a manger.'"

"Must've been a crowded manger," Walt joked. "All three of them in there."

"Oh, Grandpa, really now!" admonished Claire.

"Faith's solo at the late service was beautiful," Carol said proudly. "She did a wonderful job." Grace smiled at her mother, grateful that Carol and Walt had been at both Christmas Eve services.

David took up the account as Faith smiled modestly. "She sure did. It ended up to be a duet. Aaron Sullivan joined in with her. It sounded really good. I think they should do another duet sometime."

Faith blushed and said nothing, making a point of buttering a roll. Claire nudged Faith with her elbow. "Who's this Aaron, huh?"

Jackson snickered and gagged on a bite of mashed potatoes as Faith blushed deeper. "Just a guy who goes to our church. He's totally not my type, so don't get any ideas."

"That's true, he's not," Jackson choked out. "At all."

"So did Santa come last night?" Carol asked Katie, rescuing Faith from the awkward discussion.

"No, Grandma, we don't have Santa," answered Katie reproachfully. "We know he's not real."

"You know what they call someone who's afraid of Santa, don't you?" Walt asked.

"I hate to ask," Andy mumbled good-naturedly.

"A Claustrophobic," Walt quipped. Groans from the adults followed his punchline.

"I don't get it," said Katie, frowning in concentration.

"It's a pun, sweetie. You'll understand in a few years," David assured her.

"You know, it's hard to explain a pun to a kleptomaniac," Walt said with a wink at Katie. "They take things literally."

Amid more groans, David asked Andy, "So how was church this morning?

"Oh! I have to tell you the funniest story!" Andy replied.

"I want to tell it!" Olivia argued.

"He asked me! I get to tell it!"

Jason intervened. "Mom! Dad! *I'll* tell it if you're gonna fight."

"No!" exclaimed Andy, quickly launching in before his wife had a chance. "So there we were confessing the Creed this morning, and Joe Mitchell—"

"Mind you, it was the *Nicene* Creed," Olivia interrupted.

"I've got it!" assured Andy. "We're saying the Creed together, and Joe, whose voice is the loudest one in the congregation—"

"I mean, you can hear him over the organ, he's so loud—"

"Got mixed up and started saying the Apostles' Creed instead—" Andy continued as if Olivia hadn't even spoken.

"And he just kept going!" exclaimed Olivia.

"Refused to admit he was on the wrong Creed," Andy said, laughing. "So the whole congregation ended up finishing the Apostles' Creed with him!"

"Even Pastor!" they finished together.

By now, the rest of the family was in stitches, as much from their retelling of the story as from the account itself. Olivia and Andy certainly had a flair for the dramatic.

After the meal, Olivia insisted everyone leave the dishes until later so they could do the gift exchange, a suggestion which everyone heartily supported. There was a flurry of activity as gifts were unwrapped, and everyone talked and exclaimed at once.

Once the presents were opened and the chaos started to abate, Grace glanced at David, who nodded encouragingly. She cleared her throat and spoke. "Okay, everyone. I have one more gift. Mom, it's for you."

She walked over to her mother and handed her a small box. Carol looked surprised but opened the present nonetheless. Inside the box was a sheet of paper, which she unfolded and read silently, her eyes widening as she registered the import of the message.

"*Really*?!" she asked excitedly. "Grace, that's wonderful!"

She quickly stood to hug her daughter, who was wiping happy tears from her cheeks. Grace figured the other adults had deduced what was going on, but Olivia snatched up the paper to be sure, reading the words out loud.

Coming next August:
Baby Neunaber
Congratulations, Grandma!

Olivia squealed and ran to Grace as well, while Andy and

Walt grinned and thumped David on the back. Erwin, once clued in, smiled and nodded as he shook his finger knowingly at David, and the McNeal siblings chimed in with their own congratulations.

"Gracie!" chided Olivia. "Did you drink that whole glass of wine at dinner?"

"I took one sip and switched glasses with David when he finished his," Grace defended herself.

Katie chimed in over the cacophony, "I don't get it. Why is everyone excited?"

Laughing, Grace pulled her daughter into her lap and explained, "Mommy's going to have a baby!"

Freddie's eyes opened wide at this, and Jackson mumbled, "Yeah, great. Just what we need." Katie bounced up and down, her eyes sparkling at the news.

Faith, on the other hand, seemed adversely affected by the news. She had gone deathly white and simply stared at her mother. When the initial excitement started to die down, she stood stiffly and gave her mother a look of disdain. "That is so embarrassing," she hissed. "I cannot believe this. How pathetic." With that, she fled from the room, ran up the stairs, and slammed a door, leaving the rest of them staring after her in bewilderment.

Grace's cheeks burned, and she desperately blinked back tears at the response from her oldest daughter. An uncomfortable silence filled the room until Jackson said, "I guess *she's* not happy about it."

Claire excused herself to check on Faith while Olivia tried to patch things up. "It's a shock to her, that's all," she soothed. "None of her classmates' parents are having babies, and she's in high school. Stuff like this is awkward for her. She'll come around."

Andy heartily interjected, "Hey, let's break into that moscato, huh? We need a toast! I even have a bottle of sparkling juice for Grace and the kids. This is wonderful! We're so happy for you guys."

"And I totally called this one, did I not, Andrew McNeal?" Olivia had a triumphant gleam in her eye.

"You did, you did," her husband conceded.

"We were placing bets on whether or not you would make an announcement," Olivia explained to Grace. "I know these things." She smiled smugly at Andy.

"You guys bet on everything," complained Jason.

His twin chimed in. "Seriously. And thanks, Aunt Grace, for adding even more things for them to bet on. Gender, birthday, names..."

Everyone laughed as Andy walked in to get the bottle of wine and some glasses, the tension relieved for the time being. David reached over and took Grace's hand with a gentle squeeze. She smiled at him sadly. While she was happy about their baby, she was terribly hurt by Faith's reaction, and she had the sinking feeling that her daughter's attitude wasn't about to blow over.

The ride home that evening was mostly silent. Katie was tired from the excitement of the day, and the rest of the family still felt the tension between Faith and Grace over the outburst earlier. Although Faith had emerged from Claire's room later, she was still out of sorts, and the adults all tried to make up for this by overly cheerful attitudes on their own parts, ignoring the earlier episode.

Once they got home, David offered to put Katie down, and Grace instructed the boys to brush their teeth before approaching Faith. "We need to talk," she said firmly to her teenager. "My room."

Faith reluctantly followed, heaving a sigh.

After the door was shut behind them, Grace turned to Faith, her eyes snapping. "What in the *world* was that?" she demanded. "Do you have any idea how hurt I was by your reaction today? David and I are excited about this baby, and you were blatantly rude about it! I was humiliated by your rotten attitude, and everyone there witnessed it!"

"*You're* embarrassed? Mother, please. Do you have any idea how embarrassing it is for me to have my friends find out my *mom* is having a baby now? I mean, we know what has to happen to make a baby. You're old. I don't even want to think about it."

Grace could feel her cheeks get red and blotchy as she got more upset. "In case you've forgotten, my dear," she said in an icy voice, "we *are* married. This is hardly a shock. And I'm thirty-eight. Not what most people consider 'old.'"

Faith scoffed. "It's still embarrassing. So what is this, we aren't good enough for you anymore? Do we remind you too much of Dad? You have to have kids with David to replace us? Or aren't we good enough for *him*?"

Grace was fighting tears. "Faith! How can you say such things? You know that's not true!"

"Look, if you want me to pretend to be all excited about this baby, great. I will. Congratulations. I'm glad you're happy. But don't expect me to like it." With that, she flounced out of the room, leaving Grace to sink down on her bed, tears streaming down her cheeks.

CHAPTER

15

By the following week, Grace could tell everyone in the household was ready for a trip to Detroit. David's family always celebrated their Christmas the day before New Year's Eve. Things had been chilly at best between Faith and Grace over the past five days. Faith chose on her part to more or less ignore her mother, sleeping in and spending most of her time in her room. Although Grace had tried multiple times to approach her again, Faith had rebuffed her. To say their relationship was strained was an understatement. Grace hoped the time away would help adjust Faith's attitude.

David's mother and stepfather, Mary Anne and Greg Nichols, lived in Detroit and invited the Neunabers to stay at their house, while David's sister's family offered to stay in a hotel. Sally and Trevor's daughters, Amber and Victoria, were good friends of Faith, and for this trip the Barlowes got adjoining hotel rooms so the three girls could have their own room, staying up late to gossip and giggle.

The Neunaber clan arrived around noon on Thursday and had a pleasant lunch with Mary Anne and Greg. Sally and

Trevor were due to arrive mid-afternoon, and Mary Anne fussed over the dinner menu already, making sure they'd have enough variety. Grace volunteered herself and Faith to help in the kitchen, which Faith did grudgingly. Fortunately, she adored Mary Anne and put aside her hard feelings toward Grace to help her step-grandmother, whom the kids called "Nana."

The Barlowes arrived at four thirty with hugs all around. "How was the trip?" David asked.

"Don't ask," Sally groaned. "Not good."

"Chicago. Need I say more?" said Trevor dryly.

"We got stuck for an hour and a half this time!" exclaimed Sally.

"Well, now you can relax. Everyone wash up and come to the table," Mary Anne instructed. "I've had everything ready since four, so let's eat before the turkey dries out. We have a schedule to keep so we can get to our presents."

Everyone followed Mary Anne's instructions and hustled to do her bidding. David and Grace had decided to make their big announcement right away before Faith could make any snarky comments, so as soon as everyone had loaded their plates at the table, Grace prompted Katie, "Sweetie, don't you have something you want to tell everyone?"

All eyes turned expectantly to darling Katie, her eyes wide as she bobbed her head up and down. She took her job seriously as she announced, "Mommy's havin' a baby!"

There was a collective gasp from David's family, and questions swirled around them.

"When?"

"How long have you known?"

"Will you find out the gender?"

"How are you feeling?"

Greg, a doctor, smiled knowingly and said, "I guessed that. You have the glowing look of an expectant mother."

Grace felt herself blush, but Faith snorted beside her. David shot her a warning glance and spoke quickly. "The baby's due mid-August, as far as we can tell. Hopefully he or she won't decide to come early or Freddie might have a birthday buddy, right, pal?" He ruffled Freddie's hair.

Freddie grinned. "Right, Dad."

Faith sat silently through the rest of the meal, not making any snide comments, but not taking part in the conversation, either. Grace waffled between irritation and concern. What was Faith's problem? Couldn't she just be happy about the baby? Was it asking too much for her daughter to be supportive?

After the gift exchange following dinner, Freddie and Jackson went to the kitchen to play Sorry, the board game they'd gotten. Amber, Victoria, and Faith retreated upstairs to talk, and Katie went up with them to dress her doll in the new outfits she'd received.

As the adults helped themselves to coffee and settled down in the living room to chat, Grace asked, "So what Christmas memories do you have from growing up?" David's family loved to reminisce.

"Oh, good question!" said Sally, her eyes lighting up. "We always opened one gift on Christmas Eve and saved the rest for Christmas Day."

"That was my idea," Greg said proudly.

"Yes, that was nice," agreed Mary Anne.

David addressed his sister. "Except for the time you opened underwear."

"Hmm, now *that's* an idea. Why didn't I think of that?" Trevor asked with a mischievous smile at his wife.

"Oh, stop," Sally blushed, swatting her husband's arm playfully. "It wasn't *my* fault! I'm not the one who bought the gift!"

Mary Anne defended herself. "She wanted something fancy. I bought her pretty ruffled undies."

"Do we *have* to discuss this?" pleaded Sally. "And lest you get any ideas here, I was all of seven years old. It was a completely innocent request."

"That's why you started opening the smallest gift first, as I recall," Greg reminded her with a smile.

"Exactly! It was usually jewelry, so I could wear it for church the next morning. The best year was when I turned thirteen and opened a pair of earrings on Christmas Eve. Mom was finally allowing me to get my ears pierced!"

"Remember the year we got cross country skis?" asked David, a grin playing about his lips.

Sally burst out laughing. "Those were hilarious!" She turned to Trevor and Grace to explain. "We got these little plastic skis, and we were so excited to use them, but there was no snow that Christmas! We shuffled around the yard on the grass instead just so we could use them."

Everyone laughed, and Greg spoke up next. "Remember the year our electricity was out?"

All four laughed, and Grace grinned at Trevor. They loved hearing the family retell stories.

"There was an ice storm on Christmas Eve morning," Mary Anne said. "Half the city was out of electricity. Ice formed on the tree branches and made them so heavy a lot of limbs broke off, pulling down power lines. There was nothing they could do to hasten the process of getting the power back on. We were out for thirty-six hours."

"We had a huge fire going in the fireplace to keep warm,"

continued Sally. "The living room was the only place that was tolerable. It was so cold that ice formed on the inside of the windows. Upstairs we could see our breath it was so cold."

"Church lost power too," Greg said, "and the roads were so icy they issued a Level Three emergency or something. Only emergency vehicles were allowed out, so church was cancelled. Sally played a few Christmas carols for us on the piano, and we sang the rest of the hymns acapella."

"You read the Christmas story from Luke," David told Greg, "and then we had our Christmas Eve feast."

"Roasted hot dogs and s'mores!" said Sally. "We cooked them in the fireplace!"

"I was so disappointed," Mary Anne said. "I had planned such a nice Christmas dinner and here we ended up eating hot dogs."

"Then we all piled in the living room with sleeping bags for the night. We didn't dare venture too far from the fire," said David.

"And in the morning we opened our presents," Sally remembered, "and our big gift that year was an Atari! We were so bummed because we didn't have power so we couldn't even try it out!"

"That certainly dates the story," chuckled Trevor. "I doubt kids today would even know what an Atari is."

"Could you imagine how mortified Jackson would be if I still had *that* thing?" David asked Grace. "He's embarrassed enough that I have an 'old school' Nintendo."

"It's not old school. It's *vintage*," Sally insisted. "It's all in the semantics, brother dearest. Tell him it's worth more money that way." She gave her older brother a conspiratorial grin, then returned to the topic at hand. "I tell you what, though. That Christmas seemed like a complete disaster, but looking back I'd have to say it was probably my favorite one."

Greg, Mary Anne, and David nodded in agreement. "Certainly the most memorable too!" said Greg as they laughed.

"Who needs more coffee?" asked Mary Anne. "Or how about some Christmas cookies? I'll go make a variety tray so we can nibble on them."

"I'll help," offered Grace, but her mother-in-law stopped her firmly.

"You will do no such thing, young lady. You take it easy. You're pregnant. Your husband is perfectly capable of helping his mother. David, you come with me," she commanded.

"Yes, Mother," he said meekly, rising to follow her as the others chuckled.

Sally turned to Grace as the two left the room and asked, "So are the kids excited about the baby?"

Grace sighed. "Katie and Freddie are excited," she said. "Jackson, who knows? He does like babies, but he'd never admit it. And Faith… Oh, Faith. I don't know what's going on with her, but she's been downright hostile to me about it. She's openly scornful, and the things she says to me are almost hateful! I just don't know what to do about it. Every time I try to talk to her she shuts me out. It really hurts."

"Oh, Grace, I'm so sorry," Sally replied, reaching over to squeeze Grace's hand. "That must be so painful for you. I've had a few ugly confrontations with Amber and Victoria, so I know how frustrating and complicated the mother-daughter relationship can be. I can't even imagine how they'd respond if I found out I was pregnant now."

"Hmm…" mused Trevor with a sly grin.

"Don't you even *think* about it, Trevor Barlowe!" commanded Sally. "There is no way on God's green earth I want to have another baby now! And neither do you. You wouldn't want to take the chance that we'd have a boy."

"This is true," conceded her husband with a shudder.

"You remember Trevor's full name, don't you, Grace?" asked Sally.

"I know it's pretty laborious," said Grace.

"Trevor Alexander Barlowe III," Trevor informed her. "Who wants to pass that along to a son?"

Grace laughed. "I'm with you. But I'm hoping this weekend will do Faith some good," she continued, addressing Sally. "She loves spending time with your girls. Maybe if they're excited about the baby, it'll rub off on Faith."

"I'll talk to Victoria on the side," Sally promised. "But Faith is probably just embarrassed. You know how it is for teenagers. They don't want to think their parents even have the word 'romance' in their vocabulary. She's probably still getting over having newlyweds for parents, and now this. Give her time. I think she'll come around."

"That's what my sister said too. I hope you're both right. Faith and I have had such a close relationship in the past, though, so her meanness now especially hurts. I just wish she'd be happy for us."

Mary Anne bustled back into the room just then with a tray of cookies, David following behind with another tray, and Jackson and Freddie following him. Grace chuckled. "You're like the Pied Piper!" she exclaimed. "They'll follow you anywhere as long as you have cookies!"

The adults laughed, and Greg went upstairs to invite the girls down as well. The rest of the evening passed amicably as everyone chatted and munched on cookies. When Katie started to rub her eyes, Sally and Trevor stood.

"We'd better get to the hotel," said Trevor. "We didn't even check in yet. Faith, you have your suitcase?"

"Yeah, right there by the front closet."

"Then let's get going. We have our annual Monopoly marathon tomorrow. We need our rest."

"In case the continental breakfast isn't sufficient, I'll have muffins and cinnamon rolls here in the morning too," Mary Anne offered.

"You had me at 'cinnamon rolls,'" Trevor said, patting his ample stomach. "I'll definitely save room for a couple of those!"

The Barlowes made their exit with Faith, and Grace was glad to see her daughter conversing easily with her step-cousins. She could almost believe Faith was back to her normal self again. If only that would last.

CHAPTER

16

When the Barlowes arrived back the next morning, the adults were all in jovial moods. Grace noted that the girls looked exhausted. They must have stayed up until the wee hours of the morning.

"All right, guys! Let's get started!" said David excitedly, rubbing his hands together. "We have everything set up in the living room. Let's go!"

"I thought you said we could have cinnamon rolls," Trevor complained. "All I had at the hotel was a cup of weak coffee and some yogurt."

"Ah, yes!" Mary Anne exclaimed. "Let's bring those out here. Amber, dear, come help me in the kitchen, will you? Go on in. I'll be right there as soon as I hang up this coat."

Amber turned to do what her grandmother requested, and a moment later she let out an excited squeal, followed by a small commotion in the kitchen. Grace exchanged a knowing look with Sally. Soon thereafter, Amber came back out, her face lit up in a huge smile. Justin McNeal was with her, holding her hand and sporting a smile that was big enough to rival hers.

"Look who I found!" she chirped happily. "He drove over to surprise me!" She gave Justin a dazzling smile.

"Ah, Justin! Good to see you again!" exclaimed Trevor, extending his hand for Justin to shake.

Sally hugged him in welcome. "I think she liked the surprise," she said cheerfully. "We're so excited to go to your house on Monday! It'll be lovely to see your parents again, and to see David's 'new' house." They hadn't been to Grace's house since David had moved in after the wedding.

"You came all the way over here for *her?*" Jackson asked.

"Jackson!" exclaimed Grace, embarrassed by her son's tactlessness. "How rude!"

"Well, no, I mean, she's going to his house in, like, three days. What's the point?"

"Someday you'll understand, kiddo," Justin told his younger cousin with a grin. "So are we playing Monopoly or what?"

There was a flurry of activity as everyone found seats and argued good-naturedly over which pawn to use. The six adults played one game, and the six older kids played another. Katie was the floater, on Grace's team when she was at their table, and on Faith's team while at the kids' table. When she got bored, she left to go play elsewhere.

The day passed quickly with friendly banter, cheers, groans, and laughter all around. From Grace's position at the adult game, she could see Faith at the other table, and she noticed her daughter studying Amber and Justin as they interacted. Grace couldn't read the expression in Faith's eyes, but she rather suspected Faith was a bit jealous at how happy they were together. She still wasn't the same after breaking up with Spencer and seemed more emotional than she ought to be, given the fact that more than a month had passed. Grace personally thought Faith should be over it by now, but she would never dare voice that to her eldest child.

The group paused for snacks and meals during the day, but otherwise played straight until eleven. At that point, everyone counted money and properties, and the winners were announced. Greg won the adult game, and Victoria narrowly beat Jackson in the other game. Jackson, predictably, was upset and vowed he'd never play this stupid game again. He always seemed to lose by a few hundred dollars, continually wounding his pride.

"Okay, everyone, let's get out the munchies as we get ready to watch the ball drop," Mary Anne instructed. "Girls, come on in here with me to bring stuff out."

Amber, Victoria, and Faith went in to help bring out bowls of chips and Chex mix, plus plates of crackers and cheese, cookies, and veggies.

"Remember the year Mom let us toast the New Year with sparkling grape juice?" Sally asked David with a twinkle in her eye.

"How could we forget?" asked Greg dryly. "Wasn't exactly the way we thought we'd ring in the New Year."

"What happened?" Trevor prompted.

"David dropped his glass and spilled juice all over the carpet," Sally said. "About a minute and a half before the ball dropped."

"So instead of kissing my wife to usher in the New Year, we found ourselves desperately blotting up purple juice from the beige carpet at midnight," Greg said.

"Hey, I couldn't help it!" insisted David.

"Oh, yes you could!" Sally contradicted. "You were showing off, trying to balance your glass on the palm of your hand. It was bound to happen!"

Everyone laughed, and David said, "Well, I promise not to

do anything like that tonight. I'd much rather kiss my wife than clean up a spill." He glanced at Grace, who nodded in agreement.

"So, let's do our year in review," Greg suggested. "Think back over the past year to see what events we can recall from each month. Start with January—go!"

"My birthday!" exclaimed Katie. Grace had allowed her to stay up until the New Year for the first time, and Grace could tell she was trying very hard not to show how tired she was.

"No, it has to be something *important*," Jackson inserted. "That doesn't count."

"It certainly does!" Greg defended quickly. "A birthday is a very important event indeed!"

Jackson snorted. "Then I guess for February I can say my basketball tournament. I scored more than half the points for our team."

The family continued through the year, chiming in as they recalled events. For June, Sally offered, "Amber's high school graduation! She graduated with honors!" Her eyes shone with motherly pride.

"Justin did too," bragged Grace.

"And Jason at least graduated," said Justin with a grin.

Grace and David laughed. Jason was not known for good grades. He thought the sole purpose of high school was socializing.

"And of course, the highlight of my year was our wedding at the end of June," David said.

"Ditto that!" said Grace. "And then our honeymoon at the beginning of July."

When they got to October, Jackson spoke up. "If Katie got to say her birthday, I get to say mine for October," he insisted. "Oh, and Homecoming too. It was the same weekend as my party."

He said this with a cruel smile at Faith. Grace knew it reminded her of going to the dance with Spencer. Faith turned red and glowered at her younger brother, who simply grinned at her. It was probably his own way of getting back at her for the gift of the math flashcards, which still sat unopened in their box.

"November was definitely the U of M game." David spoke up before Faith could respond. "They won in overtime! We sure got our money's worth on that one, right, Jackson?"

"Totally! I hope you get me tickets to another game for my birthday next year!"

"November was also Thanksgiving," said Sally. "We got to host Justin and Jason at our place."

"That was wonderful," Justin agreed.

"Yes, and the Lions had a meltdown in their Thanksgiving game," Trevor pointed out smugly to David. Having grown up in Wisconsin, he was a staunch Green Bay Packers fan and had no use whatsoever for the Detroit Lions.

"Thanks for the reminder," said David indignantly. "These are supposed to be *good* memories, you know."

"December would be David and Grace's exciting news," Sally laughed, getting the conversation back on track, "as well as this whole day. Just being together is a gift in and of itself."

"Hear, hear!" Greg seconded. "And with that, it's time to get our glasses for a toast. I hope no one expects champagne tonight. I personally can't stand the stuff. So we have a nice bottle of white wine for the adults and some sparkling *white* grape juice for our underage friends. I don't want any more purple stains on this carpet."

Everyone hastened to get their glasses ready. The ball drop was only four minutes away. As the clock ticked down, all eyes were on the TV as they reported live from Times Square. At last, everyone chimed in with the final countdown.

"...Three, two, one! Happy New Year!"

Each of the couples kissed, and then everyone clinked glasses for a toast, full of hope and expectation for the coming year.

"This will be another eventful year, I'm sure," Grace murmured to David as she linked arms with him. "Especially with the baby coming. You sure you're ready for this?"

"Do we have a choice?" he asked, his eyes teasing. She chuckled, and he continued. "I don't know what this year will hold, Grace Neunaber, but I know we'll be facing it together, and that's all that matters."

CHAPTER

17

Grace lay on the bed, exhausted. It was only nine o'clock, but she felt like it was midnight.

David entered the room and asked, "Are you going to bed already?"

"I think I'd better," she replied with a yawn. "This weekend wore me out."

Katie's sixth birthday party had been more difficult than Grace had anticipated. Cleaning the house, planning the menu, baking the cake, and organizing the gifts had been inordinately harder than usual. Her energy level was next to nothing thanks to the pregnancy. While she'd never been one to get morning sickness, the first trimester was always difficult because she felt lethargic throughout.

"I know," said David apologetically. "I was afraid of that. We should have taken Olivia up on her offer to host it at her place." He walked to the bed as he spoke and sat down next to her.

"True. But she just had Christmas. I didn't think it would be fair."

"Well, she gets Easter. No question about that."

"Definitely."

"Hey, any word on your grandma?" he asked gently, taking her hand in his.

"Nothing new. It's just a matter of time. She was sick at Christmas, but now that she has pneumonia…" Grace's voice caught, and she swallowed hard. "Mom called her brother and sister to come say their goodbyes."

"I'm glad we were able to see her before she got sick."

"Me too. I'm not about to expose myself or the kids to pneumonia. But it was special to spend that one last time with her."

"It was," David agreed.

The two lapsed into silence until Grace sighed and said, "I'm worried about Gram."

David's brow furrowed slightly. "That's natural with her being so sick and all…"

"No, that's not what I mean. I… I'm worried about her spiritually. She doesn't even know who Jesus is anymore," she said. "She's been a Christian her entire life, but now she can't even understand that Jesus is her Savior. Will she still go to heaven?" She looked at her husband, her vision blurred with tears as she waited for him to answer.

"Does our faith rest upon our own reason and strength, or does it rest upon God's grace and mercy?" David prodded gently.

"On God."

"That's right. Remember when you discussed the Third Article of the Creed in adult instruction class? About how the Holy Spirit calls us to faith?"

Grace nodded. She and Faith had taken the class two and a half years ago shortly after they'd become Christians, and

Pastor Lixon had instructed them in what Lutherans believe and why.

David continued. "It's never because of our own *reason* that we come to the faith or remain in it. The Holy Spirit calls us into the faith, and He *keeps* us in that faith. He does so for the entire Christian Church on earth. Your grandmother is part of that Church, even when she's not aware of it. Think of it like this. If you were to die in your sleep, say, would you go to heaven?"

"Of course."

"Yet when you're sleeping you're not actively aware of your faith, either, right?"

Grace had never considered that before. "Good point."

"And what about our baby?"

"What *about* our baby?" she asked.

"Are we going to have him or her baptized?"

"Absolutely!"

"Why? That baby won't be able to comprehend faith for some time."

"Because we believe God works faith in their hearts through baptism."

"Exactly. Babies are born sinful and therefore need the promises God offers through baptism. But even so, they aren't aware of that faith at such a young age. It's purely based on God's grace and promises. If God can work faith in a newborn, He can certainly hold one of His aged saints in her faith at life's end."

"That's true," whispered Grace. "Thanks, David. I feel like I have so much yet to learn. I don't want you to think I'm stupid, asking you questions like this."

"I don't think you're stupid," he assured her. "I'm glad to answer your questions. Learning is a lifelong thing. Even after years in a parochial school and college, I still have a lot to learn when it comes to the Bible. You're doing remarkably well, especially for someone who didn't grow up Christian."

Grace smiled at the compliment. Her husband was too kind. "Then it's a good thing this little one will grow up in a Christian household, isn't it?" She patted her stomach as she said this.

"Oh, man, I totally forgot to ask. How did your appointment go?"

"Oh, *that*," she said dejectedly.

David looked at her in alarm. "Is everything okay?"

"Yeah, physically. I mean, the baby's fine. I heard the heartbeat today and everything."

"That's great! I can't wait to hear it myself!" he encouraged. "But...?"

She sighed. "I just feel so... *old* this time around. Faith is right. I'm too old to be having a baby."

"Grace, women have babies well into their forties. You're hardly old."

"Maybe. But my OB told me today that I'm considered 'high risk' because of my age."

"Are you serious?"

"Oh, yes. If you're over thirty-five, it's considered advanced maternal age."

"That's the most ridiculous thing I've ever heard!"

"I know." Grace had been humiliated when her doctor had explained the concept of advanced maternal age. She already felt keenly the age difference between herself and the other mothers in the waiting room, most of them in their twenties.

"David, I'm the oldest mother there," she said. "Even my OB is younger than I am. I like Dr. Langston well enough, but I miss Dr. Stafford. I had him for all my other kids, but he retired a few years ago. I know *he* wouldn't have tried to talk me into a special three-hour-long ultrasound for high risk pregnancies."

David's eyebrows shot up. "What exactly would be the point of that?"

"To find potential problems, I guess."

"And my question still stands."

Grace rolled her eyes. Her husband was clueless sometimes. "What do you think? So if there's something wrong, we can 'decide accordingly.'"

David sucked in a gasp. "So that's standard procedure?"

"Apparently so. I said I had no interest whatsoever in this special 3D ultrasound. A plain old black and white one will be just fine. I told her even if there's something terribly wrong, we're keeping the baby. Period."

"Good for you."

"But she's right about one thing. I *am* old. I feel it, David. This time around is much harder than any of the others. I feel drained. Spent. I get tired so much faster, and I'm already starting to pudge out. I'm officially calling this my 'Sarah' pregnancy. I can't even imagine how that poor woman managed a pregnancy at ninety! That would be like Gram having a baby!"

"Well, I'm not an entire decade older than you, so I won't call myself Abraham just yet," David teased. "Besides, to me you're still a spring chicken. I robbed the cradle when I married you."

She laughed. She'd known couples with more than six years separating them. "That's true. If I'm advanced maternal age, you're practically ancient!"

"Then we make a good pair," he smiled.

"Yes, we do," she said. "And there's no one I'd rather be geriatric with than you."

FAITH ALONE

CHAPTER

18

Faith was in her room when her mother knocked on the door. "Faith? Can I come in?"

She groaned. *Great.* Her mom probably wanted to try another heart-to-heart. Grace was still after her to be excited about the baby, but Faith was tired of it. She was sick of hearing her mother gush on and on and give David those sappy looks. It was embarrassing to have newlyweds for parents. They were so lovey-dovey. And now word was getting out at church, which meant everyone there was excited and congratulating them too, making it even worse. Her mom was acting just like a giddy teenager, and Faith wanted none of it.

"Yeah, Mom, whatever. Come in."

As Grace entered, Faith could see she'd been crying. *Even better.* That was another thing. Grace was so emotional lately that practically anything set her off. It was getting old. Her mom drew in a ragged breath and sat down on Katie's bed. "Gram died," she said simply.

Instantly, Faith felt ashamed. She should have known. They'd all been awaiting word since she'd been placed on

143

hospice a week and a half ago. "Oh, Mom…" For a moment, she dropped her hostility. "I'm sorry. She was so sweet. I'll miss her. I've been visiting her every Saturday."

Grace looked surprised. "You have? I had no idea!"

"I didn't want everyone to know. I wasn't doing it to look good. But remember back when she fell and broke her hip and you made me come to the hospital with you?"

Her face warmed even as she asked. Neither of them was likely to forget. That had been the weekend she'd snuck out of the house to meet a boy, and her mother had taken her to the hospital when Gram was admitted.

"I started to realize something then," Faith continued. "I like old people." She cringed at her choice of wording and hurried on. "No, what I mean is that I like spending time with them. Working with them. Their slower pace doesn't bother me. I kinda like it, actually. They're so… patient. Totally not like kids my age. Old people take the time to listen to you without checking their phones every ten seconds, and they're really interesting if you give them a chance."

Her mom studied her but didn't say anything, which made Faith feel the need to explain herself further. "Gramps and I talked about his childhood when we were at the hospital, and it was really neat. He told me what it was like in America during World War II. It was like reading a history book that was actually interesting. So after Gram went to the nursing home, I started visiting her there and talking to some of the other residents. I think maybe I might want to go into geriatrics someday. I'd like to work with elderly people."

She could see by the look on Grace's face that her mother was impressed. Faith hadn't mentioned any of this before.

"Sweetie, that's wonderful!" enthused her mom. "I think you'd be great at that. You were so good with Gramps at the hospital that day. I was proud of you. Why didn't you tell me you were still visiting Gram? I thought you were going to Chelsea's to study and do homework."

"I don't know… I was self-conscious about it, I guess. I didn't want it to be a big deal."

"Well, it *is* a big deal. I'm so proud of you, Faith. You've always had such a tender heart."

Faith grimaced. Lately she hadn't had a tender heart toward her mother, that's for sure. "So when is the funeral?" she asked, changing the subject.

"Thursday at eleven. It'll be at the funeral home since Gram doesn't really have a home church anymore. Her old one is too far away, and she's been in the nursing home the last few years. But Pastor Kleinschmidt from Andy and Olivia's congregation has been visiting her on a regular basis, so he'll do the funeral."

"So I'll have to get out of school?"

"Yes. I'll have David arrange things with the teachers for Freddie and Katie, and I'll contact Jackson's school tomorrow, but I'll just write a note for you and trust you to get the assignments you'll miss. We'll pick you up at ten fifteen. After the funeral, Uncle Doug wants to take us all out for lunch, so you could probably still make it back for a couple hours in the afternoon."

"Okay. I can arrange that."

"Thanks."

Her mother rose and walked over to kiss her on top of the head, then quickly let herself out of the room. It was as if she feared her daughter would snap at her if she lingered there too long. Faith's shoulders sagged as she realized with a twinge of guilt that that was the best exchange she'd had with her mom since Christmas. And it had only taken a funeral to get to this point.

***

The funeral home had a solemn and dignified atmosphere. Quiet organ music piped in through the speakers as the family assembled before the funeral. Carol stood staunchly by the coffin with her husband, her eyes red from crying. Grace knew she still blamed herself for Edna's demise. Edna and Erwin had moved in with them when Edna's dementia became apparent, and the poor woman had snuck out the house one morning for a walk only to fall and break her hip. She'd never returned home after that.

Carol's siblings and their families were in town for the funeral, a somber occasion for a family reunion. The only ones not able to attend were the McNeal twins. It was too much for them to make the eight-hour trip in winter weather for a single day.

As eleven o'clock approached, the family shuffled into the folding chairs set up in the chapel. Grace watched her mother carefully. Carol had grown up Christian in Edna and Erwin's household, but had left the church when she'd married Dennis Williams right out of high school. Pastor Kleinschmidt was aware of the situation and would preach accordingly. Grace hoped her mother would really listen.

The service began with the singing of "I Am Jesus' Little Lamb." The parlor organ with its awful tremolo was a far cry from the beautiful pipe organ at St. John, but as their tiny congregation sang the hymn with strong voices, Grace choked up. She couldn't even finish the last verse.

... And when my short life is ended, By His angel host attended, He shall fold me to His breast, There within His arms to rest.

Edna was resting in her Savior's arms now. Grace couldn't

even imagine the joy of being in heaven.

After the Bible readings and another hymn, Pastor Kleinschmidt took his place at the podium for the sermon. He said a brief prayer and began.

"If someone asked you who Edna was, what would you tell them? I suppose that depends on your perspective. I've only known Edna for a year and a half out of her ninety-two years on this earth. I've only seen her in the context of a nursing home, battling dementia. Although I came to see her on a regular basis, she didn't remember me from one visit to the next. Nor did she remember her own family by the end. Alzheimer's is a cruel disease that attacks the mind. But that disease didn't define Edna's whole life. So again I pose the question: if someone asked you who Edna was, what would you say?"

He paused momentarily, as if to allow family members time to formulate their own answers. Grace thought of Gram as she'd been years ago, before her sickness and before she'd been confined to bed. *That's* the way she wanted to remember Gram, as a sweet, soft-spoken lady with a constant smile on her face.

Pastor continued. "Erwin, you would undoubtedly label Edna as 'devoted wife.' You remember her as your young bride, excited to begin your life together as you worked on your orchards and raised your family. Doug, Carol, and Lou, you may answer that she was a 'loving mother.' You recall the way she read to you, sang to you, cooked for you, and taught you as you grew up. Edna's grandchildren and great-grandchildren may call her 'Grandma' or 'Gram.' They may remember how she baked sugar cookies for them whenever they came over, the hugs she gave them, and how she kept a jar of coffee-flavored candy in the kitchen for visitors."

Grace laughed even as tears sprang to her eyes. She exchanged a small smile with Olivia, remembering how much she'd loved sneaking a piece of that candy whenever she could.

"Perhaps the nurses who worked with Edna in the nursing home thought of her only as a patient. Maybe her medical charts defined her simply as an elderly hip fracture patient suffering from Alzheimer's. But any and all of these descriptions are incomplete. In the end, they don't matter. For you see, she had a far more important label: *daughter*.

"Now, don't get me wrong. I'm not talking about her relationship to her earthly parents, as meaningful as that relationship was. I'm talking about the fact that God called Edna to be His own daughter. She was His. The very God of the universe loved Edna so much that He sent His Son to live a perfect life for her, to die an innocent death for her, and to rise again for her, all so that she could be His precious child. As we just sang in our sermon hymn, she was one of the 'Children of the Heavenly Father.' 1 John 3:1 says it like this: 'See what kind of love the Father has given to us, that we should be called children of God; and so we are.'

"The apostle John further drives home that point in John 1:12-13. 'But to all who did receive him, who believed in his name, he gave the right to become children of God, who were born, not of blood nor of the will of the flesh nor of the will of man, but of God.' Edna did 'believe in his name.' She believed that her Savior had taken her sins upon Himself by His grace."

Grace snuck a glance at her mother. She seemed to be attentive, which was a good sign. She needed to hear this Gospel message.

"Every one of us here needs God's grace. There isn't a soul alive on this earth that doesn't. Edna was sweet and kind and loving, yes, but that didn't earn her a spot in heaven. She knew she was sinful. We all are. And as such, none of us deserves heaven. We can never get there on our own merit. Edna knew that, but she also believed that her Savior had already won eternity for her on the cross and by the empty tomb. She had the faith Peter talks about in today's epistle, where he says, 'Though you have not seen him, you love him. Though you do not now see him, you believe in him...'

"Dear family, I have good news for you. Edna *has* now seen Him. She is experiencing the 'inexpressible joy' of which Peter speaks, for she is obtaining the outcome of her faith, the salvation of her soul. Edna is even now beholding her risen and glorified Savior, who died to remove her every sin. She no longer needs faith, because she sees Jesus with her own eyes."

The tears that had been swimming in her eyes spilled over as Grace thought of Gram in heaven, worshipping her Savior. There was no greater comfort to be offered a grieving family than the assurance of salvation.

"Someday, all of us will die. We will face our Maker. Those of us who believe in Jesus will be welcomed into heaven with Him. We will see Edna again, her mind fully restored. I pray that each of us will one day be there together. We all have many titles that describe who we are—spouse, parent, student, worker, and so on. But on our final day, God grant that we may be welcomed by Him as His own son or daughter into our eternal dwelling. Amen."

Although almost everyone was wiping away tears, Grace noticed that both Carol and Faith seemed particularly moved by the message. As Pastor Kleinschmidt led them in the prayers, Grace prayed silently that her mother would take the message to heart. Funerals were a particularly good time to witness, since the mourners were there desperately seeking hope and comfort. If only Carol would come to know that hope and comfort in Jesus.

The ceremony closed with the hymn "Abide With Me," and the family sang together, their voices wavering as they reached the final verse.

Hold Thou Thy cross before my closing eyes;
Shine through the gloom, and point me to the skies.
Heaven's morning breaks, and earth's vain shadows flee;
In life, in death, O Lord, abide with me.

The funeral over, the family filed out to the lobby. Grace gave her mother a hug, and Carol leaned on her shoulder, quiet sobs racking her body.

"It's okay, Mom. Gram's with Jesus now," she whispered.

"I know," Carol said, her voice breaking.

Grace's heart skipped a beat. She wasn't sure what her mother meant by the affirmation, but at the very least, it was promising. Her mom wasn't completely scoffing at the message of the Gospel. She closed her eyes as she hugged her mother fiercely, praying that in time Carol would also bear the label of *daughter.*

CHAPTER

19

Faith groaned as she saw Aaron lingering around after the Sunday morning Youth Bible Class. She knew he was waiting for her. Since he'd jumped in on the solo at Christmas, the two of them had been on more friendly terms. He really was a nice guy. Not the best-looking kid in the world, but he had a good heart, and Faith was perceptive enough to discern that.

After the January Youth Group meeting last Sunday afternoon, he'd walked her back to her house half a block away, a fact that did not escape the notice of her mother. Grace had seemed a little too excited when Aaron delivered Faith to the door, and Faith didn't want to give her mom any more ideas. Nor did she want to encourage *him*. While she considered him a friend and liked him as such, she wasn't interested in him in any other way. If only she could find a way to communicate that to him.

"Hey, Faith," he said eagerly as she approached. "Good discussion today, huh?"

"Yes, it was," she replied. "Revelation is so confusing to me. It's neat to hear it explained in a way that makes sense. It's not as scary as I used to think it was."

"And it's nothing like the Judgment Day movies and books out there."

"I know, right? And that's a good thing. I wouldn't want to be left behind."

They chuckled together before he asked, "Do you still want to sing a duet for Lent? I was looking through the hymnal and have a few I think would be good. Maybe we can get together sometime to run through some stuff and see if it would work?" He looked hopeful.

Faith cringed. She shouldn't have made that offer on Christmas Eve. She'd been giddy with the spirit of the season, but now she wished she hadn't been so jubilant. Still, she didn't want to make him feel bad, so she forced a smile. "Maybe," she hedged.

"Great!" Apparently ambiguity was as good as an affirmative answer for him. "My dad has a finance meeting here on Thursday evening. I know Lent is still a month away, but we can at least run through some stuff now. That month will go fast. I can come with my dad and pick you up? I know enough piano to at least play our parts."

"I'll meet you here. You don't have to go to the trouble to come get me," she assured him hastily. Good grief, the last thing she needed was for him to come fetch her like this was a date. She'd never hear the end of it.

"It's no problem. The meeting is at seven. Dad usually gets here about ten minutes early."

"Tell you what—if I'm not here when you guys arrive, you can come get me. Deal?"

"Deal," he grinned, obviously relieved. "See you at school."

She waved a goodbye as he hurried upstairs, and Faith shook her head. She'd come at six thirty if she had to. There was no way she was going to let him pick her up.

When Thursday came, Faith was ready. She told her mom she was going to practice Lenten music at church, and thankfully Grace hadn't questioned her too much about it. She must have assumed Faith was meeting with Mrs. Wilcox. Faith left the house at six twenty-five and got to church just as Aaron and his dad were pulling into the parking lot. Sheesh. Aaron had probably convinced his dad to get there early so he would have an excuse to pick her up.

They greeted each other at the doors as Mr. Sullivan unlocked the church for them. Aaron led the way to the music room, which had a decent piano. Secretly, Faith was relieved. The sanctuary was so big and shadowy at night that she was nervous about going in there. The music room was much more comfortable.

After shrugging off their coats, Aaron grabbed two hymnals from a bookshelf and handed one to Faith. She sat in one of the plastic choir chairs, and he sat next to her, leafing aimlessly through pages as though he needed to occupy his hands. Finally he seemed to gather his courage and shut his hymnal, turning toward her but still looking down.

"Say, I was wondering," he began nervously, and Faith felt the blood drain from her face. He was going to ask her out. She knew it intuitively and closed her eyes.

This is not happening, she thought. *No, Aaron, don't do it.*

He took a deep breath and went on, carefully studying the hymnal cover to avoid looking at her face. "Um, I wondered if maybe you'd… um… like to go to the Valentine's Dance with me."

Aaron waited nervously for her answer, his heart pounding so hard he could feel it in his head. It had taken all of his courage to voice the question, and there was no going back now. Faith remained silent a long moment, and he finally looked at her, his expression almost pleading. When he saw the look on her face he knew the answer. Feeling suddenly very, very foolish, he hurried to fill the awkward void.

"I mean… well… I know I'm probably not really your type, but I know you and Spencer broke up a while ago, and I thought maybe you'd like to… you know, we could… maybe go as friends."

Faith had turned away and was shaking her head. Aaron's face flushed with shame. He shouldn't have asked her. What was he thinking? She was nice, sure, but school and church were different. It was one thing to be friends at church. It was another matter entirely to go to a school dance where everyone would see them together. She was way out of his league, and everyone at school knew it.

At length, Faith drew in a shaky breath and turned to face him again. Aaron was surprised to see a tear on her cheek. "You don't want to go out with me," she whispered, more tears pooling in her brown eyes.

What? Where did that come from? he wondered. He was too dumbfounded to speak, so he just sat there with his mouth slightly open, waiting for her to elaborate.

"Can I trust you? Can you keep a secret?" she asked. Her eyes searched his as though she could find the answer there.

Aaron nodded, still unable to speak.

"Promise you won't tell anyone?"

Another nod.

Now it was Faith's turn to avert her eyes as she stared down at the carpet. "Aaron, I'm pregnant," she whispered, her cheeks turning crimson at the confession.

He felt like the wind had been knocked out of him as he

sank back against the hard plastic chair. He could hardly breathe. And he had no idea what to say. His mind swirled with questions, and many emotions vied for the upper hand. He was at once devastated, angry, embarrassed, confused, and exceedingly sad.

She peeked at him out of the corner of her eye. "Say something," she pleaded in a tiny voice.

"I... I don't... This... Wow. Spencer?" He wanted to kick himself for such an obvious question.

"Mm-hmm." Her cheeks were still aflame.

"Is that why you two broke up?"

"More or less."

Aaron rubbed the back of his neck and tried to make sense of it all. He didn't think much of Spencer to begin with. Too cocky and self-assured. Thought he was God's gift to women. Aaron had never liked the fact that Faith was going out with Spencer. Now knowing what had been going on between the two of them... He was upset and dreadfully disappointed in Faith for making such a dumb decision in the first place, but he was furious with Spencer, who obviously wasn't going to man up and take responsibility for his part. Instead, he was going to leave Faith out in the cold to deal with the problem.

The problem. This thought made Aaron sit up straight. "What are you going to do now?" he asked, almost harshly.

"I don't know," she wailed. "There's no good answer here. I don't want to have an abortion, but Spencer is convinced that's the best option. Mom and David would kill me if they found out I was pregnant. And my mom is pregnant herself, as embarrassing as *that* is. It would totally mess things up if I have a baby now. Maybe Spencer's right. It would probably be best if no one ever found out..." She trailed off, and Aaron's heart started hammering again.

"Faith, listen," he commanded, grabbing her hand in earnest. "Don't do anything rash here. Please don't make any decisions you'll regret later. This is a huge shock, yeah, but you can do this. Look, if you don't want the baby, give it up for adoption. Just please, please, don't get an abortion. Please."

"What do *you* care?" she hissed as she yanked her hand from his grasp. "It's not your baby. It's none of your concern!"

"Faith... " he groaned, but she stopped him coldly.

"Aaron, you told me you can keep a secret. I'm trusting you. Other than Spencer, you're the only person who knows. I didn't even tell Chelsea. I know Spencer won't tell anyone. He told me to take care of it so no one ever finds out. So if anyone *does* find out, I'll know you broke your promise." Her eyes were both accusing him and pleading with him.

Instead of answering, he pulled her into a hug. She was taken aback, but accepted his hug as her tears started anew. Silently they sat there, each lost in thought, the music completely forgotten.

CHAPTER

20

Taking a deep breath for courage, Aaron knocked on the partially open door of David's office. His stomach was in knots, and he felt like he might throw up.

"Come in!" came the invitation from the other side of the door.

Aaron let himself in and asked politely, "Do you have a few minutes, Mr. Neunaber? I'm sorry to bother you, but this is really important."

Faith's stepfather looked surprised to see him but gestured him in and motioned to a chair nonetheless. Shutting the door behind him, Aaron sat down on the very front of the chair. Mr. Neunaber's brow furrowed. Aaron guessed he could tell something was wrong.

"The office looks different since the last time I was in here," he began, evading the topic he'd come to discuss. "Not like I was ever in here because I was in trouble, but I mean when I went to school here the principal was still Mr. Kaiser. He left the summer after I graduated. It looks different with your stuff instead of his." Aaron knew he was babbling, and Mr.

Neunaber was waiting patiently for him to get to the point. He cleared his throat. It was now or never.

"Um, sir, I need to tell you something that I'm not supposed to tell you," he started, then rushed to explain. "Oh, um… what I mean is, I made a promise not to tell anyone. I don't want to break a promise, but I'm afraid something terrible will happen if I don't."

David looked a bit confused, but answered, "Well, son, sometimes we have to break a confidence if we fear the results otherwise. But are you sure you want to tell me? Would you rather talk to Pastor?"

"Oh, no, sir. No, it has to be you."

"Alright then, Aaron. Tell me." The look in his eye had changed to one of slight alarm.

Aaron took a deep breath. "It's about Faith."

He saw Mr. Neunaber clench his jaw, and an expression he couldn't read flitted across his face.

"She's pregnant."

The blood drained from Mr. Neunaber's face, and he quickly stood and turned away, walking to the window as he rubbed his hand over his hair. A sudden thought occurred to Aaron, and his eyes widened in horror as he hastened on, heat flooding his cheeks. "Oh, I mean, I'm not the… It's not my… I, uh, didn't get her pregnant, just so you know. She told me last night. When we came over here to practice music. I… um, well… I asked her out," he admitted sheepishly, embarrassed to confide this to her stepfather. "She told me I wouldn't want her because… Well, she made me promise not to tell anyone, but then she told me she was pregnant. She doesn't want anyone to know. But I'm afraid if I don't tell someone she might do something stupid." He reddened even more at his choice of words. Faith had already crossed that line in his opinion. He was botching this up.

Mr. Neunaber appeared to know what he meant. "You mean you're afraid she'll abort the baby," he said quietly, turning to face him once again.

Aaron nodded in confirmation.

Mr. Neunaber sighed wearily, rubbing his forehead with the tips of his fingers. "Son, you did the right thing coming to me. I'm sure Faith will be mad at you when she finds out, but you did it for her own good, even if she can't see that yet. I'd say the fact that you broke your promise makes you all the more trustworthy in this case. It shows that you *can* be trusted to do the right thing, even when it's difficult. You're a good man, Aaron. And a good friend to Faith."

A wave of relief washed over him at the compliment, and he said, "I hope so, sir. I like her a whole lot." Then he rushed on, aghast that he'd just admitted such a thing out loud. "I know you're probably really mad at her. But be careful with her. I mean… Well, she's already really emotional as it is. Like, sensitive about it or whatever. So I think if you yell at her or… well… Like, if you overreact, maybe she'll rebel against that and do something just to spite you, if you know what I mean. I'm not… I'm not trying to tell you what to do, but I know when my parents come down hard on me, my gut reaction is to fight back and hurt them in return. So I think you… I think Faith needs support now more than punishment," he finished lamely. He kicked himself for bringing it up at all. He knew he stammered when he got nervous.

Fortunately, Mr. Neunaber didn't seem to notice. Instead, he replied, "I'll keep that in mind. Thanks for the perspective." He appeared to be lost in thought, considering what Aaron had said.

Aaron stood to go then. He had nothing more to say. Mr.

Neunaber looked up with a start, as if he'd forgotten Aaron was even there. He walked over to shake Aaron's hand, and as the two locked gazes, a look of understanding passed between them. For a moment it was no longer a principal and an awkward teenager standing there, but two men with a shared secret and a mutual concern for Faith.

"Shouldn't you be in school?" David asked suspiciously as he opened his office door to let him out. It wasn't even three o'clock yet.

Aaron ducked his head. "My last period is study hall. I told the teacher I wasn't feeling well, and she let me leave. I drove over here to be sure to catch you before you left for the day."

"Ah." He smiled slightly. "Good plan."

"Thanks for taking the time to see me, sir. Please tell Faith I didn't break my promise to be mean or tattle on her. And please, do go easy on her. Whatever the circumstances, that's your grandchild she's carrying." He stopped abruptly, then hastily turned to make his escape.

David watched Aaron rush down the hall, as if he couldn't wait to get out of the building. Slowly, he shut the door again and crossed back to his office chair. The numbers he'd been crunching now seemed very insignificant. He felt like his whole world has just been turned upside down. It was a good thing Faith wasn't home yet. His first impulse was to rush over there and give her a piece of his mind. He was furious that she would compromise herself like that, and the possibility that she'd gotten pregnant in their own home made his stomach turn. He'd always been uneasy with Faith dating Spencer anyhow. A boy who would sneak into his girlfriend's room wasn't the kind of guy he could trust.

A crushing sense of guilt enveloped him as he realized he should have addressed that very issue with Faith. He'd let his wife deal with it instead, and he hadn't said so much as one word to Faith about boys and relationships. As her stepfather, shouldn't he have done something? At the very least, he should have talked with Grace to establish some family rules and boundaries for dating. He had vowed to protect his family, but he'd failed to protect Faith in her very first dating relationship. He'd failed *her*.

But he was not going to let her down again. Besides Aaron, he was the only other person who knew of Faith's condition. He had to address the situation before she had a chance to make a rash decision to end the pregnancy, which meant he had to move quickly. Tonight he would tell Grace so they could decide how best to proceed from here.

The very thought of Grace made him break into a clammy sweat. How was he going to break the news to her? How would she react? How should he react?

Sighing, David took off his glasses and closed his eyes as he put his head into his hands. Now he had a pregnant wife *and* a pregnant daughter. Everything had suddenly gotten quite complicated.

David lay on the bed, staring at the ceiling. He knew he had to tell Grace, but he had no idea how to broach the subject. He'd rehearsed a dozen different ways in his mind, but none of them seemed right.

After Aaron had left his office earlier that afternoon, David sat in his chair just staring out the window, his mind racing. He didn't think he should deal with Faith right away, so he'd texted Grace to let her know he had some work to finish up and would be home later. It was a blatant lie, but he didn't trust himself enough to look Faith in the eye knowing what he now knew. He'd timed it so he walked in the door right as the family was sitting down to dinner, trying his best to be pleasant and pretend nothing was wrong.

David was grateful Katie was so talkative, making it that much easier for him to remain silent. He hadn't even dared to glance at Faith the entire meal, but he'd noted that she had three helpings and wondered if Grace noticed too. Grace was constantly hungry in her first trimester, and apparently so was Faith. After dinner, Faith went to bed earlier than usual. The rest of the evening, he'd managed to interact with the other kids and help get them to bed, but now he waited in the room he shared with Grace, a sense of dread enveloping him as he waited for her to finish brushing her teeth.

Just then she entered the room and walked over to flop down next to him on the bed. She flung an arm across his chest and said, "I don't know if I can make it through the first trimester. I am so tired. All. The. Time."

Without thinking, he replied, "No wonder Faith sleeps so much."

Grace quickly pushed herself up on one elbow and gave him a hard look. "What is *that* supposed to mean?" she demanded.

David shut his eyes. He'd stepped in it. Now he had no choice but to tell her, and this was not the way he'd planned to lead into the discussion.

"David?" Her voice sounded desperate.

With a resigned sigh, he pushed himself up to a cross-legged position. Quietly, he admitted, "Faith is pregnant."

Grace's breath caught in her throat. She pushed herself all the way up to a sitting position as well. "David, that is *not* funny," she said harshly.

"I wouldn't joke about this, hon. Aaron Sullivan came to talk to me today after school. Apparently, Faith confided in him, making him promise not to tell anyone. He was really conflicted about it. He didn't want to break her trust, but he's afraid she'll…" His voice faltered, and he cleared his throat to try again. "He's afraid she won't keep the baby if no one else knows about it."

Grace had gone deathly white. David feared she might faint. He scooted over to her side of the bed and swung her around so they were sitting side by side, their legs dangling off the bed. He put his arm around her back to support her in case she did faint. For a long moment neither of them spoke.

Finally, Grace whispered, "What are we going to do?"

David didn't have an answer. "I… I don't know. I just don't know."

"I can't believe she would do this. She should know better! For crying out loud, David, she's only sixteen!" Grace sounded panicked, and her voice had risen an octave.

"You were eighteen when you got pregnant," he reminded her.

"Oh, nice, David. Very nice." Her voice was cold. "Rub salt in a wound, why don't you? The apple doesn't fall far from the tree, right? Like mother, like daughter. Remind me again what a terrible a person I was!"

"No, Grace, that's not what I meant," David cut in hastily. "Hey, look at me." He gently pulled her chin so she was facing him. "Sweetheart, that's *not* what I meant. That came out badly. I'm not blaming you or trying to start a fight. I just meant that right now I think your experiences could be… could… help, I guess," he floundered. "Faith probably feels scared and alone right now. She probably thinks that we'll disown her, and she's afraid of what will happen to her reputation if her classmates find out. You can relate to her in a way I can't. You know the feelings and doubts she's having. And maybe if you share with her your decision and how much you regret it now, it will prevent her from making that same choice."

He held his breath, knowing he was treading on thin ice. Grace had aborted her baby when she'd gotten pregnant at eighteen, and although she knew God had forgiven her, she had a hard time forgiving herself.

There was a long moment of silence while he let Grace digest his words. At last she sagged against him and spoke in a whisper. "You might be right. But I don't know if I can tell her the truth."

He pulled her into a hug from the side, resting his chin on the top of her head. "That's your decision, honey. I won't try to talk you into it if you aren't ready. But one thing is certain: we need to talk to Faith. Sooner than later."

Grace started weeping then, silent tears that made her shoulders shake. "How could she do this? I talked with her about maintaining boundaries! I told her she should never be alone in a room with a boy. Did she learn *nothing* from sneaking Spencer in?" She sucked in a gasp. "Or do you think that's when she got pregnant?"

"That thought crossed my mind too, but I highly doubt it. That was seven months ago. This has to be a much more recent development."

"But do you think she was still sneaking him in, even after she got in trouble?"

"Perhaps."

"David, did she get pregnant *here*? In our own house?"

He sighed. "I don't know, Grace. I suppose it's possible. But at the same time, it doesn't really matter. There's no use speculating on how or where it happened. What's important is how we respond now. Look, I'm upset about this too. Trust me, I was furious when Aaron told me. But Aaron, bless his heart, gave me some perspective. He said when his parents yell at him it makes him want to get even or hurt them back. So if we punish her maybe she'd run out and get an abortion anyhow just to spite us. And no matter the circumstances, that is our grandchild in her womb right now." He stole the line straight from Aaron's mouth.

"I'm so not ready for this," Grace blubbered. "Me, a grandma before forty! What are we going to do? How can I even talk to her about this? She's been so hostile to me lately."

David hesitated to voice his idea, but finally proposed, "What if I had a talk with her?" He was long since overdue. It was high time he step up as the spiritual head of the household.

"You?" Grace pulled away so she could look into his face as she wiped the tears from her own. She sounded incredulous.

"Yeah, well, I... you know... I mean, I'm not exactly an expert at dealing with teenage girls, but I do have a unique perspective. Remember, my mom got pregnant with me at a college party." His face burned just mentioning it. "She didn't even know my birth father. And by all rights, she very easily could have aborted me. She considered it. But she didn't go through with it. And now she's a faithful Christian woman who is secure in the knowledge that her Savior has forgiven her. Her past does not define her. Maybe if I share that with Faith, it might... I don't know... reach her somehow..." He trailed off uncertainly. He probably sounded idiotic to his wife. What did he know, after all, about talking to a teenager about such delicate matters as pregnancy?

Grace reached up to touch his cheek with her palm. "Oh, David," she whispered, tears still glistening in her eyes. "You have no idea how much I love you for making such an offer. The fact that you're willing to talk to Faith to help her out... I hardly know what to say." She kissed him and laid her cheek against his chest, wrapping her arms around his waist before continuing. "I think that may be our best course of action for now. Then once you've talked to her, I can broach the subject with her as well. I don't know if I'll tell her about the abortion, but she knows Bob and I weren't married when she was born. She's aware of the fact that I don't have a spotless reputation myself. Maybe my experiences can help me relate to her too."

"So when do you want me to talk to her?" he asked.

Grace blew out a long breath of air, then replied, "This weekend? Tomorrow? I don't want to put you on the spot or anything, but I don't want her sneaking off and doing something she might live to regret, either. Tomorrow is Saturday. I can take the other kids to the library so you can have privacy to talk to her here."

"Sounds good. In the meantime, let's pray, shall we?"

Grace nodded, and they clasped their hands and bowed their heads in unison to speak to their Heavenly Father.

CHAPTER

21

"Faith? Can I come in?"

David knocked on her door and waited, his heart beating so loudly he could hear it in his ears. He and Grace had prayed together again that morning, and he'd been praying almost nonstop himself, but he was still petrified.

He heard rustling as Faith rolled off her bed. After a few moments, the door opened and she looked out warily. "What do *you* want?" she demanded.

"I just wanted to talk to you for a few minutes, if you don't mind."

She rolled her eyes and opened the door wider. "Fine. Whatever. Let's have a heart-to-heart. Great bonding time to impress Mom, huh?" Her voice dripped with sarcasm.

David took a deep breath and offered another silent petition for patience as he entered the room she shared with Katie. Faith threw herself down on her bed and glared at him as he stood there feeling gangly. As principal, he could stand in front of a room of parents feeling confident and poised, but here in the presence of a hostile teenager, he felt like an awkward adolescent himself.

Uncertainly, he perched on the edge of Katie's bed and tried his best to appear casual. "Hey, I just wanted to ask you what's on your mind. Lately you've seemed kind of distant, and your mom and I are concerned."

She heaved an impatient sigh but didn't answer. David gritted his teeth and tried again. "Is there something bothering you, Faith?"

After an interminable silence, she sat up on her bed and spoke, her voice still hard. "That would be a real feather in your cap, wouldn't it? Find out what's wrong with me. Swoop in like Mom's knight in shining armor. Neither of you have time for me anymore anyhow. What difference does it make to you?" Her voice had risen to a near shout, and she was fighting back tears. "All you ever talk about is that stupid baby. Well, you know what?" Her voice was a full shout now. "I don't even want that baby!"

With that, she turned around and flung herself face down down on her bed, sobs racking her body. David knew she would resent it if he tried to pat her back or offer sympathy, so he simply sat there until her bawling lessened to a whimper. Then he inquired quietly, "Are you talking about our baby or yours?"

Faith went completely still, then ever so slowly sat up to face him. Tears stained her cheeks, and her eyes held an expression of panic. "What did you say?" she hissed.

"You heard me," he returned levelly.

"What are you even talking about?" She tried to scoff at the very idea, but David held his ground.

"We know you're pregnant, Faith. And we want you to know that no matter what, we love you. Nothing can change that. But this does pose some major challenges. We'll be there with you through those challenges, but it'll still be tough on you."

He saw a mixture of emotions flit across her face. Her eyes flashed anger, then fear, shame, and confusion. David was sure he was the last person Faith would have expected to confront her over the matter. Patiently, he waited her out until she whispered fiercely, "He told you. He *promised* not to, but he did anyhow."

"Yes, Faith. Aaron came to me privately to tell me. But he didn't do it because he wanted to hurt you or betray your trust. He did it because he cares about you and about the baby. He wants to make sure you'll be okay—physically and emotionally. He doesn't want you to make any rash decisions on your own."

Faith's cheeks were splotchy red. "What I do with my body is hardly your business."

"Ah, but it's *not* your body. Already that baby has a beating heart. He or she is a real person, not a part of your body."

"Don't go preaching to me! I don't need you giving me a guilt trip!" She glared at him fiercely.

David leaned forward and put his elbows on his knees. "I don't want to preach to you. But I do want to tell you something, and all I ask is that you hear me out, okay? I mean really listen. Will you do that?"

She reluctantly nodded, glaring at him suspiciously out of the corner of her eye.

Taking a deep breath, David plunged in. "My mother got pregnant with me in college. She wasn't married. And the guy who got her pregnant wasn't even her boyfriend. She got drunk at a party and slept with someone she didn't know. In human terms, I was a complete accident."

Faith looked startled. She adored David's mother and thought of her as "Nana." Mary Anne was a strong Christian woman who was heavily involved in her church, and David was certain Faith couldn't picture her doing something like that. Even he found it difficult to reconcile the idea with the woman he knew.

"When she got pregnant, she knew her boyfriend wasn't the father," David continued. "She actually considered abortion, wanting to make it all go away. I was a 'problem' to be solved. But for whatever the reason, she ended up keeping me. She and her boyfriend rushed into a wedding so they could be married when I was born. She told him I was his child." David's attempt at a smile fell flat. He couldn't believe he was sharing this so openly with Faith. Still, he forged ahead with the sordid tale.

"Her husband didn't even know the truth until some years later, when she became a Christian and admitted it to him. He didn't take it well. He went out and had an affair of his own to get back at her, and then he left her anyhow. We lived with my grandparents for a few years while my mom struggled to get back on her feet, and then she met and married my stepfather, and they've had a great marriage. He knows the whole story, and they both know that her past is forgiven in Jesus."

He stopped, and Faith said, "I... I had no idea. That's crazy. I can't even picture your mom getting pregnant like that. She's so... *good* now."

"But that's just it, Faith. We all make mistakes. We all sin. But too often we try to cover up one sin with another sin. Think of what would have happened if she had chosen to abort me. I wouldn't be here now, and in all likelihood your mom would still be raising the four of you by herself. And it's entirely possible that none of you would be Christians, either. Remember, it was mainly to humor me that she even started reading the Bible in the first place."

Faith nodded slowly, obviously considering the implications in her own mind. David went on. "When I found out the truth about my biological father, it threw me for a loop. I felt ashamed, confused, even worthless. So I talked to Pastor about it, and he reminded me of an incredible truth. Even if I was an accident in earthly terms, I was no accident to God. Paul says in Ephesians that God chose us in Christ before the foundation of the world. Think of what that means! Before He even created the world, God knew you would be His someday. He chose you and knew you before He made Adam and Eve. And He chose your baby too, Faith. This baby is no surprise to God."

Tears were spilling down her cheeks now, and she wiped them away impatiently. "It's easy for you to talk like this, you know," she said accusingly. "You're married. People are *happy* that you and Mom are having a baby. I mean, you're both old, but whatever. People are excited for you. They think it's cute and sweet and romantic. But me? I'm a teenager. I'm not married. It's not cute or romantic. It's scandalous. My reputation is shot. I'll be forever labelled as a tramp. I'm sixteen! My baby sister or brother will be the same age as my own baby. How pathetic is that?"

David cautiously rose and walked the few steps across the room to sit next to her on her bed. He pulled her into a hug and let her cry on his shoulder. He didn't know what to say, so he gingerly patted her shoulder and waited for her to speak again. After a few minutes she pulled away and looked at the floor.

"So I guess you and Mom are pretty mad at me, huh?" she asked dully.

"We're still trying to work through our emotions," he admitted, trying to be as diplomatic as possible. "But we love you, and we'll get through this. I know you think right now that this will tarnish your reputation forever, but speaking from an adult perspective I can tell you that's not so. You wouldn't consider my mom to be a 'tramp,' would you? Even knowing how she got pregnant with me?" Faith shook her head, and he continued. "It's amazing what forgiveness can do. God specializes in new beginnings."

She breathed out a mirthless laugh. "Aren't you at all worried that this will reflect badly on you or Mom?"

David hated to admit, even to himself, that she had a point. People *would* talk, and loose lips often did much damage. He *did* worry about what people would say and how they would react when her condition became public knowledge. There were a few on the school board in particular who would be appalled.

Pushing those thoughts aside, he answered, "We can't base our decisions on what other people might think or say. People will gossip. We can't stop them. But don't let your desire for a good reputation trump the desire to do what's right in God's eyes."

Faith nodded, her eyes still focused on the carpet. David gave her another hug and said, "If you ever want to talk, please know that both your mom and I are available anytime. We love you, and we're both proud of you."

With that, he kissed the top of her head and made his exit, closing the door quietly behind him. He wasn't at all sure he had handled the situation properly, but he'd done his best. Now all he could do was wait. And pray.

CHAPTER

22

The five-minute warning bell had just rung when Aaron looked up from his locker to see Faith marching toward him, her eyes flashing. He'd known this was coming. Clearly Mr. Neunaber hadn't wasted any time addressing the situation.

She charged up to him and shoved him in the chest with both hands. He fell back against the lockers, and she leaned close to hiss into his face, "How *dare* you! I told you my secret in confidence, and you *promised* not to tell anyone. You promised, Aaron! And then, just like that, you turned around and told David? Really? Have you no decency at all? You have *no* idea how hurt I am that you betrayed me like that. I thought I could trust you!"

"Faith, I—"

"Don't bother!" she interrupted. "I don't want to hear your lame excuses. Who else are you going to tell, huh, Aaron? Want to tell the Youth Group? All our classmates here? I never should have told you in the first place. That's what I get for thinking you were my friend. Now I know better." Aaron was well aware of the fact that they were drawing attention. He wondered what their classmates thought of the bizarre scene playing out in the school hallway.

Faith lowered her voice even more. "You've put me in a terrible place. My mom and David know I'm pregnant now, and they're giving me the whole, 'We'll get through this—just keep the baby' spiel. So now I'm stuck. Thanks a lot. Thanks for *nothing!*"

Her face was red, but she had managed to keep her voice low enough that other students couldn't hear the exchange. It was obvious she was chewing him out, so people looked at them curiously, but Aaron felt confident no one knew why as they rushed past on their way to class. She spun around on her heel, stomping off to her first class as other students looked away and pretended not to notice. Aaron stared after her forlornly. He had known she'd be mad, but he'd had to do it for her own good. He only hoped that in time she would come to realize that as well.

Grace was waiting for her daughter at the front door when she got home from school. Jackson had basketball practice, and David kept Freddie and Katie after school at St. John, allowing them the novelty of staying with the latchkey kids for their snack. Faith and Grace had the house to themselves.

"We need to talk, young lady," she said firmly, leaving no room for argument. "Come sit on the couch with me."

Faith's eyes held a look of dull resignation as she followed. Grace hadn't seen her daughter since Saturday morning. After the talk with David, Faith had snuck out of the house, presumably calling Chelsea for a ride. When they'd realized Faith was missing, Grace had called Chelsea's mom frantically, and Chelsea admitted she'd dropped her off at the McNeals' house. Grace then called her sister and begged her to keep a close eye on Faith and not to let her go anywhere unsupervised. She knew Olivia was dying of curiosity, but she wasn't ready to explain the situation to her yet.

Plopping down on the couch, Faith leaned her head back against the cushions. She closed her eyes and said, "Go ahead. Yell at me. Tell me what a stupid thing I did and how I messed up everything for everyone. Ground me for a year. Whatever. I don't even care anymore."

Grace studied her daughter's face before responding. She had struggled all weekend with this talk and whether or not to tell Faith about the abortion. Right now, she knew Faith was only looking at the short-term picture. She needed to know that abortion wasn't a quick fix that solved everything in a neat little package. But she was terrified to reveal her secret to her daughter.

"I'm not going to yell at you, Faith. I'm not even going to ground you. I think you're punishing yourself enough as it is. In case you don't remember, you were born before I was married, and I was pregnant with Jackson at my wedding. I'm no poster child for abstinence."

"Sure, but you were in your twenties. You were young back then, but not a teenage mother."

"Yes, but I *was* a teenager when I got pregnant the first time," Grace confessed, her voice just above a whisper. She could barely get the words out.

Faith's head shot up, and she looked at her mom in shock. Grace's pulse raced, but she locked gazes with her daughter and soldiered on. "I was eighteen. Your father and I were in college, living together in an apartment off campus. It was only our freshman year. I thought a baby would mess up my plans for the future, so I had an abortion, thinking it would solve everything. But it didn't, honey. I was such a mess afterward that I quit college anyhow. I couldn't deal with the emotional fallout and the guilt. I don't want you to have to live through that like I did. I've lived with guilt over that decision ever since. That baby would be twenty right now. Maybe in college herself. I've always thought of the baby as a girl. I wonder who she would have been and what she would have looked like. I wonder what talents she would have had, and what her personality would be like. Yes, God has forgiven me, but still I wonder. Every day I think about it. Sweetie, I don't want that for you."

She had silent tears coursing down her cheeks as Faith responded quietly. "Mom, I... I don't even know what to say... Does David know?"

Grace nodded. "I told him before we even started dating. I wanted to be upfront with him from the start. Pastor knows about it as well." A look of surprise flitted across Faith's face, and Grace continued gently. "And I think you should talk to Pastor yourself."

Color flooded Faith's cheeks and she replied hotly, "No way. Never."

Taking Faith's hand, Grace said, "Soon enough it will become obvious anyhow. He will find out whether you tell him or not. I can go with you if you want or you can go alone. But I do want you to talk to him."

Faith started crying. "Oh, Mom, I don't want to do this! Any of it!" Grace reached for her daughter and hugged her fiercely, her heart aching. Faith went on. "Look, I know it was wrong. I knew it then too. But after Homecoming everyone else was doing it. Spencer was on the Homecoming court, and all the others had plans. Some even had rooms reserved and stuff. I didn't want to be a prude. Then once we did it the first time, it wasn't as big a deal the next time. It only happened twice, I swear!"

Grace felt nauseous to hear the details. It was one thing to speculate, but quite another to know for certain when her daughter had decided to give away her chastity. Nor had she realized it had happened more than once. She could have done without knowing that particular detail.

Continuing, Faith said, "But I knew we shouldn't have been sleeping together at all, and before Thanksgiving I told Spencer I didn't want to anymore. That's why he broke up with me. I was crushed, but I didn't realize then that I was pregnant. I mean, we used… Well, you know. We were careful." Grace knew her cheeks matched the color of Faith's. They'd never had such a personal discussion before. "But when I missed my period in December, I started to worry. I'm not always regular, so I hoped it was a fluke. When I still hadn't gotten it by Katie's birthday, I was pretty panicked. So I took a home pregnancy test after her party that Saturday. Two of them, actually, to be sure it wasn't a false positive the first time."

She paused and reached for a tissue on the end table to blow her nose. Softly, Grace said, "Oh, sweetie. You were dealing with all of this alone right when I made the announcement that I was expecting too. No wonder you distanced yourself from me after that." It was far easier to talk about Faith's attitude than to address the intimate things Faith had just revealed.

Faith curled up and put her head in Grace's lap, looking very much like a vulnerable child rather than a young woman who would soon have a baby of her own. Grace stroked her long, silky hair as they both sat in silence for some time.

Finally, Grace asked, "Did you tell Spencer?"

Her daughter closed her eyes, but tears escaped anyway. "Yes, I did," she said in a small voice. "I went to his house a few weeks ago. He was mad. Told me it was my fault and my problem. He said that unless I wanted to ruin my life I should just get rid of the problem."

Anger flared up inside Grace, and she fought the almost overwhelming urge to say a few choice words about Spencer. For him to be so callous and cold upset Grace more than Faith getting pregnant in the first place. She took a few deep breaths and tried to speak calmly. "Do you want me to talk to his parents? Don't you think they ought to know?"

"I don't know, Mom. That would make him even more mad."

Grace didn't really care how mad he got. He needed to take responsibility for his own actions. But she'd deal with that later. Right now she needed to focus on her daughter.

"Sweetie, I know how it feels to think you're madly in love with someone. That's how I felt in college with your father. We thought we knew what true love was, and we'd found it in each other. Like you, I got pregnant out of wedlock. But I've since come to understand something very important. God gives us the gift of physical intimacy, but He wants that to be used within the safe boundaries of marriage. He wants to spare us the pain of what can happen if we abuse that gift outside a lifelong commitment. I know you thought you were in love with Spencer, but from the way he reacted to everything, he obviously didn't love you in return. He was... Well, he was kind of using you. He was attracted to you physically, but beyond that... I'm so sorry, hon. I really am."

Faith moaned, "It's too late for me now anyway. No decent guy would want to think twice about me anymore, knowing I got pregnant in high school."

"Do you think David is a decent guy?"

"Yeah, he is. One of the nicest guys I've ever known."

"Yet he fell in love with me knowing I had an abortion

when I was eighteen, knowing I had you and conceived Jackson before I was married, and knowing I was divorced. That's a lot of strikes against me. But forgiveness goes a long way."

"I guess," sighed Faith. "But I don't want to wait until I'm as old as you to find the right guy."

Grace bit back a smile. She'd be thirty-nine in a few weeks. Apparently that was ancient. "God will send the right person at the right time, Faith. I would have preferred not to have been a single mom for so long, but David was worth the wait. Now, back to the subject at hand. Do I have your word that you won't sneak out and get an abortion?"

Faith sat up and blew her nose again. "Yeah," she mumbled half-heartedly.

Grace turned her daughter's face to look into her eyes. "That hardly puts my mind at ease. Do you promise?"

"Yes, I promise. I'll keep the baby, Mom."

"Good. As for what to do once the baby is born, we'll pray about that and decide later. I don't know if we should look into adoption or not. I do want you to be able to go to college and everything, but I don't want to raise the baby myself. Babies require a lot of work, and I'll have this one by then anyhow."

She patted her stomach, which was already starting to swell. Faith's stomach was still taut and flat, but Grace was on her fifth pregnancy. She was wearing elastic waistbands more often than not even though she was just starting her second trimester.

"Mom, I've been in the baby room at daycare. I know what I'm doing. I can take care of a baby." The dismissive tone in her daughter's voice alarmed Grace. It was similar to the discussion they'd had about dating and marriage a few months ago. Faith seemed to think babies were usually cute and cuddly. There was no way she could possibly fathom the time and energy it would take to raise a child, especially as a single mother.

"Yes, but having your own baby is completely different from watching one for a few hours," she objected. "Your entire schedule will have to revolve around your baby's. I don't want to scare you, but I also don't think you realize how much this is going to change your life, assuming you don't give it up for adoption. This isn't playing house with a sweet little baby."

"Mom, I *know*."

"I don't think you do. Honey, until you experience it for yourself, there's no way to describe to you how much effort is required to care for a newborn. When your baby is up half the night with an ear infection, you'll still have to drag yourself out of bed the next morning to take him to the doctor. No matter how many times you're up during the night, you'll still have to go to school the next day. It will be challenging enough to fit school and homework around a baby. Volleyball next year is out of the question."

The look in Faith's eyes indicated that she hadn't even considered this. "But it will be my senior year!" she protested.

"I know. But you'll have to sacrifice time and a few of the things you love in order to care for this baby. Children are indeed a blessing, but they require so much time it's exhausting, especially as a new mom who's getting woken up every couple hours to feed your baby every night."

"You sound like you want me to give it up for adoption."

Grace paused. *Is that what I want?* She honestly didn't know. "Right now it's still too fresh to decide anything, honey. All I'm saying is that I want you to have a realistic view of what's involved. But in the meantime, there are some more immediate practical issues we need to deal with. First, we need to get you to the OB. I can schedule you an appointment with

Dr. Langston. She's really nice. I think you'll like her." For the first time, Grace was glad Dr. Stafford had retired after all. She knew a teenage girl would be far more comfortable with a female obstetrician.

"Next, think about how you want to handle school," she continued. "In another couple of months you'll start showing, and yes, kids will gossip. If you don't want to go to school and deal with that, we could check into completing your assignments here. Maybe your teachers would be willing to do private tutoring after school. We can inquire about it discreetly."

Grace snuck a glance at Faith to gauge her reaction so far. That was the easy stuff. Now she needed to get more personal, and she wanted to make sure her daughter was up for the discussion. Deciding Faith looked receptive enough, she went on.

"Another thing we need to do is tell the family. If you prefer, I can tell your siblings. They may take it better coming from me than from you. But I want you to tell Grandma and Grandpa and Livy and Andy yourself. They'll be supportive of you. And you should tell Nana and Papa too."

She hesitated before mentioning the last item. She knew she was asking a lot of Faith, but she also knew from personal experience how important this step would be.

"Lastly, you do need to talk to Pastor. Trust me, it'll be uncomfortable, but he won't judge you. He will assure you of God's forgiveness and give solid biblical advice. You can ask him about attending church and taking communion when you start showing. Some people are pretty touchy about stuff like that and might not take kindly to an unwed pregnant teenager at the communion rail, even though you have repented."

Faith's shoulders sagged, but she said in a small voice,

"Okay. I'll talk to him."

"Good enough. Faith, look at me." Faith met her mom's eyes tentatively. "I am very proud of you. I want you to know that. You stood up for your convictions and told Spencer you weren't going to sleep with him anymore. That takes a lot of courage and a lot of character. I know how strong peer pressure is, especially when you're feeling that pressure from your boyfriend. I'm not so old that I don't remember. You were very brave to put a stop to your physical intimacy, and you're very brave now. I couldn't be any prouder of you."

Breathing out a short laugh of astonishment, Faith said, "I sure wasn't expecting that. I figured I'd be grounded for life."

Grace pulled her into a hug and whispered into her hair, "No matter what, I will always love you."

They sat there clinging to each other, while Grace prayed silently for strength for Faith in the months ahead. She was certainly going to need it.

CHAPTER

23

Later that week Faith sat in Pastor Lixon's office, spent from the ordeal of revealing her secret yet again. Her cheeks burned, her eyes were downcast, and her heart heavy. She waited apprehensively to hear how he would respond.

Pastor let a few moments pass before saying, "Faith, thank you for gathering the courage to tell me this. I appreciate your honesty. Now I need to ask you something. Are you truly sorry for your sin, or just sorry you got caught?"

Faith dared to glance at him, a bit taken aback by the directness of the question. "Both, I guess. I really don't want to deal with a baby now, and I think it's unfair. A lot of my classmates are sleeping with their boyfriends, and none of them have gotten pregnant. Why did I have to? But I knew all along that I shouldn't have been messing around. I knew it was wrong, and yes, I'm sorry for that. I wish I could go back and tell him no from the very beginning. I wasted my vir—" She stopped abruptly, her cheeks flaming even more, aghast that she had almost spoken the word out loud to her pastor, of all people.

Pastor's cheeks, likewise, were suspiciously pink. Faith guessed he wasn't entirely comfortable with the topic of discussion, either. "Well, ah…" He cleared his throat and started again. "Let's begin with the first issue. Since you are repentant, I proclaim to you by Christ's authority that you are forgiven. Your sins have been washed white by the blood of the Lamb."

"Thank you," she whispered hoarsely.

"Don't thank me," he said gently. "I'm just the messenger. Thank Jesus for removing your sins from you. Now, I also wanted to address your other concern that you are no longer a… um, that you have already been unchaste." Pastor fiddled with a pen on his desk as he continued. "I don't know if you've heard of this or not, but there is something called secondary chastity. It's basically a vow—a promise—to abstain from now until you get married. Just because you slept with your boyfriend a few times in the past doesn't mean you have to continue that pattern. The vow is a marvelous idea and emphasizes the beauty of the Gospel where God gives us a fresh start. I know a few youth who have done this. Even adults."

Faith nodded, averting her own eyes. "But now what?" she asked. "What should I do in the meantime? About going to church? Communion? Should I even go? I'm sure some people would be offended standing next to an obviously pregnant teenager at the rail." Her mom had made that point, although Faith had a different concern. She didn't so much care if other people were offended, but she cared what they thought of her. She didn't want to see the looks of judgment in their eyes.

"Yes, you're probably right," Pastor conceded. "But it's your decision. It depends on what you're comfortable with. In my mind, you've confessed your sins. You've received absolution.

You have no reason to refrain from the assembly of believers or the communion rail. If you choose to come forward for communion and anyone takes issue with it, I will tell them exactly what I just told you. But if you're uncomfortable, that's understandable too. You could always come to Monday evening services, which are sparsely attended. Or I could give you private communion afterward. It's up to you."

"I'm not sure at this point," she said. "Until I start showing, I'll come with my family like normal. But once people start noticing... I don't know..."

"Cross that bridge when you come to it. I'm fine either way. But you bring up a good point. People *will* find out eventually. You may get nasty looks or comments from classmates, church members, even strangers. That hurts. It won't be easy. But remind yourself that God has forgiven you. Period. When He looks at you, He sees Christ's sinlessness. It's called the Great Exchange. 2 Corinthians 5:21 tells us, 'For our sake he made him to be sin who knew no sin, so that in him we might become the righteousness of God.' You are clean."

Through her tear-filled eyes, Faith smiled at Pastor. "Incredible. What a wonderful God we have."

"Indeed," agreed Pastor, as he stood to usher her out.

Grace was waiting outside Pastor's office, and she rushed forward to hug Faith when she emerged. A look of understanding and peace passed between the two—the confidence of sins forgiven. Grace thanked Pastor and shook his hand, then walked with Faith arm in arm out the door.

CHAPTER

24

Grace took a sip of water to steady her nerves. "Kids, before we leave the table, I have to tell you something," she began. "It's important, and I need you to listen. I don't want to have to explain myself three times." Jackson, Freddie, and Katie slowly quieted down and looked at her as she continued. "You need to know something that is going to be a big surprise. It's about Faith. But before I tell you, I need you to know that this is *not* something you can make fun of her for when she returns from Chelsea's. We're going to be supportive of her and show her we love her. Understand?"

Katie frowned slightly and Freddie's expression was blank. Jackson muttered under his breath, "Boy, she must have done something really stupid."

"Jackson, that is exactly the type of thing I'm talking about," reprimanded Grace. "We don't need you making snide comments. Got it?"

"Got it," he mumbled back.

"Good." Grace fixed her eyes on her water glass as she broke the news. "Faith is pregnant too. She's going to have a baby like I am."

There was dead silence after this announcement, and all three kids stared at Grace, looks of shock on their faces.

At length, Jackson said quietly, "*Told* you she did something really stupid."

Katie scrunched her brow in concentration, trying to make sense of it all. "But how can she have a baby?" she asked in confusion. "She's not married."

"Dummy, you don't have to be married to have a baby," Jackson informed her in a superior voice. "You just have to have—"

"Jackson Robert!" interrupted David loudly. "That is *quite* enough! Your siblings do not need a biology lesson right now!"

Katie was still frowning. "But she doesn't have a daddy!"

"Yeah, she does," Jackson corrected. "We all have a dad. You mean she doesn't have a husband. But her baby still has a daddy. Probably Spencer."

"Jackson!" Grace exclaimed, almost pleading. She wished she'd thought to tell him privately. Turning to Katie, she said, "Sweetie, I know it's confusing. And you're right—people *should* be married before they have a baby, but—"

"*You* weren't," inserted Jackson.

Grace considered strangling her second-born. "No, that's true, Jackson," she said through clenched teeth. "Thank you for pointing that out." She blew out a long breath before continuing. "Faith was born when I wasn't married, and I was pregnant with Jackson before I married your father. Now Faith is in the same boat. Yes, it was wrong of her to get pregnant like this. It was wrong of me too. But I know God has forgiven me, and He has also forgiven Faith. We need to let her know we love her and that we *aren't* going to tease her or make fun of her about this. Right?" She fixed Jackson with a hard stare.

Freddie surprised her by speaking up. "I think it'll be neat. Her baby and your baby can play together. They'll be good friends."

"What a lovely way of looking at things, Freddie!" she exclaimed. "I hadn't even thought of that."

Jackson snorted. "Well, *I* won't go off and do something dumb like that in high school."

"How could you?" Katie asked, genuinely confused now. "Boys can't have babies anyway!"

"No, but I'm not gonna get a girl—"

"*Jackson!*" David and Grace chorused in unison. "That's enough!"

"Well, I won't," he muttered. "Just saying…"

"Okay!" Grace said in an overly cheery voice, ready for the conversation to be over. "Thank you all for listening. Please don't talk to anyone about it unless they mention it to you first. And if anyone tries to make fun of Faith, stick up for her and tell them that she knows Jesus forgives her. Okay?"

Her children nodded at her, and she excused them from the table. David caught Jackson by the arm as he passed and looked him in the eye. "Just so we're clear, young man, you do *not* need to explain the process to Freddie or Katie," he warned in a low voice. "They don't need to hear the details from you. If they have questions, tell them to ask me or your mother. Do I make myself clear?"

"Yeah, okay," mumbled Jackson, averting his eyes.

"Jackson!" David's voice was firm.

"I *get* it. I promise," Jackson said, more convincingly this time as he made eye contact.

"Thank you." He released Jackson's arm so he could slink back to his room, then turned to Grace. "Well?" he asked.

She shook her head in exasperation. "We should have told

Jackson separately," she said. "I mean, really, should we have expected anything else?"

"No," he admitted ruefully. "He responded exactly the way I imagined he would. And I have a feeling we're going to have to have the birds and the bees talk with Freddie and/or Katie before too long."

"I know," Grace said grimly. "I was able to hold off explaining it to Jackson until he was about ten. Wanna know what he said when I was done?" She grinned at the memory. "He said, 'Gross! You had to do that *four times* so you could have us?'"

David burst out laughing, and she smiled. "It still cracks me up too. But I'm glad at least the kids know about Faith," she said, getting the conversation back on track. "Now we have to deal with our families. Faith said she'd call your parents tomorrow. Amber and Victoria too. You can call Sally to let her and Trevor know. And I invited my whole family over for Sunday dinner to clue them in too. I'll be glad when the weekend is over."

"Ditto. And these are the people we *know* will be supportive. Just wait until other people start finding out and aren't as understanding. I shudder to think of what poor Faith will have to face at school and even at church."

"There's also the issue of the Youngs. Should we tell them? I doubt Spencer will tell his parents, but don't you think they should know? Wouldn't we want to know if Jackson fathered a child?"

"Yes," sighed David wearily. "I suppose we would, although he's already assured us that won't be an issue." They both chuckled, and David went on. "But you're right. We'd want to know if that was the case, so I suppose we ought to afford Spencer's parents the same courtesy. I'll give them a call to see if we can set up a time to meet with both of them. Mr. Young is gone quite a bit on business from what I hear, so it would behoove us to make an appointment."

"Thanks, sweetie. I appreciate you doing that. I frankly don't have the guts to call them myself."

"Neither do I. I was just trying to impress you."

He grinned, and she laughed. "What would impress me even more is if you offered to do the dishes tonight," she teased. "Remember, I'm pregnant. I need my rest."

"Well, now I'd look like a jerk if I said no. Very clever of you to trick me into it."

"Mm-hmm," she said sweetly, walking over to give him a kiss. "How thoughtful of you, my love. Thanks for the offer. You're the best." She patted his cheek and scooted away, glad that the conversation with the kids was over. She knew it was incredibly petty, but she was also grateful she'd married a man who knew how to do the dishes.

Sunday found Grace's family over for dinner. Grace had told them beforehand that they needed to discuss something with everyone, so naturally they were all curious. Olivia had been pestering her since she walked in the door, worried that something was wrong with Grace's baby. Although they'd planned to have Faith tell them after dinner, Grace now realized they needed to do it beforehand. She popped in a DVD on David's laptop and sent Jackson, Freddie, and Katie into the master bedroom to watch a movie while the adults talked in the living room.

Olivia and Carol were both concerned as they assembled, and even Andy was unusually quiet. Clearly, everyone could sense something was wrong.

"We may as well get this over with before we eat," Grace

began. "You need to know something, and you need to hear it from us."

Olivia had gone deathly white. "Oh, my gosh, it's the baby, isn't it?" she whispered. "Something's wrong."

Faith surprised Grace by speaking up. "No, Aunt Livy, it's not *their* baby we're talking about. It's mine. I'm pregnant."

All eyes turned to stare at Faith, who was studying her hands in her lap, avoiding eye contact with anyone as she continued. "I know it was a stupid thing to do, and I'm really sorry. I wish I could go back and do everything differently. But I can't, so here I am, pregnant, and I'm trying to make the best of the situation, so, yeah… I guess I wanted to be the one to tell you guys before you hear it from someone else. I'm sorry I disappointed you." She bit her lip and blinked furiously.

For a moment no one spoke, but then Olivia swooped across the room to engulf her niece in a hug. "Oh, sweetie, but you *didn't* disappoint us. You're doing a very brave thing to keep the baby. Thank you for telling us. That was really brave of you too. You just tell us what you need, and we'll help with anything we can. We're behind you one hundred percent."

Faith cried on her aunt's shoulder, and Grace saw Carol wiping her eyes too. Grace silently thanked her sister for the supportive response.

Carol came over to sit next to her granddaughter and give her a hug as well. She whispered something into Faith's ear, and Faith nodded. Walt fidgeted awkwardly, unsure of what to say, and Erwin sat in confusion. His hearing aid needed new batteries, so Carol and Walt would need to explain things to him later.

When Olivia gave up her spot on the floor in front of Faith, Andy came over to pull Faith up. "Come here, kiddo," he said, giving her another hug. "Ditto everything Liv said. Come on down to the pharmacy sometime. I'll hook you up with a good prenatal vitamin."

"Thanks, everyone," sniffled Faith as she wiped her cheeks with the edge of her sleeve. "I'm glad I have such a supportive family."

Perceiving that Faith wanted to end the conversation, Grace broke in. "So am I," she agreed. "But now it's time for dinner. We have two pregnant women here, after all, who are always hungry. Let's eat!"

Everyone chuckled nervously, and Faith excused herself to go to the bathroom to wash her face. David went back to their room to fetch the other kids for supper, and Olivia approached Grace to give her a hug.

"Oh, Gracie," she murmured. "I'm so sorry. I don't even know what to say."

"Me neither," confessed Grace. "We just found out last weekend, so it's still pretty new. I'm starting to accept the fact that she's pregnant, but sometimes I just start to panic. I'm a mess anyhow, with all these pregnancy hormones, so this is almost too much."

"I'm sure," Olivia said, giving her sister's elbow a gentle squeeze. "But I'll bet this is why she was so hostile about your announcement at Christmas. She was suspecting she was pregnant herself, and your news gave her an excuse to lash out at someone."

"Yes, that's true. Poor Faith. This is going to be really tough on her. Physically and emotionally."

"And now last weekend makes perfect sense," continued Olivia. "When Faith showed up at our door and asked if she could stay the weekend, I figured the two of you had a fight. But then when you called frantically and asked me to keep a close eye on her, I was more curious than ever."

"Yeah, that's when we found out, and we were scared she would sneak over to Planned Parenthood," Grace said quietly. "It makes me so mad. She can't even take an aspirin at school without me signing a consent form, but she can waltz in and get an abortion without any parental knowledge whatsoever. How is that fair to anyone involved?"

Just then, Jackson came in the kitchen. "So are we eating or not?" he demanded. "David came to get us, but nothing's on the table!"

"Yes, we are," replied Grace, "and thank you for offering to set the table for me. Here." She handed him the stack of plates and silverware. "When you're done with that, come back in for the glasses."

Mumbling under his breath, Jackson took the dishes to the table while Olivia and Carol helped get the food on. The meal was much more subdued than normal, the adults all contemplative. Katie did most of the talking, even though no one really bothered to listen. Their minds were still on Faith's news.

When everyone left that evening, Grace turned to David with a sigh. "Well, that was tough, but at least it's over."

They exchanged a glance, and he pulled her into a hug. Grace was pretty sure they were both thinking the same thing. Even though the conversation with their families was behind them, the situation was far from over. On the contrary, it had just begun.

CHAPTER

25

"Are you sure it's Spencer's?"

Vivian Young picked an imaginary piece of lint off her silk blouse and asked the question as casually as if they were discussing the weather.

Grace bristled next to David as they sat on the white couch in the Young's lavishly decorated living room. Before she could make a sharp remark, David grabbed her hand and held it firmly, speaking for her.

"Yes. It's Spencer's child. Faith wouldn't lie about this, and he's the only boyfriend she's had."

"Perhaps," Vivian said in a voice that sounded like she was speaking to a hopelessly naïve child, "but they did break up, you know."

"Yes, they did. Because of this," insisted David.

There was a moment of uncomfortable silence as Vivian and Leonard Young exchanged a glance. As distressing as the news had been to Faith's parents, it was obvious the Youngs did not feel the same way.

Leonard spoke with a frown. "I told him to be careful," he

said. "I was afraid this would happen otherwise. We'll need to have a talk with him."

Grace's grip tightened on David's hand. Apparently the Youngs had a very different idea of morality than they did.

"Is she going to keep it?" Vivian asked in a breezy voice.

The Neunabers stared at her in astonishment. "Of course!" they exclaimed in unison.

"Don't you think it would be easier if the problem just went away quietly?" pressed Vivian.

David's hand was losing circulation because Grace was squeezing it so hard, and her nails dug into his skin. He was fighting for control himself. Maybe they shouldn't have come after all.

"You mean to tell me you think she should have an abortion?" he asked in a tight voice.

Vivian sniffed. "It makes more sense than asking a high schooler to have a baby. Besides, I hear you're going to have one yourself before too long. Another baby is hardly the thing you need at this point."

"Abortion is not an option, no matter the circumstances," David said firmly.

"If it's a matter of cost, we'd be more than happy to help you cover it," Leonard said affably, as if offering to buy him a beer at the bar.

Though Leonard Young would probably be more of a single malt whiskey kind of guy, David thought with more than a hint of disdain. Clearly the Youngs believed money could solve any problem.

"Cost has nothing to do with it. This is your *grandchild* we are talking about!" David practically exploded. "As upset as Grace and I are with Faith, she is carrying a *life* in her womb right now, and we would never support ending that life because it would be more 'convenient' to do so!" He sucked in a slow breath and continued in a more level voice. "We came over here because as Spencer's parents you have the right to know. Rather than suggest ways to evade responsibility, I think we should discuss how to make both of them step up and accept the consequences for their actions. I'd say ideally we should split the medical costs, and once the baby is born, Faith will need help with childcare, especially come next school year. She still has a year left of high school. Spencer should be expected to take some responsibility as well."

"Oh, he'll have to answer to us, all right," promised Leonard. "We'll discuss this with him and come up with a plan. And rest assured that we will cover any expenses."

Money again.

David had nothing further to say, so he simply stood, pulling Grace up with him. "Thank you for your time," he said in a voice that sounded robotic even to his own ears. "We will be in touch."

Vivian stood to escort them out as her husband pulled out his phone and started tapping away. At the door, Vivian spoke. "Thank you for stopping by to discuss this with us. We…" Her voice faltered slightly. "I'm sorry this happened in the first place. I'm very disappointed in Spencer, though unfortunately not surprised. I doubt he'll be of much help to Faith, but I'm glad she has supportive parents like you. She needs that." Her eyes registered a fleeting look of sorrow mixed with longing, and then she quickly shut the door, as if fearing she'd said too much.

David took Grace's hand and left. Neither of them spoke the entire ride home. David was deeply saddened by the whole exchange. He did appreciate the Youngs' offer to help with finances, but their flippant attitude about the pregnancy and the baby had shaken him deeply. He suddenly felt quite sorry for Spencer. Despite his privileged lifestyle and opulent surroundings, Spencer Young was rather poor indeed.

Grace couldn't get the conversation with the Youngs out of her mind. When the kids got home from school that afternoon, she wrapped her arms around each of them in turn and simply wept. She knew they thought she was crazy, but humored her and chalked it up to pregnancy hormones. But it was so much more than that. She was deeply grateful for her family. No, they weren't perfect, and yes, they drove each other insane at times, but they all loved and supported each other. There was never a question of that. Plus they were Christians, secure in their faith and in the knowledge of their Savior.

Never would she wish to trade places with Vivian Young. She'd much rather have her cluttered house than Vivian's professionally decorated mini mansion. She'd take the glorious mess that was her own life over Vivian's polished façade any day. The glimpse of the Youngs' family life, albeit a small one, had showed her enough to know for certain that money couldn't buy happiness.

After the kids were down for the night, she curled up on the couch next to David and welcomed his arm around her and his cheek against her head. Both sat quietly for a few moments until he spoke. "You know, back in my day, if I would have gotten a girl pregnant, my parents would have pushed for me to marry her," he mused. "Not that I would have done such a thing in the first place," he hastened to assure her, "but that was the mentality. Frankly, though, I don't *want* Faith to marry Spencer. He's not the kind of guy I'd want taking care of her and supporting our grandchildren. I really don't want him involved in this baby's life at all."

"I think he'd agree with you on that," answered Grace dryly. "I don't think that boy has ever had to accept responsibility for anything in his life. Heaven forbid he start now."

"I got that distinct impression as well. He may be charming and handsome and rich, but his character is sorely lacking."

"Very true. I wish we could go back and do everything again. We should never have let Faith date him in the first place. We both had a bad feeling about it, and now look where we are!"

"If we would have forbid her, she probably would have done it anyhow just to spite us. We can't torture ourselves with 'should haves.'"

"I guess," she said dejectedly. "But now what? We really didn't settle anything with the Youngs today. I assume Spencer will be off to college next year shortly after the baby is born. He won't be around to watch the baby as it is. But should we ask or expect him to come on weekends or anything? I hate the idea of joint custody, because it's so hard on kids to have to split their time like that. But at the same time, I know firsthand how hard it is to be a single mom."

"Honestly? I'm wondering if he could completely sign away any parental rights so if someday he decides he wants to try to get the child back, he couldn't. He wanted Faith to abort the baby anyhow. In my mind, he's already writing himself out of the equation. We may as well keep it that way."

"But what about financial support?"

There was a thoughtful pause as David considered the question. "I'd even maybe say no to that. He could theoretically use it as leverage later to hurt either the baby or Faith, claiming he's better equipped to take care of the child. I don't know that we want to take that chance."

Grace mulled that over in her mind. She knew how

concerned David was about their budget. For him to refuse monetary support when it should be expected was serious business indeed.

"I don't know what I think about that," she answered. "Babies are expensive, and I'm not just talking medical costs. There's also diapers, clothes, equipment, and in Faith's case, formula. I can't see a high schooler keeping up a nursing schedule. And she'll probably need her own car as well. I'll help her watch the baby in a pinch, but I don't want to raise it for her. I think part of taking responsibility on her part should be arranging child care, which is another potential expense. I'm sure Mom and Liv will help out too, but when there are gaps, she may have to do daycare. Maybe they'll give her an employee discount from her summer job," she finished wryly.

David breathed out a laugh. "I hadn't even thought about all that yet," he confessed. "And you make a good point about the car. Maybe the Youngs can throw in a Mustang, and we'll call it even?"

Now it was Grace's turn to chuckle. "Dream on, babe." Then she turned serious again. "This is all just so confusing right now. I'm still trying to process everything. And that exchange with the Youngs didn't go at all how I expected. I guess I assumed they'd be more like-minded. I'm not sure how to proceed from here as far as they're concerned."

"Same here. I'm sort of thinking we just won't do anything for now. I mean, we told them the news. Now if they decide to step up and offer support, we'll take it into consideration at that point. But I think now we should just lay low and not contact them anymore. If we never hear from them again, so be it."

"I'm leaning toward that myself. And if we decide in the future that we *do* want them involved, financially or otherwise, we can always contact them again. This doesn't have to be a one-time permanent decision."

"Agreed." David exhaled a deep, weary sigh. "I honestly never saw this one coming. Any of this."

"Nor I," Grace murmured quietly. "Yet at the same time, as I slowly get used to the idea of Faith being pregnant, something is shifting in my own mentality. When you first told me, I was really mad at her. I was in denial, hoping I'd wake up and find it to be a bad dream. But while we were talking to the Youngs today, I felt a surge of loyalty for the baby."

Had she really just said that? *A surge of loyalty?* What a dumb way to express her emotions. Maybe pregnancy brain was already getting to her. She hastened on. "No, it's so much more than that. I felt fiercely protective of the baby, and hearing the Youngs discuss the pregnancy so callously almost made my heart break. I know we've mentioned the possibility of giving the baby up for adoption, but I can't do it. It's not the way I would have chosen to obtain a grandchild, but I love that little baby already, David!"

David pulled her closer and rested his chin on top of her head. "So do I, sweetheart," he whispered hoarsely. "So do I."

"Faith!"

She turned at the familiar sound of Spencer's voice in the parking lot as she and Chelsea made their way to Chelsea's car.

"Go on," Faith told her. "I'll be right there."

"Good luck," mumbled Chelsea. "He doesn't look happy."

Indeed he did not. Spencer's eyes were hard as he glared at Faith through narrowed eyelids.

"What gives?" he demanded as he reached her in the parking lot. "I thought we discussed this and decided to get an abortion. Now I find out you're keeping the baby *and* your parents came over to talk to mine? Are you kidding me?"

Faith was grateful her mother had told her about the visit beforehand so she wasn't caught off guard now. "No, Spencer. *We* didn't decide anything. You told me to abort. I decided not to."

"Well, great. And you had your parents go tattle to mine like we're back in second grade? My dad took away my car for a month!"

"Oh, no! How will you ever survive?" Faith's voice dripped with sarcasm and scorn. "That's not even a slap on the wrist! I have to carry this baby for nine months, give birth, and then take care of it after that! This is my *life*, Spencer! And *you* can't drive for one whole month? Pathetic!" She fixed him with the most withering look she could muster, half wishing that looks really could kill.

"If it's going to mess up your life so much, why keep it? What will you tell everyone when it becomes obvious? You want everyone to know you sleep around?"

She slapped him across the face so hard that other students walking to their cars glanced over in surprise. "How *dare* you, Spencer Young! I'm ashamed of myself for ever falling for you in the first place. You might be handsome and charming, but beneath that you have *nothing*! No character, no integrity, nothing! You're a stupid, selfish, arrogant, immature, shallow, no-good, rotten *jerk*!" She was yelling by now, and the other students nearby grinned at the scene.

Faith shoved him in the chest for effect, spun around on her heel, and stomped to Chelsea's car. She got in and slammed the door, and Chelsea turned the ignition and started driving. Only after they turned out of the parking lot did Chelsea voice what was on her mind.

"He had it coming," she said with a grin. "Good for you!"

CHAPTER

26

After much inner debate, Faith worked up the nerve to ask Mr. Sanders, the Youth Group leader, if she could have a few minutes after their Sunday morning Bible class. She knew word would eventually get around that she was pregnant, and she'd rather be the one to share it with the high schoolers who went to her church. Maybe she could get them on her side so they wouldn't make fun of her at school when everyone else started finding out.

"Okay, guys," Mr. Sanders announced. "We're gonna call it quits for the day because Faith asked to share something with us all. She's already told me what she wants to say, and I ask that you listen and respond like the young Christians you are. Faith?"

She squirmed as all eyes turned to her, wishing she hadn't been quite so eager to share this after all. Maybe she should have fled to Olivia's church for the duration of her pregnancy where no one knew her. But it was too late. Nine pairs of eyes peered at her curiously, so she plunged in before she lost her nerve.

"I want to tell you guys something that will probably shock you," she began hesitantly. Although she'd rehearsed her little speech hundreds of times in her head, her mind drew a blank now. "It's something that's a taboo subject in the church, and I know a lot of people are going to think a whole lot less of me because of it, but..." She sucked in a breath and looked up. "I'm pregnant."

Aaron Sullivan was sitting across the room, and he nodded at her, his eyes willing her to go on. The other kids sat there with wide eyes, but no one made any snide comments or snickered, which gave her a small boost of confidence.

"I know what I did was wrong. We've talked about it in class before, and I never thought I would give in to that temptation, but... well, obviously I did." She attempted a short laugh before continuing. "But you should know that this could happen to you too. I mean, I didn't plan this. I thought I'd wait until I was married, but abstinence is a lot harder than you might think."

Her face was burning, but she pressed on. "After I found out about the baby, I was really mad. Mad at God for letting this happen. You guys know how many kids are sleeping around, and of all the people, *I'm* the one to get pregnant? It seemed really unfair. And I didn't want this baby at first. I... I actually considered getting an abortion," she confessed in a near whisper, her eyes on the carpet in front of her. "If it wasn't for a good friend, I may have made that mistake too. But my friend told David what was going on, and he and my mom helped me see that abortion wasn't going to solve anything. It would just create more problems and hurt. My mom and stepfather have been really supportive, even with my mom expecting too, and I'm really glad I have such a loving family. And glad to have such a good friend." She peeked covertly at Aaron out of the corner of her eye.

"So I guess I just wanted to tell you guys first before everyone at school finds out. Maybe my example can keep you from making the same mistake. I don't know…" She trailed off, not knowing how to conclude.

Mr. Sanders spoke up before anyone else. "Thank you, Faith, for being so honest with us. It takes a lot of courage to speak up like that about such a personal matter, and I, for one, respect you for taking responsibility for your actions. And we all know that there is no sin too big for God to forgive, right, guys?"

They all nodded, and Bree Robertson came over to sit next to Faith and pulled her into a hug. Faith started crying then. "You're doing the right thing, Faith," she whispered. "Thanks for telling us. If there's anything I can do to help, let me know, okay?"

Faith nodded, unable to respond, and then Mr. Sanders led them in prayer before dismissing the class. Faith breathed a sigh of relief. At least *that* was over.

She turned to grab her Bible before leaving, and was surprised to find Aaron still there. She'd avoided him since he'd told David her news, and it flustered her that he was waiting for her now. They spoke at the same time.

"Aaron—"

"Faith—"

They both laughed, and Aaron said, "Ladies first. Go ahead."

"Well, I… um… I just wanted to… you know…" She shook her head and paused for a moment to envision what she needed to say. "I'm sorry I've been so mean to you this past month. I was really, really mad at you for telling David after you promised you wouldn't, but…" She took a deep breath.

"But I've come to realize that you were being a true friend, looking out for me when I was too blind to think clearly. You know you were the friend I mentioned. I owe you a thank you. And an apology. Truce?"

Aaron broke into a huge grin. "Truce. And I want you to know that I'm really proud of you. Not only for keeping the baby but for being honest with everyone here. That was really brave."

Faith breathed out a disbelieving laugh. "Trust me, I'm not brave at all. I'm scared to death. I'm totally not ready to have a baby at this age. But Mom and David really are supportive, and that counts for a lot. I know Spencer won't be. He's mad I didn't get an abortion."

"Yeah, I figured as much. I heard about your fight in the parking lot. You slapped him pretty hard, huh?"

"Oh, man. If you know, *everyone* must know," she groaned.

He laughed. "Hey, it's not every day Spencer gets slapped by a girl. That's big news for sure. It was all over social media within three minutes. I think a lot of people were secretly jealous of you."

Now it was her turn to laugh. "As bad as it sounds to say it out loud, it *did* give me immense satisfaction."

He chuckled and reached for her Bible. "You guys were in the early service today too. Let me walk you home."

Faith was slightly embarrassed but didn't protest. Aaron really was a good guy, and she was glad they were back on friendly terms. Maybe in time she'd even sing a duet with him again.

CHAPTER

27

David could feel the tension in the air as he walked into the school board meeting the first Tuesday in March. He exchanged a look with Pastor, who looked grim at best. David found out the reason soon enough. As soon as Pastor led them in prayer, Clay Henderson, the school board president, stood and looked directly at David.

"Before we call this meeting to order, is there anything you'd like to report, Mr. Neunaber?" His voice barely concealed his scorn.

David intuitively knew Clay was talking about Faith. He had intended to inform the school board of the situation tonight so they wouldn't think he was trying to hide anything. But apparently, Clay had beaten him to the punch.

"I always have things to report, Clay. To what, specifically, are you referring?" he returned in a level voice.

"I hear your stepdaughter has some interesting news."

"This is hardly the time or place to discuss my stepdaughter."

"Oh, I disagree. Besides, we haven't officially started the

meeting yet. Please, do tell."

David bit back a hot reply and decided honesty was the best policy. "Alright, then. It would appear many of you are already in the know about this anyhow. But just to make sure we're all on the same page, you should know that Faith is expecting."

"A baby?" asked the school board secretary.

"Yes. A baby. She's pregnant."

Gasps went up around the room, while Clay continued to stare at David with a steely look in his eyes. "And why might that be?" he asked.

"I don't think I need to give a biology lesson here, Clay."

"You know what I mean," he retorted. "How could you allow this to happen?"

David felt the heat creeping up his neck and into his face. He had to physically bite his tongue to keep from saying something he'd later regret. After a long, slow breath, he responded, using the speech he'd already planned. "This is not the direction I hoped Faith's life would take at this point, and I'm deeply saddened by the opportunities she will miss out on now. A high school pregnancy will change the course of her life, and I can't help but wonder what I could have done to protect her from this. It will be a challenge for all of us, but we are supporting her decision to keep the baby." He glanced around the room, trying to gauge the reactions of the other school board members.

"Nothing like this ever happened when Mr. Kaiser was here," Clay pressed on, not even acknowledging David's words. "And I believe the Bible says that our leaders are to be above reproach. That they are to have control over their household and their children, isn't that so? Then I ask you this, how can we as a church and school stand behind a principal whose teenage daughter is pregnant? The Bible says that if a man can't manage his own household, he can't lead those in the church."

"I believe the passage to which you refer is the one from Paul to Timothy, and speaks of pastors and deacons, does it not, Pastor?" asked David coldly, bristling at Clay's tone and pompous attitude.

"That's correct," Pastor replied. "And I must interrupt. This line of questioning is inappropriate. Mr. Neunaber cannot be held responsible for a choice his stepdaughter made. All of us in this room have made mistakes in the past, as have our children. It's unfair and unreasonable to blame him for this."

Several of the other members nodded in agreement at Pastor's comment.

"That's true," Clay admitted to Pastor, then turned back to look at David. "And maybe this sort of thing is why Paul also says church leaders ought not to marry recent converts to the faith."

David's blood was boiling as he stood to meet Clay's gaze. "Do *not* insult my wife or bring her into this!" he said in a low and menacing voice. "My entire family is Christian, secure in the knowledge that *all* sins are forgiven. Yes, Faith obviously sinned when she got pregnant, but she is choosing to keep the baby rather than cover up one sin with another. Now if you'll excuse me, I'm leaving. You have copies of my report printed out. I will not stay here while you insult my family."

With that, he tossed his report on the table and walked swiftly from the room, using all his willpower not to slam the door behind him. The looks of disdain and judgment he'd seen on some of the faces in that room was more than a bit distressing. If this was how church members were going to react, how in the world would Faith's classmates respond?

As he reached the front doors and walked out into the chilly evening air, David had an even more sinking realization. Although some of Faith's classmates would taunt her, many would probably be more understanding than the members of his own school board.

Later that evening, a quiet knock on the front door elicited a groan from David. He'd been so angry after he stormed out of the meeting that he'd walked around the block four times to calm down before going home. Only after walking in the front door did he realize he'd left his coat at school. So be it. He told Grace about the meeting, but he hadn't mentioned the unfair barb about marrying a recent convert. She didn't need that hanging over her head.

David opened the door and found Pastor Lixon there, holding his coat out to him. Silently, David took the coat and motioned him in before asking quietly, "How bad was it?"

Pastor sat on the couch with a nod of greeting to Grace before speaking. "I hate school board meetings," he said with a deep sigh.

"That makes two of us," agreed David wryly as he sat next to Grace and put his arm around her. "I'm sorry I left like that. I just couldn't stay any longer. I would have said something I'd regret. Or worse. I was sorely tempted to let my fist do the talking."

"Oh, I assure you, I was too!" Pastor concurred heartily. "I'm really sorry you were blindsided like that."

"Well, honestly, we both knew someone would make an issue out of it sooner or later," David said, glancing at Grace, who nodded in affirmation.

"Perhaps. But I handled the situation poorly myself," admitted Pastor. "I should have spoken up as soon as Clay started in on you. I shouldn't have let it get out of hand."

David tried to shrug it off. "It's not your place to be the referee."

"In this case, it was," argued Pastor. "I knew what he was up to, and I should have stopped the discussion. Clay is an excellent chairperson—well organized, detail-oriented, and efficient at running the meetings. But this isn't the first time he's made a scene. He can be very vindictive at times." Pastor stopped abruptly and pressed his lips into a thin line, then shut his eyes and gave a curt shake of his head. "That was unkind," he said. "I'm sorry."

Not knowing how to respond, David merely nodded to acknowledge Pastor's apology. He'd certainly harbored worse thoughts against Clay than "vindictive."

"It's just unfortunate that church members can be so judgmental," continued Pastor. "I did my best to smooth things over at the meeting, and I do think the majority of the school board members are understanding and supportive. They realize people make mistakes and that God's forgiveness covers every sin. They just don't want to speak up in front of everyone."

David sighed. "But honestly, Clay makes a valid point. The Bible *does* say that church leaders are to have control of their households. I've already been struggling with this, which is perhaps why Clay's accusation hurt so much tonight. I feel like I've failed Faith. I should have spoken to her about boys and relationships well before this. I know Grace has talked to her," he said, squeezing her shoulder, "but as the spiritual head of the household, it was my duty to do so as well. In a sense, I allowed this to happen by my silence."

Pastor paused for a moment, as if weighing his words before he spoke. "Regret is only natural," he said at last. "And I can't say one way or the other whether you failed in this area. Should you have talked to her about appropriate behavior for dating?

Probably so. But even if you had, that's no guarantee she would have made a different choice."

"No, but at least I would have made the effort. I would have fulfilled my responsibility as her father figure." David tried to keep his voice even. An overwhelming sense of guilt told him that he'd let his stepdaughter down. He had so much to learn about parenting.

"Then take this to the Lord in prayer, David," Pastor suggested gently. "Only He can judge your heart and intentions. If this is a sin of omission—doing nothing when you should have done something—He will forgive you for that and give you peace in His perfect timing. Sometimes guilt can be productive, when it prompts you to make changes in your life. Now that this has happened with Faith, perhaps you'll be more proactive about speaking to your other kids about dating relationships and physical intimacy. It's always an awkward talk, but you are correct—as the spiritual head of the household, it's your duty to look for their best interests."

David nodded glumly. He knew Pastor's advice to pray was solid, but he still wished he could somehow reverse the clock and do things differently. Faith had lost her innocence at the tender age of sixteen, and that galled him to no end. He and Grace had both known Faith was playing with fire when she'd allowed Spencer to sneak into her room, but what had he done about it? Nothing at all. Instead, he'd let his wife deal with the situation on her own. He'd failed as a husband and as a father.

Pastor spoke, interrupting his reverie. "In the meantime, you can't change what's happened." It was as if he'd read David's thoughts. "But you can help Faith moving forward. She needs love and support now, rather than judgment and disdain."

"Agreed. And she's getting that support from her family

and close friends. But beyond that, what can we do? We can't control how other people react."

"No, we can't," conceded Pastor. "But how about the people who are already supportive? Paul Sanders told me Faith let the Youth Group know a week or two ago. They took it pretty well, from what he tells me. Probably better than the school board. Maybe encourage her to surround herself with friends like that at school who won't tease her or make fun of her. She knows you guys are supportive, of course, but in public it helps to have someone else standing behind her too. Do what you can to shield her from anyone who would give her the evil eye or exhibit a holier-than-thou attitude. Act as her bodyguard, if you will. Steer her toward 'safe' people."

Grace spoke then. "I'm starting to think she should start going to Monday evening services rather than Sunday church. If it's too distracting and causing other people to gossip when they should be worshipping, maybe she should come on Mondays instead."

"That's completely up to you," Pastor said. "As I told her back when she first came to me, in my mind, she has no reason to remove herself from the fellowship of believers for a sin she's already confessed and for which she's been forgiven." He glanced at his watch and stood. "It's late. Ann will be wondering where I am. She hates school board meetings almost as much as I do! I'm always late coming home, and when I do, I'm usually in a bad mood." He shook his head and started toward the front door. David followed to see him out.

At the door, Pastor turned and spoke softly. "One last thing. I spoke with Clay afterward to ask him to patch things up between the two of you. I don't know that he will, but I want you to be aware of that. In case he does apologize, I encourage you to be receptive, even if it's less than sincere on one or both of your parts. I'd hate for this to cause a major rift with people taking sides. I've seen that happen before, and it is not a pretty sight. The devil works hardest amongst the people of God, using his full arsenal to pit us against each other, discredit our witness to the rest of the world, and even turn us away from God."

"That's for sure," David agreed. "Thanks for the heads up. I'm not in the best frame of mind to make peace with him at this exact moment, but we still need to work together in future meetings. We need to act like adults and get past this so we can be civil to one another. And hey, next month's meeting *has* to be better than tonight's, right?"

"Oh, it better be!" Pastor exclaimed, then shook David's hand before letting himself out.

Walking back to the living room, David sank down next to Grace on the couch. She wrapped her arms around his waist and laid her cheek against his chest. "I'm so sorry," she said.

"For what?" he asked incredulously.

"All this," she answered, drawing in a shaky breath. "Faith is *my* daughter. I'm the one who should have been instilling strong morals in her, and here you are taking the heat for this now. It's not fair to you. We're making you look bad. You were better off without us."

"Hey, look at me," he said adamantly, pulling her chin up so he could meet her eyes. "That is *not* true. Don't ever think that, Grace. I love all of you, and I have *never* thought I'd be better off without you. You guys are the best earthly thing that's ever happened to me, and I thank God every day that He brought you into my life." He kissed her before pulling her against his chest again. He was crestfallen that she would even think he harbored second thoughts about marrying her.

"But when you were talking to Pastor earlier, you said you

should have spoken to Faith yourself," Grace said, pulling out of the embrace so she could meet his eyes. "David, that's *my* job. That's what I should have been doing all along. You've only been her stepfather half a year. I doubt she would have taken kindly to an abstinence talk from you anyhow. You can't blame yourself."

"It looks like we're *both* blaming ourselves, doesn't it?" he asked with a sad smile. "I suppose it's only natural, given the circumstances. But this isn't getting us anywhere. Let's just both accept that we could have or should have done more, but ultimately Faith is the one who made the decision. As Pastor said, we can't change that. What's important is that we're here for Faith now. That's what she needs from us."

"I suppose." Grace did not sound convinced. She rested her head against his shoulder, and the two sat in silence until David spoke again. "You know that Bible verse that says God works all things for the good of those who love Him? I've seen that promise fulfilled with other families before. We have to cling to that promise too, even when we can't see how that's possible."

Grace shifted slightly to look into his eyes as he continued. "There was a family at my last church who found out their teenage son was addicted to meth. That was quite the scandal, especially since the family was one of the pillars of the church. They got him into rehab and he got clean, and now he's working for a rehab place himself. He can relate to the people who come through there because he went through the same thing. He's helped dozens of people get clean and stay clean. At the time, his addiction seemed like a terrible and pointless tragedy, with no possible good coming from it. But now, looking back, his family admits God used that for His good."

He gently brushed a stray curl from Grace's forehead. "As

for us, we're at the front lines right now. This is still new, we're all overwhelmed, and it's our church's own scandal of the year. But God promises to work good through any situation, and I'll bet you that years from now we'll look back and realize a number of blessings that came from all this."

"I hope you're right," whispered Grace. The two lapsed back into reflective silence for a few minutes until they heard a bedroom door open and footsteps approaching. Shortly, Faith appeared in the doorway.

"Hi, sweetie," Grace said in a tender voice. "Come join us." She patted the cushion next to her and reached behind her to grab the blanket hanging on the back of the couch. Faith sat next to her mother and helped arrange the blanket so it was covering their laps.

"It was a pretty bad meeting, then, huh?" Faith finally asked in a tiny voice. "Because of me."

"Were you eavesdropping?" Grace asked, arching an eyebrow.

"Maybe a little," admitted Faith. "I wanted to know why Pastor was coming over at nine thirty at night."

David smiled at the comment. "That's true. Not a normal time for a pastoral visit."

"I heard what you guys were talking about for Monday evening services, and I think that's a good idea. But I have an even better one. I'll ask Grandma to go with me."

David exchanged a startled glance with Grace. Clearly, the thought hadn't crossed her mind either.

"Why is that?" Grace asked.

"When I told the family I was pregnant a few weeks ago, Grandma told me if I needed her to do anything at all, I should just ask. So I figure this way, she really can't say no. I'll tell her I want someone to be there with me besides you guys. And this way she can be in church each week."

"Oh, Faith." Grace pulled her daughter into a hug. "You're an amazing young lady, you know that? I never would have thought of that, but I think it's a wonderful idea. At Gram's funeral, I told her Gram was with Jesus now, and Grandma said, 'I know.' I'm not sure what she meant by that, but it would be good to get her back in church while that's still fairly fresh in her mind."

David was humbled by Faith's suggestion. She was using her less-than-ideal situation to reach out to her grandmother, while she easily could have chosen to shut herself off from the world. How remarkable.

"I'll call her tomorrow," Faith promised. "Maybe we can start next week. But I would still like to go to Youth Bible Class on Sunday mornings. I don't mind facing the kids. It's the adults I dread."

David grimaced at the sad commentary as Faith stood and stretched. Then she turned to kiss Grace on top of the head before heading back to her room.

Grace shifted the blanket to cover both David and herself and snuggled closer to him. After a few moments, David said, "Then again, maybe it won't take years for us to discern blessings that come as a result of Faith's pregnancy. If your mom starts going to church with her, who knows what can happen? Monday evening church with Faith is far less intimidating than a full Sunday service. I'm proud of Faith for thinking of it. Perhaps we're seeing one of the hidden blessings already."

CHAPTER
28

"Grace?"

The smiling nurse summoned her back to the exam room. Grace rose from her chair in the waiting room, and David stood with her. He felt hopelessly out of place compared to the others in the waiting room. Most were women, at least fifteen years his junior. There was but one other male in the waiting room, sitting with his female counterpart, both absorbed in their phones as they waited. David now understood Grace's discomfort about her "advanced maternal age." He gave her hand an encouraging squeeze before falling into step behind her.

Grace followed the nurse to get her weight check and blood pressure before entering Exam Room #2. David tagged along feeling rather conspicuous. After a few obligatory questions, the nurse left, promising them the doctor would be in shortly. Fifteen minutes later, the OB knocked and let herself in.

"Good morning!" she chirped. "How's everything going?"

Grace was right. The doctor was younger than she. Barely pushing thirty. For all David knew, this was her first post right out of med school. She'd better know what she was doing. He knew he was being unfair, but her cheery attitude somehow rubbed him the wrong way. It was almost like she was humoring the two of them. But he also knew Faith really liked her and had a good rapport with her, so that somewhat mollified him.

"I'm Doctor Langston," she introduced herself as she held out her hand to David.

He returned the handshake and replied, "David Neunaber. Grace's husband."

"So I figured," she said lightly. "Glad you could make it today. Are we going to find out the baby's gender?" she asked as she washed her hands.

No, "we" are not, he thought resentfully. *You won't even be in the ultrasound room with us.* He still couldn't forgive her for being as young as she was.

Fortunately, Grace took the question in stride. "No, we want it to be a surprise," she said.

"Ooh! Exciting! You're braver than I am. I don't think I could stand the suspense!" Dr. Langston laughed, then got down to business. "You're feeling okay?" she addressed Grace.

"Mm-hmm. I'm finally getting over the tiredness from the first trimester. I actually have energy again, which is a good feeling."

"Excellent! And still no morning sickness?"

"Not a bit of it."

"Good. Well, you're gaining weight accordingly. Maybe a bit too much, in fact. It's not a huge deal at this point, but it is something to keep an eye on. Make sure you're eating well and getting physical activity in as much as possible. Now that spring is finally in sight, try to get out more for walks and fresh air. It'll do you and the baby good."

David was aghast that the doctor had made such a tactless comment about Grace's weight. She was pregnant, for crying out loud. Of course she was gaining weight. And his poor wife's cheeks had reddened considerably. David's opinion of the young doctor lowered yet another notch.

"Have you felt the baby move yet?" Dr. Langston asked.

"I don't think so," Grace said. "The first movements are always hard to tell for sure. They're so light."

"Enjoy it while you can. By the end you'll be feeling those little elbows and knees all over. Okay!" the doctor continued briskly. "Let's take a listen, shall we? Go ahead and lay back."

Grace slowly reclined on the exam table as Dr. Langston grabbed the gel and fetal Doppler to hear the baby's heartbeat. She squeezed a glob of gel onto Grace's stomach and moved around the probe. David heard nothing but swooshing, but suddenly, there it was. The sound of a heartbeat, much faster than he'd thought it would be.

He stared at Grace with a smile of awe on his face. It was the first time he'd ever heard a baby's heartbeat, and to think it was his own child in his wife's womb was an incredible feeling. As they listened, he took her hand and murmured, "It's the most beautiful sound in the world." She beamed back at him in agreement.

Doctor Langston nodded after a few seconds. "One hundred thirty," she said.

"Is that normal?" asked David with a bit of concern. "It seems awfully high."

"Perfectly normal," she assured. "Babies in utero have a much higher heart rate than adults. Everything sounds just fine." She wiped Grace's stomach with a rag to pick up as much gel as she could, then offered her hand to Grace to help her back to a sitting position.

"Let's get you two over to the ultrasound lab," she said. "We scheduled it so you can go right over. I'll walk you there. The ultrasound tech on duty today is Maggie Harris. She'll take good care of you."

David and Grace looked at one another in surprise as they followed Dr. Langston down the hallway. Maggie Harris was a member at St. John, although neither of them knew her very well.

Dr. Langston showed them to a small seating area outside the ultrasound room and knocked to announce their arrival. Within two minutes, Maggie was ushering them into the darkened room, her face wreathed in smiles. David felt instantly more comfortable with Maggie. She was older than they were, perhaps in her early fifties, and looked genuinely excited to see them there.

"I'm so glad I'm the one working today!" she bubbled. "When I saw your name on the list, it made my day! Bill and I are so happy for you two. So happy. What a blessing!"

Her excitement was contagious, and Grace laughed. "Yes, it is," she agreed. "Although my doctor seems to think I'm high risk because I'm *so* old. I'm calling this my Sarah pregnancy."

Maggie laughed and waved her hand dismissively. "Oh, phooey. Doctors always have to be cautious like that. But you'll be just fine. The Lord has you covered."

She grinned at them and turned to her screen. By now Grace was lying down on the exam table, and Maggie prepared the gel for her stomach once again.

"Do you want to find out the gender?" she inquired.

"No," Grace answered firmly. "We want it to be a surprise."

"Good for you! I know I'm old-fashioned, but I always think the element of surprise is best when it comes to babies." She started moving the probe across Grace's belly, and the grainy black and white picture appeared on the screen.

"That's incredible!" gasped David. "I've never seen the likes of it!"

Maggie smiled but didn't comment as she studied the screen in front of her. She leaned forward and squinted slightly. "Oh, my," she murmured.

David, likewise, stared at the screen, his heart nearly stopping. "Um, Maggie, I'm not an expert at reading these things, but am I seeing what I think I'm seeing?"

"Indeed you are," she confirmed. She turned to Grace. "Sweetie, this isn't your Sarah pregnancy after all. This is your Rebekah pregnancy."

"*Twins?!*"

Olivia shrieked the word on the other line. Grace had called her in the car after the appointment, which had turned out to be much longer than anticipated after the surprise of learning she was carrying two babies instead of one. Olivia was so loud Grace knew David could hear her from his position behind the wheel.

"Oh, yes. Unmistakably so."

"I guess it runs in the family!"

"I thought twins were supposed to come from the father's side."

"Then it's David's fault!"

"Sure is," Grace said. She hadn't gotten over the shock yet, and was overwhelmed by the sudden revelation. How on earth would she ever manage two babies at once? Three, really, with Faith's baby added to the equation.

"Hey, sweetie, listen to me. I know it's a surprise. But you can do this. I'll help when they're born. The first few months are brutal."

"Thanks for the encouragement."

"Well, they are. But the first few months are tough with any new baby."

"Liv, we are going to have *three* newborns in the house at the same time! Plus four other kids! We can't even fit into one vehicle anymore. We're gonna have to get a bus!" She was starting to panic.

"Whoa, whoa, whoa. Take it one step at a time, Gracie. Yes, it'll be a challenge, but Mom and I will help. Send Faith and her baby over here if you need to. Our house is too empty now that the kids are all off to college."

Grace felt a stab of envy. An empty house didn't sound so terrible at this point.

"So are they fraternal or identical?" prompted her sister.

"Fraternal. As far as twins go, ours are the least risky, although the fact that I have twins at all puts me at higher risk than I was before. The doctor told me they have two placentas and two sacs."

"That's good. Justin and Jason had one placenta and one sac. My doctor was watching me like a hawk the entire time. I don't know who was happier when they were finally born—me or him! We both cried when they were delivered!"

Grace breathed a small laugh, and Olivia continued. "But that moves your due date up, doesn't it? Full term for twins is thirty-seven or thirty-eight weeks."

"Yes," agreed Grace despondently. "My new due date is July 29."

"Oh, Gracie," sighed Olivia. "Just when Faith is due. Wow. I don't even know what to say."

"Neither do I. There are no words to express how I feel right now."

"How did David react, or can't you talk about it now?"

"He's excited. That makes exactly one of us," she said glumly, looking at her husband, who grinned sideways at her and gave her knee a quick squeeze.

"Give yourself time, honey," Olivia encouraged. "I cried for three days when I found out I was pregnant with twins. But Mom helped a lot after they were born, and she and I can help you too. Twins are tough as babies, but when they get older they have a natural playmate. They'll amuse themselves in time. And they can share clothes too, unless you get one of each."

Grace laughed shakily. "I guess."

"I know it's a shock. Go home and let yourself cry. Then take a good long nap. Make David worry about dinner. You deserve a break. It's hard work carrying twins."

"Got that right," sighed Grace. "I need to go now. We're just pulling into the driveway."

"Gotcha. Hey, congrats, Gracie. Twins are a blessing once you get used to the idea."

"Thanks, Liv. Talk to you later."

They hung up, and David and Grace walked together into the quiet house. The kids were all in school.

"Want me to make lunch?" offered David. "That appointment took longer than we thought it would. You must be famished."

"Sure, hon. Thanks. I'm going to lie down for a while first," she said. "Give me about twenty minutes."

He kissed her hair and went to the kitchen to see what was available. Grace walked unsteadily back to their room. She was going to take her sister's advice. She needed a good long cry.

"We need a bigger house," Grace stated flatly to David that night as they lay in bed.

"I know. I was thinking the very same thing. We're about to

experience a fifty percent increase in the members of this household."

Grace groaned. David was always throwing around numbers. The very thought made her even more depressed. There was no way they could afford a new house. She squeezed her eyes shut but couldn't stop a tear from sliding down each cheek. She sniffled, and David realized she was crying.

"Hey, hey. Come here, sweetheart," he soothed softly, pulling her onto his chest in a hug. She accepted his embrace as he rubbed her neck and let her cry.

"David, I can't do this. We learn about a new baby every other month! I was so excited when I took the pregnancy test back in December, and then at the beginning of February we found out Faith was pregnant. Now here we are in March and I find out—surprise! We get twins! I'm starting to get paranoid that maybe they missed something at Faith's ultrasound, and she has twins too!"

"Yeah, wouldn't that be something?"

"It would be just our luck," she said sardonically. "Wouldn't surprise me a bit at this point. Hey, may as well be triplets."

"I wouldn't go that far…"

"I just don't know how we're going to do it. We can't stay here indefinitely. Faith and her baby need their own room, the boys can still share, and the babies will eventually need a room too. That leaves Katie and us. That's five rooms! If we had to, I suppose we could squeeze into four and make the twins share with Katie, but still, there's no way we can afford a larger house. Especially if I'm quitting my job. It would cost more for childcare for twins than I'd make anyhow. But that means our grocery money is gone. It'll totally mess up whatever budget you have," she finished with a hint of sarcasm.

"That's okay. It'll require a lot of changes all around, but we'll make it work."

Grace snorted in disbelief, but her husband was undeterred. "And hey, one financial bonus is that we're guaranteed to make our deductible now! May as well schedule as many doctor visits and procedures as we can this year!"

"Oh, brother. You *would* think of that. But that doesn't help with a house."

"I'm already on it. Even if we didn't have twins, we'd need more space. A three-bedroom house with all of us just isn't enough."

"Too bad we can't swap houses with the Youngs," Grace said wryly.

David chuckled. "I have a few leads, actually. I found a house five miles from church that could work. There's another one seven miles away, slightly more expensive, but maybe a better fit. We can go look at them tomorrow if you want."

"When did you do all this?" Grace asked in surprise. "While I was napping?"

"No, I started inquiring a few weeks ago. One of the school moms is a realtor. I enlisted her help."

Grace was impressed. He was a step ahead of her. "Okay. Let's do it. If we're going to move, we may as well get cracking while I have energy in the second trimester. Once the third trimester hits, I'll be waddling around not wanting to do anything. What about this house, though?"

"Mary said she'd do her best to sell it, but admittedly there isn't a huge demand in Mapleport at present for houses. She does more of her work in Forest Springs and Muskegon. But you never can tell. Hopefully it'll sell sooner than later."

"David, how will we ever pay for two mortgages?"

"We'll cross that bridge if and when we come to it. Remember, I was a bachelor for years, and even on a teacher's oalary I was able to put a lot into savings. We have plenty in our account, and if we can't contribute to college funds for a while, so be it. That's why scholarships and student loans are available. God will provide for us. He's never let us down before."

"You're right, of course. I can't help but worry, though. I'm still in complete shock that we're having twins."

"Me too, but hey, look at it like this—you only have to deal with one pregnancy this way, and get twice the results!"

She laughed. "Not thinking I'd exactly put it that way, but sure."

"Sweetheart, I know this wasn't what you were planning. It'll take a while to get used to the idea. But honestly, I'm thrilled. We'll double the number of Neunabers in our household in one day when they're born!"

Again, Grace giggled, then snuggled into the crook of his arm and felt herself drifting off to sleep. At least David was excited about the twins. Hopefully in time she'd catch his excitement as well.

CHAPTER

29

True to his word, the following day David arranged a tour of both houses he'd mentioned. Immediately following Grace's shift at the cafeteria, they met the realtor at St. John. Mary took them in her car, chatting about the advantages of each house as she drove. Grace turned from her position in the passenger seat to exchange a smile with her husband. Mary was certainly good at what she did.

As they entered the first house, Mary gushed about how open and roomy it was, but Grace found she didn't like it at all. It was a four-bedroom house, with a study that Mary insisted could work as a bedroom in a pinch. But something about the layout of the house didn't feel right to Grace. The vaulted ceiling in the living room seemed like it would carry too much sound to the bedrooms upstairs, and the office on the main floor opened right into the living room. They *could* make it work if they had to, but she wasn't entirely convinced. She didn't want to rush into a decision now only to regret it later. She was polite but noncommittal about the house, and David must have picked up on the fact that she didn't like it, because he asked if they could see the other house.

Mary drove to the next house, raving over how wonderful it was and how she secretly liked it better than the previous one anyhow. But the second house was more expensive, since it had five official bedrooms. It was a two-story house with four bedrooms upstairs, a master bedroom on the first floor, and a partially finished basement. It had plenty of space, and Grace could picture them there, but David seemed concerned when he asked Mary if the owners might come down on the price.

"Of course we always make a lower offer, but I'm not sure this couple would take it. They put a lot of work into the house and installed a new furnace just a year ago. They don't want to lose money on their investment. And the new furnace is much more efficient. It would save you money during the winter because it's so effective. It even has three separate heating zones so you aren't wasting money trying to keep the whole house the same temperature. If no one is in the basement, you can just turn that one off. It may be a more expensive house at first, but it'll pay for itself over time."

"We'll consider both houses and get back to you, Mary," David said. "In the meantime, we'd better get back to school so we can get the kids and you can get Bailey."

They piled into Mary's car and drove back, although Grace didn't listen to Mary as she prattled on. She was grateful when they reached St. John.

"Thank you so much for your time, Mary. We really appreciate this. We'll talk things over and let you know what we decide," David said to her as they left the car. She waved a cheery farewell and drove to the end of the car pick-up line.

"Well?" David turned to Grace as they entered his office.

"I'm not sure I can see us in either of those houses," she confessed. "The first one was just one big open space. I dubbed it the 'uni-room.' If Andy and Olivia were over in the evening, their loud talking and laughing would keep the kids up all night the way the rooms are set up. It looks nice, but it's not practical for a family with so many kids."

"Probably true," he conceded. "I actually liked the open spaces. Makes it feel bigger. But you have a point. That's why you need a woman's perspective. What about the second one?"

"I like that one a lot better. But I'm not sure you do. I saw the look on your face when you were discussing the cost with Mary. It's fifteen thousand more than the other one to begin with, and she's not hopeful they'd come down much or at all. Unless we knew for sure our own house would sell right away, I don't think it's wise for us to make that big of a commitment."

"That's my thought too," David said. "But I do like the setup of that one. Everyone who needs to could have their own rooms, and if the boys ever get sick of sharing a room, we could throw one of them into the basement in a pinch."

Grace laughed. "Which side?" she teased.

"Depends on how well they behave," he joked back. "That unfinished half wasn't so bad. Cold concrete floors in the dead of winter build stamina."

They chuckled together. "Let's sit on it over the weekend and come back to it on Sunday evening. We can call Mary on Monday if we decide anything," Grace suggested.

"Good idea. In the meantime, are you up to telling the kids the big news tonight?"

Grace hadn't worked up the courage to tell the kids about the twins the night before, but today she was starting to feel better about the situation. "Sure. Let's do it."

"Great! I'll order pizza. That'll put them in an automatic good mood anyhow."

"Perfect!" she laughed. "It'll put me in a good mood too! I

don't have to cook. Just as long as my half gets mushrooms, I'm happy."

David made a face. "How you can eat fungus on pizza is beyond me," he retorted, just as Freddie walked into the office.

"Yay! Pizza night!" he cheered, overhearing the comment. "You guys are the best!"

Grace grinned at her husband. It was going to be a good night.

A few hours later, the kids were happily munching the last of the two pizzas when David gave Grace a nod. It was time.

"Kids, we need to tell you something. Quiet down!" she called over their noise. As the chatter died down, she continued. "You know we went to the doctor yesterday to see the baby on the ultrasound, right? Remember when Faith did that a few weeks ago and found out that her baby is a boy? Well, we found out what we're having too. Any guesses?"

"It better be a boy," Jackson said vehemently. "No *way* I'm changing diapers for a baby girl."

"I want a sister," said Katie. "I think it's a girl."

"I vote sister," said Freddie. Grace hid a smile. She was certain he only said that to defy Jackson.

Faith looked at her mother suspiciously. "I thought you weren't going to find out the gender."

"We didn't."

"Then what's the point?" demanded Jackson. "This is stupid."

"Oh, trust me. I think you'll be interested to find out what we *did* learn." She paused for effect to make sure she had their full attention. "We're having twins."

There was a moment of dead silence as everyone digested this. Then Faith let out a little moan of sympathy or dread,

Grace wasn't sure which. Freddie slapped his hand to his forehead. Katie's eyes were as big as saucers as she whispered, "Two?"

Grace nodded to confirm her six-year-old's question, and Jackson let out a dramatic sigh. "That's *it*. I'm moving in with Grandma and Grandpa. Every time I turn around there's another baby coming. We're like a circus family in a clown car. Just when you think the last one is out, another one comes along."

The adults both laughed. The kid had a point. "But isn't it exciting?" prompted David. "Just think of it—you'll be so experienced with babies by the time you're an adult that your future wife will be impressed."

"I'm never getting married," Jackson snorted. "I don't want all these babies running around like you guys."

David smiled knowingly at him. "I have a feeling you'll change your mind before then. But for now, you'll be a wonderful helper with your new siblings and nephew. I know how good you are with babies already."

Jackson flushed at the praise and tried to brush it off. "You don't have to keep adding more babies just to prove the point. Where is everyone supposed to sleep, anyhow? No way I'm sharing my room with crying babies."

"Your mother and I are already looking at new houses," David said. "It may even be possible that we move before any of the babies are born."

"Cool!" Now Jackson was excited. "I have dibs on my own room! I've never had my own room before. I deserve one now."

"I hate to burst your bubble, but you and Freddie still have to share a room," Grace said. "Don't get your hopes up."

"That's not fair!"

David counted off on his fingers the rooms they'd need.

"Faith and her baby, you and Freddie, the twins, Katie, and your mom and me. That's already five rooms, Jackson. Most houses only have three or four. We're pushing it as it is."

"Great," moaned Jackson. "Then I really will stay with Grandma and Grandpa. At least then I can get my own room!"

"Or maybe they'd make you share with Gramps so they still have a guest room," Freddie inserted with a sly grin.

Everyone laughed as Jackson scowled at his brother. Grace looked at David and exchanged a smile. That hadn't been too hard breaking the news. Maybe things would be okay after all.

CHAPTER

30

"Mom! What are you doing here? Is everything okay?"

It was Saturday morning, and Carol had just rung the doorbell. Grace was still in her bathrobe since they'd had a late breakfast of scrambled eggs and sausage. It was unusual for Carol to just drop by, and it alarmed Grace.

"Oh, yes, everything's fine. I'm sorry to barge in like this, but I wanted to see and talk to you in person. I want to hug my daughter who's pregnant with twins." She gave Grace a tight hug and whispered, "Congratulations, sweetie."

"Thanks, Mom." She knew her mother had picked up on her apprehension about carrying twins. Carol was probably here now to make sure she wasn't in the throes of depression.

"Do you think you can spare an hour or two? Could David watch the kids? I want to take you out for coffee."

That took Grace aback. Her mom didn't do things like this. She must really be worried. "Oh! Um, yeah, I think that'll work. Hang on. Let me go talk to him and get dressed. Come on into the living room. You can have Katie read to you. She's getting pretty good at it."

Half an hour later, after hurriedly getting dressed and leaving the kids in David's care, the two ladies were sitting at a table in The Java House, Carol sipping a cappuccino as Grace blew on a caramel steamer. They made small talk for a while until Carol put her cup down and looked at Grace.

"Olivia told me you were starting to house shop," she said.

"Yes, that's true. There's no way we can all fit into our current house." Grace wondered where this conversation was going. Maybe Jackson really would get his wish and Carol would offer to take him in.

"Can you afford that?"

"Mom, really now," she protested, embarrassed by her mother's directness. "We'll manage."

"But it'll be difficult, right?" Carol pressed.

Grace shrugged.

"Honey, I know David doesn't have a huge salary. Parochial teachers aren't in it for the money, that's for sure. And I don't know what his savings account was coming into your marriage, but I know you didn't have a whole lot saved up. You're going to have seven kids in the house soon enough. That's a lot of mouths to feed. I'm perceptive enough to realize that you need money if you want to buy a good house that'll hold your growing family."

Having no idea how to respond, Grace simply stared at her mother and waited for her to get to the point.

Carol leaned forward and said, "Gramps wants you to have your portion of his money now."

Grace felt the blood drain from her face. "Mom, no!" she objected. "That's not right! I can't do that. It's sweet of him to offer, but... No. I just can't." By now, the blood had reversed course and was rushing to her face. She could feel herself turning red.

"Sweetie, he *wants* you to have it now. He and Gram saved a lot of money over the years. Their orchards were really successful, and he was a shrewd businessman. When he sold the orchard to Martin last year, he got good money from that as well. A lot of Gram's medical expenses were taken care of with insurance, and even after he paid the rest of them, they still have a substantial amount left over. Their will directs that Doug, Lou, and I each get twenty percent of their assets. Ten percent goes to the church. The remaining thirty percent is to be split equally between the grandkids. They have four grandkids, so each of you gets seven and a half percent. That doesn't sound like much, but like I said, they've done really well. Here's your portion."

Carol handed Grace a check. She took it and unfolded it, her eyes widening in shock. "Mother!" she gasped. "That's almost as much as David makes in a whole year! Are you sure about that?"

"Absolutely. We checked and double checked the figures. Dad's an accountant, you know. He verified the numbers and graphed everything on a spreadsheet. Gramps wants you to use it for a down payment on a house, and he wants you to use it now so he can see it while he's still with us."

Grace felt tears spring to her eyes. "I don't even know what to say, Mom! This is a total shock. I didn't expect anything at all, especially not when Gramps is still alive and well. This... I... I can't even process this yet."

Carol looked pleased by her daughter's reaction. "Gramps wants to help," she whispered. "He's sweet like that. He just wants you to be happy."

"But, Mom, I *am* happy," Grace assured her, tears now streaming down her cheeks. "Come on, don't I *look* happy?"

They laughed together, and Grace grabbed her mom's hand

across the table. "I hardly know what to say, Mom. This will really help a lot. I don't know how I can ever thank Gramps."

"Your happiness is all the thanks he needs," Carol assured her. "Now, let's get you back so you can talk about this with your husband. I'll stay with the kids if you want to go out and discuss it privately."

Less than an hour later, David and Grace were in his office at school, calling Mary to authorize her to make an offer on the five-bedroom house. Mary assured them that she'd contact the owners and get back to them.

David hung up the phone and swung Grace around in a circle. "I'm still getting over this surprise," he said. "We're going to have to take your grandpa out to Le Poisson or something. We owe him a major thank you."

Grace giggled at the thought of dragging Gramps to the upscale restaurant. "Can you imagine us sitting there with him? Waiting for him to make his choice on what to order? And then waiting for him to actually finish it?" Her grandpa was a dreadfully slow eater and could make a small meal last an hour and a half if he was so inclined.

They laughed together, and Grace leaned against her husband's chest, sighing with contentment. This was the best she'd felt in days. David's phone rang just then, causing them both to jump. It was Mary. He answered excitedly, Grace still close enough to hear Mary's voice on the other end.

"I'm so sorry, David, but they just accepted an offer on the house last night. Leslie Nelson Realty beat us to it. I'm terribly sorry. It's sold."

David thanked her and hung up the phone somberly. Grace swallowed over the lump of disappointment in her throat and said, "I guess we're right back to square one."

CHAPTER

31

Faith straightened her shoulders as she exited the lunch line and prepared to find a table. Her best friend, Chelsea, was out sick today, and Faith felt lost without her there. Her other friends had different lunch hours, so she had no one to sit with now. She glanced with nostalgia at the popular kids' table. She had given up her envious position with them long ago. The elite crowd didn't get pregnant, and if they did, they took care of it to make sure no one ever found out. Faith had violated the rules and was therefore an outsider again.

As she walked by their table, she held her head high and tried to pretend she didn't see them, but she saw their glances and heard their whispers and snickers. They were laughing at her.

Although she was gaining weight, it wasn't immediately obvious to the casual observer that she was expecting. It was nearing the end of March, and she was almost twenty-two weeks along. According to Dr. Langston, her baby was almost the size of a papaya. For now, she could still wear loose shirts and keep her jeans unbuttoned.

However, after her parking lot fight with Spencer, word started getting around about her condition. Not only that, but the circulating rumor was that the baby wasn't even Spencer's. She knew he had started it to spite her. But as mad as she was at him, she refused to stoop to his level. She didn't bother to correct the fallacy or fight back. Instead she ignored everyone and pretended she didn't care. The problem was, she *did* care. It hurt.

Spying an empty table in the corner, Faith sighed and made her way there. She realized now how shallow her friendships had been before. Chelsea had been loyal, yes, as had most of her volleyball friends. But all her other so-called friends had left her in the dust after she broke up with Spencer, some of them shamelessly vying for his attention themselves. The fact that she was pregnant was the icing on the cake. Now they had an excuse to shun her.

She put her tray down and pulled out a chair, feeling very lonely indeed as she poked at the food on her plate.

"Can I sit with you?" a voice asked. Faith looked up into the kind eyes of Bree Robertson, and felt tears prick her own. She gestured to the chair across from her, and Bree sat down. "Don't let them bother you," she said in a low voice, indicating the popular crowd. "They're using you as a scapegoat. They're glad it's not *them* dealing with all this. And I think their consciences are pricked that you actually chose to keep the baby. It's not an automatic for a lot of people."

Faith shrugged. "I try not to let them bother me, but it's hard. I see how they look at me. I know the kinds of things they say about me."

"Yeah, but what do the people who *really* matter in your life say about it? Like your mom and stepdad? Pastor? Mr. Sanders? They're all really proud of you. Remember that."

Suddenly another tray was placed on the table next to Faith, and she looked up to see Aaron Sullivan pulling out the chair next to her while his friend Brian White pulled out the chair beside Bree. Faith laughed. "Do I really look that pathetic?" she teased. "I must have been throwing a whopper of a pity party to have half the Youth Group join me!"

Bree giggled. "We just want you to know we're standing beside you, even in the landmine otherwise known as the school cafeteria." Everyone laughed, and Bree asked Faith, "So is it strange having your mom remarry? To have Mr. Neunaber living with you guys now? I think I'd be totally weirded out."

"It *was* super awkward at first," she confessed, "especially right after they got back from their honeymoon. I was scared to death I'd run into him in the middle of the night in the bathroom or something. And I totally didn't want to see him in pajamas. Or even worse," she lowered her voice to a dramatic whisper, "without a shirt on!" She and Bree both shuddered at the thought. "But once we all got past the first week or so of, 'Oh, so *that's* how you look first thing in the morning,' it wasn't too bad."

"How about your siblings? Are they okay with the change?"

"Oh, yeah. Katie and Freddie adore him. They both call him 'Dad.' Katie was already calling him that before he and Mom were engaged. She's the little charmer of the family. She's excited to finally have a daddy, and Mom is happier than I've seen since before Dad ran off."

Faith saw Aaron and Bree exchange a look. Both of them had parents who were happily married. They probably couldn't fathom their father just leaving.

"How long ago did he leave?" asked Bree, then rushed on. "You don't have to answer if you don't want to. I'm sorry. I'm too nosy sometimes."

"No, it's fine," Faith assured. "He ran off with another chick when Mom was pregnant with Katie. She's six now, so it's been at least six and a half years."

"Wow. I never knew," Bree said softly. "I'm really sorry."

"Most of the time I'm okay with it, but sometimes it hurts. I mean, Katie never met him at all, and Freddie doesn't remember him. I wonder if he thinks about us anymore, you know? Wonders how we're doing? But if it hadn't been for all that, Mom wouldn't have met David, and we probably would never have started going to church. So I guess in the end it worked out for the best. It's just sometimes hard getting to that point where things work out."

Brian spoke up then, surprising Faith. He was one of the quietest guys in their class and seldom spoke unless specifically addressed first. "My parents got divorced when I was seven," he offered. "Neither of them remarried. My brother and I go to Dad's house every other weekend. It's hard." He stopped then as if he had more he was going to say, but decided he'd already surpassed his word quota for the day.

"I can't even imagine," said Bree when it was apparent he wasn't going to elaborate. "Sometimes I feel like I live such a sheltered life. My parents are happy together, and my sisters and I grew up in the church. I can't imagine it any other way."

"You have two sisters, right?" Faith asked, remembering that Bree sat with her parents and two other girls at church.

"Three, actually. Morgan is already in college. She hardly ever comes home. Even stays there to work and do service projects over the summer."

"So which sister are you closest to?" Faith inquired.

"Eliana. She's the youngest. She's only in eighth grade, but she and I have more in common than I do with Morgan or Ginny. Morgan is all lofty now that she's in college, like she knows everything and is an expert on every subject. Ginny is only a year younger than I am, and we fight constantly! We drive our parents crazy."

"I always wished Jackson had been a girl," Faith confessed. "I thought it would have been fun to have a sister closer in age. Katie is sweet and I love her, but she's six. I'm more like a babysitter to her than a sister. And I'm not really close to my brothers, either. Freddie is pretty quiet and reserved, and Jackson is out of control. I think he has ADHD, but Mom refuses to even consider that. She says he has a lot of enthusiasm. That's her nice way of saying he's insane."

Everyone laughed. "I'm so jealous," admitted Aaron, "hearing you guys talk about siblings and how everyone relates to each other. I always wished I had a sibling or two. It's hard being an only child. Kind of lonely."

"You can have Jackson," Faith offered hopefully. "He'd liven things up pretty fast!"

They chuckled together again, and then Bree changed the subject. "So what did you guys think of that history test today? I thought I was ready for it, but those true and false questions were terrible! Most of them were so confusing that the answer could have been true *or* false, depending on how you looked at it. I'm pretty sure I got every one of those wrong!"

They spent the rest of the period discussing classes and chatting easily. When the bell rang, Faith was amazed how quickly the time had gone. She was also very thankful for the kindness of new friends.

CHAPTER

32

Grace knocked on her mom's door to announce her presence and walked in, calling, "Hello, Gramps! It's me!"

It was the week after Carol had given Grace the check, and Grace had been waiting for an opportunity to talk to her grandfather in private. Today Walt was at work and Carol was running errands, so Grace stopped by after her cafeteria shift.

"In here, Gracie!" called her grandpa. His voice came from the den, which was exactly where Grace expected him to be. He spent much of his time in his recliner doing crossword puzzles, reading the newspaper, and dozing. She made her way there and knelt down beside his chair to give him a big hug. He accepted her embrace, and the two sat there silently for some time before Grace pulled back. Both had tears glistening in their eyes.

"Gramps, I can't even begin to thank you," she said, speaking loudly enough for him to hear. "You don't know how much this means to me. To *us*. You're the sweetest, most thoughtful man I know."

"You deserve it, honey. The money isn't doing me any good

just sitting there, so I figured I may as well give it to you now so I can see it put to good use. You deserve a good house to hold all them babies." He winked at her and smiled proudly.

Grace pulled over the footstool to perch on so she wasn't kneeling on the floor. She took his frail hand in hers and gave it a gentle squeeze. "Well, it was very kind of you. We've been looking at houses already, but the one we liked was sold by the time we made an offer. Our realtor told us there were a few in Forest Springs, and we may have to do that. It's a further drive to school for David, and I'm not sure what that would mean for school districts for the kids, but it may be worth considering. There aren't a lot of houses for sale in Mapleport big enough for our family."

"Now, sweetie, don't be hasty. I know you want to get moved and settled in before the babies are born, but don't rush into anything. Now, me, I never had to worry about that sort of thing. I was born at the homestead there on the orchard, and when my daddy got too old, I took over for him. Edna moved in with me when we got married, so I lived in that house my entire life until I came here. I don't know anything at all about moving and prices and school districts. But I want your whole family to be happy about the move. If you need to wait out the market to find the right house, go ahead."

"You're probably right, Gramps. It would just be a lot easier if it happened *before* we have three newborns in the house."

He chuckled a wheezy sort of laugh that showed his age. "You were always my favorite, Gracie Lynn," he said softly, with a fond smile. "Of all my grandkids, you were the one dearest to my heart. Oh, don't get me wrong—I love all of my grands, but from the time you were a baby I had a special connection with you. I remember when you lived with us, back when your daddy passed on."

His eyes held a faraway look, as if he was seeing a time long past. Grace studied his face, wondering about the first couple years of her life. She knew it had been a difficult time for her mother, but Gramps clearly had good memories of those years.

"I used to just sit there and hold you at night," Erwin continued. "Edna would be tidying up in the kitchen, your momma would be getting Olivia ready for bed, and I'd just sit there and hold you in my arms and pray for you. Such a little baby, never even knowing her daddy. It seemed to be a heavy burden for such a little girl to bear. I knew you'd have a hard time of it in the world, 'specially with your momma not being a believer herself. I prayed and prayed that you'd come to know Jesus despite it all. It took a long time, but those prayers were answered, now, weren't they?" He looked at her with an affectionate smile.

Grace threw her arms around him. "Oh, Gramps! That's the sweetest thing I ever heard. You're something else, you know that? Thank you for your prayers. God answered them in a better way than any of us could have expected. He even threw in a godly husband for good measure, and now here I am expecting twins! Who could ask for anything more?"

They both chuckled, and she kissed his leathery cheek before pulling away. "I have to get back to unlock the house for the kids," she said reluctantly. "David has a meeting after school, so I need to be there when they walk home. But thanks again, Gramps. When we do find the house of our dreams, you'll be the first to know."

She smiled as she let herself out of the house, warmth spreading over her as she recalled Gramps' words. To be so loved and accepted was such a comforting feeling. Her grandpa was one special guy.

***

"David? Do you happen to have any free time this afternoon?"

It was Mary Kent, and David's pulse quickened as that fact registered in his brain. "I think so," he answered. "Do you have a house to show us?"

Her voice was excited. "David, it's perfect. It hasn't even gone on the market yet, but the owners contacted me about selling it, and when I went today for the walk-through, I thought of your family immediately. It's on Sheridan Road, two miles away from St. John. You could walk if you were so inclined. Good neighborhood, nice houses. This house is a four-bedroom, but the basement could serve as a bedroom too, like its own little apartment. I asked them if they'd mind someone coming to view it already, and they were more than happy to comply. Apparently they need to leave ASAP. So if you like the place, it would probably be ready within a month, which is uncommon. You could be moving in by early May."

David was catching her enthusiasm. "Sounds great! Let me double check with Grace. If Faith can stay home with the other kids, Grace and I can sneak away for awhile and still get back in time for the soup supper tonight."

Shortly thereafter, the arrangements made, David and Grace were walking into the home Mary was so excited about. She was right. It was perfect for their family. The main floor had a formal living room that David thought could double as an office area, a dining room, large family room, and a nice open kitchen that he could tell appealed to Grace. The upstairs had a large master bed and bath, two smaller rooms across the hall, a bathroom, and a large bedroom at the opposite end of the hall, directly over the garage. The basement was half finished, and the previous owners had installed a tiny bathroom as well. There was even a mini bar with a small refrigerator that was to stay with the house. The backyard was fenced in, which Grace reminded him would be useful for the three new additions who would be toddling around in time.

As they finished the tour, David exchanged glances with his wife. He could tell she was thinking the same thing as he. Although they'd toured more than a dozen houses over the past few weeks, none of them had felt right. This, however, was the "one." But neither did he want to make a hasty decision, so David spoke for both of them.

"Mary, you were right. This house would be great for us. I was wondering, though, if we could sit on it for a day or two. Maybe even bring the kids back here to check it out themselves? We just don't want to make a knee-jerk reaction."

"Absolutely. I completely understand. I'll tell them you're interested and are considering your options. I know this house is slightly more expensive than the others too, and that's assuming they'll take your counteroffer, which I think they will. They'd be happy just to be done with it and not deal with the hassle of officially putting it on the market."

David smiled conspiratorially at Grace. Thanks to Erwin, cost wasn't nearly as big a sticking point as it had been before.

The next day after school, David waited for Jackson and Faith to return from school so he could take the kids to the potential house. Grace excused herself to run an errand, promising to meet them there shortly. When she pulled up ten minutes after they had arrived, she had Gramps with her. The house tour was much more boisterous than the one the previous day. Jackson raced through the house shouting in excitement when he saw the huge closet in the bedroom over the garage, already claiming a spot for his bed and dresser in the room. Katie chattered away happily, and Faith was pleased about the prospect of her own little apartment in the basement for herself and the baby. Even Freddie was happy about the dormer window in the room he would have to share with Jackson. It would be a perfect spot for the telescope he'd received for his birthday.

When the kids were finally corralled back into the car, still shouting to be heard over each other, Grace turned to David and grinned.

"I think they like it," David told Mary. "We'll get back to you tonight."

She nodded knowingly and locked up as David got in the car to take the kids home. Grace linked arms with her grandpa and prompted, "Well?"

He smiled and patted her arm. "Now *that's* the kind of house I want my money to help you buy."

Grace grinned happily. His response was all the affirmation she needed.

CHAPTER

33

By the time Faith's seventeenth birthday occurred in early April, Olivia declared her ready for maternity clothes. Since her birthday fell on a Saturday, Olivia and Grace took her shopping. Grace, with twins, had already been wearing maternity clothes for some time now, most of them courtesy of an earlier shopping spree with Olivia. Faith, on the other hand, was five months along, but it was her first baby, and she could mostly make do with wearing loose shirts. But Olivia wanted to buy her some cute outfits, so the ladies spent the day shopping, giggling together, and enjoying each other's company.

In the last store, Grace excused herself to go to the restroom while Olivia flipped through outfits on a rack. She held up a maternity top to Faith just as two other ladies walked past, eying Faith with displeasure.

"Ugh. Teenagers," one hissed to her companion with barely concealed scorn as the other shook her head in disgust. Faith turned crimson and blinked back tears as they walked away, talking in low voices even as they snuck glances back at her.

"Don't listen to people like that," Olivia insisted in a quiet but firm voice. "Hey, *look* at me, girl!" She waited until Faith met her eyes, then continued, almost fiercely. "They don't know anything about you at all. *Nothing.* They have no idea what your circumstances are or what your personality is like or anything. They know *one* thing about you, and they're making an assessment based on that sole fact. It's a terrible way to judge a person. You deserve better than that, and those of us who know you realize this one thing doesn't define who you are. Got it?"

Faith nodded mutely, but Olivia knew the comment would stick with her. She could see her niece's heart wasn't in the shopping trip anymore, so when Grace returned from the bathroom, Olivia declared them done and the trip a success. "But let's stop at the coffee shop on the way back," she insisted, hoping to get Faith's mind off the cruel comment. "They make the most decadent brownies there. My treat."

The brownies were good, and Faith cheered up a bit while they chatted over the gooey treats, but she was still a bit reserved, glancing around as if to detect other naysayers. Olivia silently seethed at the two ladies who had been so callous. Did they even realize the effect they'd had on Faith? Or would they even care? The three of them had been having such a wonderful day together, and now Faith could only think about those two words from a complete stranger. It was dreadfully unfair.

Swinging by to pick up Andy, Olivia drove everyone back to the Neunabers' house for Faith's birthday meal. They'd planned this deliberately so David had to cook, and they could smell the chicken curry as soon as they walked in.

"Yum! Smells great in here!" Grace complimented her husband, going over to give him a kiss.

"Hi, guys!" he greeted them. "Well, I don't think it'll taste quite like yours, Grace, but I followed the recipe as well as I could. Hope it's not too disappointing, Faith. I tried." He made a face, and she giggled.

"Hey, why don't you put on a new top for dinner, Faith?" Olivia suggested brightly. "You need to put the clothes to good use. Come on, I'll help you pick something out."

She whisked Faith back to her room with the bags of clothes, and shortly they emerged, Faith wearing a lightweight V-neck sweater with three-quarter-length sleeves. It was teal with black flecks in it and looked good against Faith's skin tone. The sweater had a seam right underneath the bust and above the baby bump, perfectly complementing the shape of a pregnant woman. Faith looked especially cute in the top, and it was Olivia's personal favorite of all the clothes they'd gotten. She hoped it would boost Faith's confidence.

While Jackson and Freddie made a deliberate point of ignoring their sister, David and Andy both oohed and aahed appropriately, but it was Katie who stole the show. She tugged on Faith's hand until her older sister squatted down to her level. "You're as pretty as an angel," she said sincerely.

Faith gave Katie a bear hug as she blinked back tears. The rest of the evening, Faith had a small smile on her face, and Olivia knew Katie had saved the day for her older sister. At that moment, she was very grateful for the power of a compliment from a six-year-old.

The last half of April ushered in a phase of frantic packing for David and Grace as they aimed to move by the middle of May. Grace sorely wished she'd already quit her job, although she knew even the small paycheck helped. Her mother and Olivia each came twice a week to help pack. It was a good excuse to purge old clothes, toys, and books, and they made more than one trip to Goodwill to make a drop off.

One afternoon Carol arrived shortly after two o'clock, just as Grace arrived home from her job. The ladies could squeeze in an hour and a half of packing before any of the kids could be expected, and they worked doggedly together to get as much done as possible. Today they tackled pictures on the walls, wrapping them carefully with bath towels and extra blankets.

When they'd been working about an hour, Carol glanced at Grace and said in a casual voice, "So I've been thinking…"

"Yes?" Grace prompted, only half listening as she tried to arrange the pictures in a box to lay flat.

"Faith asked me if I wanted to go to the early service with her on Sunday for Easter, and I think maybe I will."

Grace stopped fiddling with the pictures and gave her mother her full attention. "Are you serious?" she asked, her voice a mixture of excitement and disbelief. Carol had been going to Monday night church with Faith for about two months now but had never discussed it with Grace or expressed any interest in attending church on a Sunday morning. Grace was sure Faith had made the offer to get Carol into church for a festival service, which meant Faith would be in attendance as well. She was willing to have a packed church see her baby bump if it meant her grandmother could be there. She felt a surge of pride in her daughter.

"I… I think I'm ready," her mother confessed. "It's high time I started going back to church for real. Dad might even give it a try too. If nothing else we could take Gramps on Sundays so Liv and Andy don't have to come get him each week."

"Mom, that's great!" Grace had completely forgotten about the pictures. Her mother wasn't a terribly demonstrative woman, and religion was something private to her. Grace knew it was difficult for her to be having this discussion at all.

"I guess Gram's funeral kind of got to me," Carol confessed in a low voice, her eyes on the box in front of her. "Made me think about the purpose of life and what really happens after death. I mean, if we all just die and that's it, then what's the point of living at all, you know? But if there's something after this life… Well, then, I want to get it right."

"Oh, Mom," Grace whispered. She engulfed her mother in a hug. "I know how confusing it can be," she assured her. "I went through the process myself just two years ago. At first my hang-up was that I thought all Christians were judgmental and self-righteous and wouldn't want the likes of me in their midst. I had all sorts of excuses. But David helped me see that the Christian faith is all about forgiveness. *God's* forgiveness. Despite all the mistakes I've made in the past, God has forgiven me because of Jesus."

"I used to know all that," sniffled Carol, pulling away from the embrace. "I used to believe that. I grew up with it, remember? But when I got into high school… I don't know, it just seemed suddenly childish, like still believing in Santa or something. I didn't have any other friends who went to church, so I sort of kept it a secret that I was a Christian. And then I fell head over heels in love with Dennis, and he had no use for religion at all, making it that much easier for me to avoid church myself. And as I got older, I made some pretty big mistakes, so I figured I was beyond hope by then anyway." She blushed as she snuck a glance at her daughter. One such mistake surrounded the circumstances of Grace's birth.

"Mom, *none* of us are beyond hope," insisted Grace. "Look at Faith. She's an unwed pregnant teenager. But she knows God has forgiven her for that. And hey, what about me?" Her pulse quickened as she continued. "I had an abortion when I was eighteen." She'd never told her mother about that, but Carol needed to know how powerful forgiveness was.

"You *did*?" Carol looked and sounded astonished. "Grace! I had no idea! Sweetie, why didn't you tell me?"

"Because I was too ashamed," she said quietly, tears coursing down her cheeks. "That's why Bob and I dropped out of college. I thought you guys would kill me if you found out I was pregnant, so I never said anything to anyone about it."

"Oh, honey," moaned Carol, reaching to give her another hug. "We would have stood behind you, just like you're standing behind Faith."

"I know that now," Grace said through her tears, "but at the time I was terrified. Abortion seemed like the only option." She pulled away from her mom and wiped her face. "But, Mom, I know I'm even forgiven for *that*. David knows about it, and so does Pastor. They were both really understanding, and Pastor assured me that God has forgiven me. So if Faith and I can both have clean slates, I know you can as well."

Carol pulled out a tissue to wipe her own face. "Thanks, sweetheart," she said. "For being honest with me and for the words of encouragement. I'm still sort of figuring out what I believe, but I'll be there on Easter. You have my word. Now," she continued in a business-like tone, "we need to get these boxes done and into the garage. The kids will be back soon."

The two ladies returned to the task at hand, even though Grace's mind was a million miles away. Her heart was still pounding after telling her mother about the abortion, and she second-guessed herself for saying anything about it. What was her mom thinking of her now? She peeked at Carol's face but saw no judgment there. Sadness, perhaps. But also something else. Might it be hope? Grace remembered how it felt to be sorting through conflicting emotions, desperately wanting to believe she could be forgiven and yet at the same time afraid the Gospel message was too good to be true.

As she reached for another picture, Grace said a silent prayer for Carol, cautiously optimistic that maybe, just maybe, her mother was ready for a new start.

CHAPTER

34

The Easter Sunrise service arrived with an air of
anticipation as church members filed into the quiet sanctuary
lit only by the faint hint of dawn. Grace and David barely
managed to get everyone ready in time and sent Faith over
before them to wait for Carol and find a pew. When the rest of
them arrived one minute before the service began, they found
Faith in a pew with both Carol and Walt, looking rather
uncomfortable and out of place. Grace slid in next to her
mother and reached over to give her dad's hand a warm
squeeze as Pastor began.

As always, the Easter service radiated joy. It was easily
Grace's favorite holiday. Since it had been one of the first
services she'd attended after becoming a Christian, Easter held
a special place in her heart. She hoped the same would hold
true for her parents.

When Communion came, Carol and Walt stayed in the
pew with Jackson, who wasn't old enough to partake of the
Sacrament yet, but thought himself too old to get a blessing at
the rail. Grace stood next to Faith, who was wearing a

flattering maternity dress Olivia had gotten her. She looked cute, but Grace also noticed a few members give her looks of disapproval as they walked back to their pew, and Grace hoped Faith hadn't seen them. But others were more welcoming. Both the Sullivans and the Robertsons smiled encouragingly at her, glad to see her at a Sunday service again.

The McNeals hosted Easter dinner at their place that afternoon, since Grace and David's house was more than half packed already. The meal was a noisy affair, as always. Twelve people together in one room did not make for a quiet dinner, especially when Olivia and Andy were competing to be heard. But Grace noted that her mother, who was naturally less outgoing than either of her daughters, seemed even more reserved than usual. In fact, she seemed nervous, taking frequent sips of her water and smoothing her napkin in her lap. Finally, at a lull in the conversation, Carol seemed to work up her courage to address the group.

"So you all know that Grandpa Walt and I went to church with Grace and David's family today, and I know you're all wondering how that went but are too polite to ask. It was a lovely service, and it reminded me of going to church as a kid." She stopped and looked at her father, who nodded. "I just want to let you know that we've decided to start going to church again. I... I want to be a daughter again." She stopped, furiously blinking back tears as she intently studied her hands in her lap. The reference to Edna's funeral was not lost on the assembly. She wanted to be a daughter of the King.

"Oh, Mom," Olivia said with a catch in her voice. "That's the best news I could ever hope to hear!" She was sitting next to Carol and practically lunged at her mother to hug her, very nearly knocking over a water glass in the process. Carol laughed as she accepted her daughter's embrace, and everyone else laughed and wiped away tears simultaneously. Grace reached over to squeeze Faith's hand. She was certain God had used Faith's circumstances to reach Carol, and she was infinitely grateful.

That news buoyed Grace through the last week of April and first part of May, which were filled with constant packing. A family from church had offered use of their snowmobile trailer to move the furniture so they didn't have to rent a moving truck, so they made multiple trips back and forth between the two houses to move everything. Walt and Andy helped with the moving and lifting, while Olivia and Carol helped Grace unpack at the new house, forbidding her and Faith to lift any boxes at all. With everyone helping, the process went much faster, and by the weekend, everything had been moved out of their old house. Grace, Carol, Olivia, and Faith spent that entire Saturday cleaning the empty house, and when it was done, David brought the rest of the kids back for one last walk-through.

Grace didn't realize how much the move would affect her. They walked through each empty room, recalling memories as they went.

"Remember when Dad came over and watched *Cars* with us that first week?" Freddie asked as they stood in the empty living room.

"Or how Katie asked him if he'd spend the night here when we were eating dinner?" Jackson asked with a grin. They all laughed. It had been an innocent question, but it was the first time David had eaten dinner with them, and Grace was sure it would give him the wrong impression of her.

"I remember a few times the smoke alarm went off," David said with a sly grin as they walked into the kitchen. Grace chuckled at the memories.

Katie let out a small sigh when she walked into her old room. "I liked sharing a room with you," she said, looking at Faith with a forlorn expression. "I'll be kind of lonely all by myself." Grace swallowed hard as Faith reached down to take her little sister's hand.

"You can share with Freddie, and I'll have my own room," inserted Jackson hopefully.

"Nice try, kiddo," David told him, ruffling his hair.

"I remember when I got a Buzz Lightyear for my birthday a few years ago and Jackson was playing with it in our room when I brushed my teeth," Freddie said as they walked into the boys' empty room.

"I was not!" Jackson shot back, his face aflame. "I don't play with baby toys!" Everyone laughed. His reaction made it clear that Jackson had been doing just that.

When they entered the master bedroom, Jackson said, "I don't even *want* to know what went on in here!"

"Oh, Jackson!" admonished Grace, shaking her head. "I've had discussions with each of you in here," she reminded them. "It was sort of our private little conference room to get away from everyone else." Her kids all nodded in agreement.

They made their way back to the living room slowly, lost in the silence of memories. As they stood in the empty living room, Grace finally started to cry. "It's really been a good house, hasn't it?" she asked through her tears. "We have lots of memories here. And notice that when we were thinking of things, we only mentioned good memories. This is where we became a family. I'll miss this house. But I also know that we'll make new memories in our new house. Because really, being with all of you is what makes a house a home."

David reached over to hug her. "You're absolutely right," he said. "Of all the places I've ever lived, this house has the most meaning to me. When I've moved before, yes, I was sad to leave friends, but I honestly never thought twice about the houses I left. But this is different. This is where I met and got to know all of you, and you put up with me moving in here and changing the entire dynamic of the house. I have fond memories of this place, and I'll miss it too. But our new house will be better for all of us, and I'm glad we can settle in there before the babies are born."

Jackson spoke then, surprising Grace. "Maybe we could, like, say a prayer or something?" he asked. "To sort of say goodbye?"

"Wonderful idea, Jackson," David seconded. "Do you want to pray?"

His eyes widened in panic. "Not at all!" he answered quickly. "I figured you could do it."

David chuckled. "I'm just teasing you, buddy. I'll pray." The family formed a circle and held hands as he bowed his head. "Dear Lord, we thank You for providing us with a new house to hold our growing family. We're excited about the change, but also a bit sad to be leaving this house. Thank You for all the wonderful memories we have of our time here. Thank You for allowing us to become a family in this house. Bless whoever moves here next, that they may have good memories as well. And now please bless us in our new home, that we continue to grow together as a family. Thank You for all Your blessings. Amen."

"Amen," they echoed together before shuffling out to the van to drive to their new house. Grace and David paused at the door before locking it up.

"This seems so… final," Grace said, her voice breaking. "It's hard to believe I'll never walk through this door again." She bit her lip and fought the tears, but it was no use. They slid down her cheeks anyway.

"I know," he said, his own voice catching a bit. "I didn't think it would be this hard."

She shut the door and turned the key with a small sob, then turned to her husband and grabbed his hand. "You okay?" he asked her.

Grace nodded, and together they walked to the van, ready to begin the next chapter in their lives.

CHAPTER

35

Grace looked up in surprise as Cynthia McDowell approached her in the narthex after church. The two were cordial enough to one another, but Cynthia had never sought her out before. Grace wondered why she was doing so now.

"Do you have a few minutes?" Cynthia asked.

"Sure," she replied, even more curious.

Cynthia motioned her to a corner of the narthex where they had relative privacy. "I'd like to throw you a baby shower," Cynthia began.

Grace felt the heat rush to her face. What was she to say to such a comment?

"Now, before you object, let me tell you what I'm planning," Cynthia hastened. "I'm well aware of the fact that your family will need three of everything all at the same time. You can't just hand down a crib from one baby to the next. You need three car seats, three cribs, three dressers, three high chairs… I'm sure you've thought of these things before. Not to mention oodles of diapers and wipes and clothes. So I'm thinking we throw a shower and invite all the ladies from church and school. They'd be happy to support their principal's family. Instead of having everyone get their own gift, I'd like to coordinate so you get big ticket items you need. For example, I'd collect donations from the preschool class, say, and put those toward one crib. That way you get what you need, and you don't end up with five hundred baby blankets. May I do that for you? I love to plan this sort of thing."

Grace was at a loss. The offer was generous and certainly tempting, but she'd never felt right about accepting charity. "That's very kind of you, Cynthia," she answered. "But my sister and mother were planning to do a shower themselves. David has a large extended family and they usually do a mail-in shower when someone has a baby. We'll manage. I don't want you to go to all the trouble."

"Oh, it's no trouble at all," insisted Cynthia. "And if your sister and mother are already planning one, we can team up and combine forces. I'll need their help anyhow, to invite family and friends outside St. John. Besides, the facilities here are perfect for hosting a large group. The church ladies love things like this. Please let us do this for you."

"Well…" Grace was torn. It was sweet of Cynthia to suggest the idea, but there was one pesky concern she had to address. "What about Faith?" she asked in a low voice. She'd seen the look on George McDowell's face when he saw Faith at church on Easter. Clearly he was unhappy about her condition. She couldn't imagine Cynthia's husband being supportive of this idea.

"The shower is for her too, naturally!" Cynthia responded kindly. "We want her to know we're supporting her decision to keep the baby."

Tears pricked Grace's eyelids. Her church family was constantly surprising her. Just when she thought most of them were silently judging her family, someone like Cynthia came along to show her otherwise. "Cynthia, I hardly know what to say. I wasn't expecting anything like this at all. Thank you for the kind offer."

"You're very welcome. But if anyone asks you, it was my husband's idea." She laughed at the look on Grace's face. "I have my ways," she continued slyly. "I managed to convince him he inspired the whole thing, and now he realizes it would look worse for him if he corrects people when they ask, so he has to go along with it."

She winked, and Grace had to laugh. She would have loved to have been a fly on the wall for that conversation between George and Cynthia. "Then I'll have to thank him myself," she said.

"Please do! But I need to get moving on this shower. I may do an announcement in the bulletin and newsletter as a group invitation, but I need time to send family invitations and coordinate gifts. Could I have your sister's number? I'll give her a call and see what we can come up with. And if you don't mind, you could give me your number as well, in case I have any questions or need clarification."

"Absolutely." Grace rattled off her number as she pulled out her phone to find Olivia's. Cynthia entered the numbers in her own phone before thanking Grace and walking away, promising to be in touch.

Grace smiled as she watched her go. Olivia and Cynthia would be a dynamic duo as party planners, and it was a relief to have Cynthia on board to get church members involved. Cynthia was right—this way they could get big ticket items out of the way, something that had been weighing on Grace's mind. Now that they were in their new house, her nesting instinct had kicked in, and she longed to fill the rooms with the furniture they needed—cribs, changing tables, dressers, and a rocking chair or two. They had been so busy unpacking their own things that the baby rooms had been placed on the back burner. But now, with Cynthia's help, it appeared that was about to change.

CHAPTER

36

Aaron's heart stopped as he passed Faith's locker. Someone had taped a crude drawing on it, a stick figure with long hair and a fat stomach. Underneath was scrawled a single derogatory word to describe her.

Angrily, he ripped the drawing off, looking around to see if he could find someone who appeared suspicious or guilty. He wadded it up and stuffed it into his pocket, hoping very few other people had seen it. Poor Faith. Everyone knew about her condition by now, and no one could deny she was showing. It was May, after all, and she was six months along. Her slender body did little to hide her growing belly. Whenever she swung her backpack onto her shoulder, the gentle curve of her stomach showed an obvious baby bump whether she wore a maternity top or not. Aaron figured she was just trying to make it till the end of the school year, less than a month away. This morning, however, she was out for a doctor appointment. Apparently whoever hung the drawing was cowardly enough to put it on her locker when there was no chance she would see them do so.

The rest of the morning, Aaron seethed about the drawing, which was burning a hole in his pocket. He didn't dare throw it away, because he had the unreasonable fear that if he did someone would find it in the trashcan and pull it out again. He had to wait until he was safely home to toss it.

Sitting at his table at lunch, someone bumped his shoulder with a tray. "Oh, I'm sorry," a condescending voice said. "Didn't see you there."

Aaron looked up into the eyes of Spencer, who set his tray down and leaned over to whisper, "So did you like my artwork? Or were you the one who took it down? I worked hard on that thing, man." His eyes were glittering, almost cruel, and Aaron wondered again what Faith had ever seen in him. This guy was a class-act jerk. And a complete hypocrite. He was the reason she was pregnant in the first place, yet he dared insult her and call her names. Aaron suspected Spencer was still mad at Faith for not getting an abortion, and this was his way of getting back at her.

Unfortunately, Spencer didn't know when to quit. He leaned closer and hissed, "You're sweet on her, I know. But we both know the only reason she'd ever consider you is because no one else would have her in her present condition. I'll give you some free advice. Don't bother, man. She's so not worth it."

Spencer never saw the right hook coming until Aaron's fist met his face. He yelped in pain and staggered backward, blood gushing from his nose as he cursed loudly. Girls shrieked around them, and people jumped up from their seats to avoid the commotion. Spencer regained his balance and faced Aaron in rage, his eyes narrowed. Aaron stood up with a sense of impending doom, anticipating retaliation. He knew he was no match for Spencer. He felt every eye in the cafeteria on him as

Spencer lunged toward him and punched him in the gut.

As Aaron doubled over with pain, gasping for breath, the crowd simultaneously groaned and exclaimed out loud. Aaron couldn't even stand, but Spencer pressed his advantage and brought his fist up on the bottom of Aaron's jaw, eliciting more screams from the girls.

Thankfully, Mr. Vance stepped between them before Spencer could strike again. "That is *e-nough*! Both of you in my office. Now! Everyone else, steer clear of the blood until Mr. Reuben gets it cleaned up. Back to your lunches. The clock is still ticking for lunch period."

With that, he marched Aaron and Spencer to his office, students gawking at them the entire way. It may have been his imagination, but Aaron thought he saw looks of awe in some of his classmates' eyes as he passed. Whatever they might be feeling, he knew one thing for sure. He felt awful. He was afraid he'd throw up all over the floor, and his teeth felt like they'd been knocked loose. Maybe they had. He was in worse pain than he could imagine, but seeing Spencer pinching his nose to stop the blood gave him great pleasure, even though he knew it shouldn't. He felt a bit like George McFly punching Biff in *Back to the Future*, and he couldn't help but feel a swell of pride that he, the lowly Aaron Sullivan, had taken a shot at the mighty Spencer Young.

Later that evening, Aaron heard the doorbell as he was lying on his bed. He had a terrible headache, his jaw ached, and his stomach was killing him. Fighting was so overrated.

A light knock on his door broke his reverie, and his mom stuck her head in. "Sweetie, there's someone here to see you."

Although it was probably his buddy Brian coming over to commiserate with him, he had a fleeting moment of panic that it was Mr. Vance coming to expel him. After he and Spencer had given their sides of the story, both had been written up for fighting, and Mr. Vance personally called their parents to explain what had happened. Since Aaron hadn't been in trouble at school before, the write-up was the only consequence, although it would stay in his permanent record. Aaron thought that was terribly unfair given the circumstances, especially since he'd only thrown one punch.

Fortunately, his parents had been understanding once he'd explained things, especially after he unwadded the drawing to show them. His mom was still upset, but his dad admitted, "Sometimes words just don't work. The only way to get through to some people is with your fists. You did the right thing, standing up for Faith." And that had been the end of it.

Now Aaron emerged from his room and walked down the hall to the living room. He stopped as he caught a glimpse of his visitor, making small talk with his parents.

Faith.

Aaron's heart sank. Of *course* she'd come at a time when he looked and felt like he'd been run over by a truck.

She looked at him as he entered the room and winced as she saw the large bruise on his jaw. "Ouch," she said sympathetically.

"Yeah, well, you should see the other guy," he joked ruefully.

She laughed before getting to the point. "I'm sorry to barge in on you like this, but do you have a few minutes? I need to talk to you."

"Oh, uh, yeah," he stammered. "We can talk, um…" He shot a look at his mom, Amy, who sat in the armchair. She took her cue and stood.

"Go ahead and make yourselves comfortable out here. Dad

and I will go back to our room, right, honey?" she prompted her husband, who reluctantly rose as well. Aaron could tell his dad was dreadfully curious as to why Faith was there. He wouldn't put it past him to eavesdrop from his room.

As his parents left, Aaron turned to Faith. "Can I get you something to drink? Do you need some water or anything?"

"No, thanks," she said, settling herself more comfortably on the couch. She waited until he sat on the opposite end of the couch, then turned to face him. "I heard what happened today in the cafeteria." Aaron had figured as much. "Chelsea texted me and told me you and Spencer got into a fight, and she had a feeling it was about me…" Her voice faltered slightly before she cleared her throat and continued. "She said if that was true, I may as well not come to school at all today, so that's why I wasn't there in the afternoon. She said I should maybe just lay low and let things cool off over the weekend."

"Okay," he said, well aware that it was a lame answer.

"Aaron, what happened? Please tell me. I need to know, especially if it was about me."

He hesitated. There was no way he was going to tell her about that drawing, but if he didn't tell her, there was no compelling reason he and Spencer would have been talking in the first place.

"Aaron?"

He decided to be as vague as possible. "He passed me in the cafeteria and made a snide comment about you, and I called him out on it. Then he insulted you, and I just couldn't help myself. Before I even knew what I was doing, I punched him right in the face."

Her eyes were large, and she seemed impressed. "I can only imagine what he said about me," she said dryly. "So I guess you were defending my honor, huh?"

He shrugged. "Something like that."

"I'm so sorry, Aaron. I'm sorry this happened to you, and I'm sorry it was on my account. I feel terrible. It's all my fault."

"It's not your fault at all," he insisted. "It's Spencer's. You have no reason to apologize."

"I still feel bad. But I'm impressed. I didn't know you had it in you." She gave him a mischievous smile to let him know she was teasing.

"Oh, of course," he smiled back smugly. "I've been carefully honing my ninja skills all these years, waiting for just such an opportunity to prove myself."

Faith burst out laughing and scooted over to sit closer to him. She reached out tentatively to touch the bruise on his jaw. "Does it hurt?" she asked quietly.

He didn't dare say that her very touch sent a jolt of electricity through him that more than made up for any pain. Instead, he shrugged again and said, "Yeah, sure, but I'll live."

She smiled at him, revealing that adorable dimple on her cheek as Aaron's heart flip-flopped. She withdrew her hand and placed it on her stomach. "The baby's moving. Do you want to feel it?"

Aaron blushed to the roots of his hair that she would make such a personal suggestion. He would never be so bold as to touch her stomach. It was too… intimate.

She sensed his discomfort and giggled. "Come on," she coaxed. "It's really cool." She took his hand and placed his palm strategically over the right side of her belly, holding her own hand on top of his, pressing it firmly against her.

"There! Did you feel that?" she asked, her eyes shining. "He kicked!"

Aaron was embarrassed to admit he hadn't felt anything. Faith repositioned his hand just as the baby moved again. This time Aaron felt it.

"Whoa!" he exclaimed. "I totally felt that one! That's amazing!"

"Isn't it, though? I first felt him move about two months ago, but I wasn't sure at first. I know that sounds dumb, but it was almost like a gurgly stomach the first few times. Like butterfly wings. Really light because he was smaller. Now that he's bigger I can feel him a lot more."

"So it's a boy?"

"Yeah, a boy. Mom didn't want to find out the gender at her ultrasound, but I did. This way I know what clothes to get. There! He moved again!"

She was still holding his hand against her stomach, and he felt the baby move this time as well. He grinned at her, marvelling at the incredible miracle of life inside her womb.

After a few more seconds, she released his hand and said, "I guess he's done moving for now. Besides, I'd better go." She stood to leave, and he rose with her. "David brought me over, and he's waiting in the car. Probably dying of curiosity by now."

"I'm sure my parents are as well. It wouldn't surprise me if their ears are pressed against their door."

They laughed together, and Faith shocked him by giving him a hug. "Thank you for sticking up for me in school," she whispered in his ear. "That took a lot of courage. And it means a lot to me."

"Anything for you," he said, then grimaced as he realized how sappy that sounded.

Faith didn't seem to be put off by the comment, and kept her arms wrapped around his neck, to his great delight. The words Spencer had spoken earlier came back to taunt him—*We both know the only reason she'd ever consider you is because no one else would have her in her present condition.* He shoved the thought out of his mind.

The two stood there a few moments until Faith pulled away. He walked her to the door and waved at Mr. Neunaber. After they backed out and drove away, Aaron closed the front door and walked slowly back to his room, a huge smile on his face. All he could think about was how right it felt to have his arms around Faith. That fight this morning had been worth it after all.

CHAPTER

37

Cynthia and Olivia had certainly outdone themselves.
Streamers and balloons decorated the school gymnasium, and
each table had a "bouquet" of rolled baby diapers for a vase and
flowers made of baby socks. They'd obviously done their
homework on Pinterest. The Ladies Aid had volunteered to
provide refreshments, and the finger sandwiches and fruit trays
were just enough for a light lunch. According to Olivia, they'd
planned for a hundred and fifty ladies, but Faith estimated
closer to two hundred in attendance, a fact that surprised her.
Besides it being Memorial Day weekend, she'd figured some
women would stay away on her account, but apparently that
hadn't stopped them. The women who showed up were kind
and supportive of both Grace and Faith.

Mother and daughter sat together, each wearing a corsage
as the guests of honor. As women gathered and started eating,
Faith introduced her friends to her aunt and grandma, and they
made pleasant small talk as they enjoyed the food. While they
ate, her mother glanced around the room and stiffened. Faith
looked at her questioningly and followed her gaze. She tensed

as well. Standing by herself near the door was Vivian Young, trying to be inconspicuous.

"Why is she here?" Grace asked in a low voice.

"I have no idea. I didn't even tell her about it. And I doubt Mrs. McDowell or Aunt Livy invited her."

"What should we do?"

"I don't know. Should I… I mean… I guess I should go talk to her?"

Grace sighed. "I suppose one of us should. Want me to go?"

"No, I'll go, Mom. You stay here and chat with Grandma and Aunt Livy. I'm curious now."

Faith rose and walked over to their surprise guest. "Mrs. Young?" she asked as she reached her. "I didn't expect to see you here. I didn't realize you had gotten an invitation to the shower. Did Spencer tell you about it?" She was sure he'd heard of it from other kids in school.

"Darling, I'm well connected in the gossip circle of Mapleport," Vivian assured in her airy voice. "And I figured the least I could do was come show my support as the closet grandmother."

Faith didn't know how to respond. She wasn't sure if the comment was a jab. Vivian looked at her and continued in a less presumptuous tone.

"I'm sorry for Spencer's behavior in all this," she said, her voice wavering ever so slightly. "You have shown far more character than he by choosing to go through with the pregnancy. And I'm glad to see your church is standing behind you. It looks like you'll be well stocked." She gestured toward the stage, where an impressive collection of gifts was on display.

"Yes, we will. I'm surprised at how much support we received. The church members were shocked at first, and some of them were pretty judgmental, but most of them have come to realize that we all make mistakes, and that our mistakes don't have to define us."

Vivian smiled faintly. "What a charming way to look at it, dearie."

Again, Faith wasn't sure how to take the words. She couldn't tell if Mrs. Young was being condescending or sincere.

"Well, darling, I needn't keep you. But I wanted to tell you that if you need help with babysitting next year during school, I'd be more than happy to help."

The offer startled Faith. Vivian Young didn't seem the type to cuddle a baby. She was always dressed fashionably, with coordinating jewelry, and Faith had never seen her wear anything other than high heels. She didn't think Mrs. Young could handle a baby spitting up on her shoulder.

"Don't look so surprised, darling!" Vivian laughed. "I know a thing or two about babies. Spencer is my youngest of three, as you know. Besides, I could use the company. Leonard is gone so often on business, and Spencer will be off to Ann Arbor come fall, so it'll just be me rattling around in that big house most of the time. The cleaning lady only comes once a week. I could stand a bit more excitement."

"I'll keep that in mind," said Faith, wondering how serious the offer was. "I haven't even thought about next year yet."

"No worries, dear," said Vivian with a wave of her perfectly manicured hand. "You have our number. Just call when you need me. And here, this is for you." She pressed a sealed envelope in Faith's hand and hastened out the door.

Faith stared after her in surprise, still trying to make sense of the exchange. Then she glanced around furtively before ripping open the embossed envelope, her curiosity getting the better of her. Inside she found ten crisp one hundred dollar bills. Gasping, she stuffed the money back inside and tucked the envelope safely in her pocket before making her way back to her mother.

Before Grace could ask her anything, Cynthia stood at the microphone and clapped her hands to get everyone's attention. "Ladies, if I could ask you to quiet down, please? I need my representatives to come up here so we can present the gifts. While they're coming this way, I want to remind you that there's a sign-up sheet by the door for meals once the babies are born. Since the due dates are both late July, I have slots starting in August, three times a week. If you haven't signed up yet, please do so. We all know how hard it is to get food on the table with a newborn in the house. Now, let's show Grace and Faith their gifts, shall we?"

Faith was astonished by the sheer volume of gifts. She'd never realized how much a small baby needed. Looking at the stage, she wondered how everything would fit into their house around the rest of the family members.

"First, we start with the school classes," Mrs. McDowell continued. "Youngest to oldest. Preschool?"

Little Hannah Roth stepped shyly to the microphone Mrs. McDowell held for her and said, "We got you a crib." Everyone oohed and aahed as Olivia, on the stage, motioned to one of the three cribs on display. Olivia was obviously enjoying her role very much, playing the part of game show hostess as she ran her hands along the railings and gestured appropriately. *All she needs is the evening gown,* Faith thought with amusement.

"And we got another crib!" Katie chimed in proudly, stepping up as the kindergarten representative.

The rest of the grades presented their gifts: a double stroller, a changing table, two high chairs, and the third crib.

"Wonderful!" enthused Cynthia as the students returned to their seats amidst applause. "And now for our church organizations. As Ladies Aid president, I am pleased to present three brand-new car seats!" Olivia held one up and turned it around for all to inspect.

"And in the absence of any males, I'll present the elders' gift as well—an infant swing and an exersaucer." Women nodded approvingly around the room as Olivia displayed those items as well.

This is unbelievable, Faith thought. *I don't even know what to do with half of this stuff. I'm in way over my head.* Seeing the mountain of supplies in front of her was a vivid reminder of just how life-changing it would be to have a baby. Her mother had been right—watching a baby for a few hours was one thing. Caring for one around the clock was quite another. Now she began to perceive what Grace meant when she'd said this was more than "playing house." She felt completely overwhelmed and unequal to the enormous task ahead of her.

"Youth Group?" Cynthia prompted. Faith forced herself to focus as Mrs. McDowell handed the microphone to Bree Robertson.

"We bought a single stroller for Faith, and a Pack 'n Play so she can use it for babysitting arrangements," Bree answered. Faith blinked back tears as Bree smiled at her. There weren't a lot of kids in the Youth Group. Each must have given a significant amount to cover the cost of both items. She was touched that they cared enough to do so.

Dorothy Wilcox informed the assembly that the choir had gone in for a dresser, which matched the cribs, and Greta Roth stepped forward to announce that the school board donations had purchased another dresser.

Mrs. McDowell took her place at the microphone once

again to say, "We also took donations from Grace's out-of-town family, and were able to get the third dresser you see up there, plus two bouncy seats! And many of you wished to bring something today as well, or weren't involved in any of the organizations, so look how many diapers, wipes, and formula we were able to collect!" She motioned toward the stage. One crib was overflowing with diapers of all sizes, one held bottles and canisters of formula, and the third held an impressive number of wipes.

The entire assembly broke into applause as the gift presentation came to a close, and ladies stood to chat before starting to drift away. Many women came to congratulate and hug Faith and her mother before they left. Mr. McDowell arrived with his snowmobile trailer to transport the gifts, and David and Andy came to help load everything at the school and then unload it at the house.

Faith could tell by the smiles and laughter of those around her that the shower had been a smashing success by their standards. Everyone seemed to be in particularly jovial moods. But the shower had had the opposite effect on Faith. Instead of feeling excitement, she was apprehensive, perhaps even dreading the birth of her baby. The shower was a stark reminder that this was for real, and there was no turning back.

CHAPTER

38

After Aaron's lunchroom scuffle with Spencer, there was a shift in the dynamic between Faith and Aaron. She started sitting with him at lunch on her own accord, and he waited for her by her locker each morning to walk her to class. He did so partly to make sure no one hung any more signs on her locker. Now he somehow felt the need to shield her. She didn't need to see something like that. He even took her home once or twice when Chelsea wasn't available to do so.

Presently, however, Aaron began to notice that some of the other students were laughing at him. Not openly, of course, but he knew people gossiped about him, speculating about his relationship with Faith. And he realized that the common consensus agreed with Spencer—she only hung out with him because no one else wanted her. In other words, she was using him. And he was too much of a sucker to realize it.

Although Aaron tried to banish these thoughts, they ate away at him, planting seeds of doubt in his mind. He hated to admit it, but there was probably some truth in what everyone was saying. Under normal circumstances, Faith never would have started hanging out with him in public. Maybe everyone else was right. Maybe he was hopelessly naïve.

Finally, he couldn't stand it anymore. He had to address the topic or it would continue to consume his thoughts. So on the final Friday of school, he offered to drive her home. The following week they had half days for exam week, and then everyone was out for the summer.

Aaron let Faith do most of the talking on the drive since his stomach was in knots as he tried to work up the courage to speak what was on his mind. When they reached her house, he pulled up to the curb but stopped her before she could get out.

"Faith, wait. I need to ask you something."

She shifted awkwardly to face him, her bulging stomach making it difficult to turn with ease.

"Um, I… Look, I need to know… Do you…" Aaron stopped, his face flaming. He knew he sounded like an idiot. He inhaled deeply and blurted out, "Why are you hanging out with me?"

The blunt question seemed to surprise Faith. "What do you mean?" she asked, frowning slightly. "I like being with you. You're a good friend."

Aaron turned away so he didn't have to look into her beautiful brown eyes. He knew he couldn't look at those eyes and go through with his questions. He didn't want to hurt her, but he had to know the truth. "But would you think so if you weren't pregnant?"

Faith's breath caught in her throat. "Why would you even ask such a question?"

He turned toward her again, his face hard as he repeated the words that had haunted him since Spencer spoke them three weeks ago. "We both know the only reason you'd ever hang out with me is because no other guy would want to be seen with you in your present condition, isn't that right?"

"Aaron!"

"You're using me. You know I like you, Faith. You know I've had a crush on you forever. I was so excited when you joined the church and started going to Youth Group. And when you sang for your mom's wedding, I thought you were the prettiest girl in the whole world, wearing that purple dress, and the way you had your hair pulled up. And your voice was so beautiful. You looked and sounded like an angel."

She had tears streaming down her face, though he could only speculate as to why.

"But you wouldn't give me the time of day at school. I wasn't part of your crowd. Now that they've all deserted you, though, you figure you'll settle for me, right?"

"Aaron—" she pleaded.

"You've turned me into a laughingstock at school!"

The words hung thickly in the air, and Faith jerked back as if he'd slapped her in the face.

"I've turned *you* into a laughingstock?" she spat out. "Well, that's rich. Who's pregnant? Whose boyfriend dumped her because of that and wants nothing to do with her anymore? Who has to face the jeers and taunts of other students? If anyone here is a laughingstock, it's me!"

"Then you're bringing me down with you!"

"Aaron!" Her tone was sharp.

He knew he was out of line, but he stubbornly continued. "Answer me this, then. Remember when I asked you to the Valentine's Dance?" She fidgeted uncomfortably, and he pressed on, his eyes narrowed. "Would you have gone to the dance with me if you hadn't been pregnant? Would you even have considered it?"

She avoided his eyes and squirmed under the question.

"That's what I thought," he said quietly. "Goodbye, Faith."

"Aaron, please. I—"

"Good*bye*, Faith." He stared straight ahead out the front windshield, not daring to look at her.

For a moment the silence was oppressive, and he feared she'd try to press the issue. But at last she got out of the car and walked up the sidewalk with her back straight, never once looking back. Aaron watched her until she was safely inside, then drove away slowly, feeling very much like his heart had just been ripped out of his chest.

David and Grace looked at each other in alarm as Faith slammed the front door and rushed downstairs to her room. Her sobs were loud enough for everyone in the house to hear.

Katie looked up, scared, as Freddie said, "I guess *she* had a bad day." He shrugged and took a bite of his after-school snack, clearly not terribly concerned.

"Should I—" Grace started, but David stood and interrupted her.

"No, I've got it," he assured. "Let me check on her first."

As he approached the basement door, he wondered why in the world he had volunteered in the first place. He wasn't sure Faith would talk to him, but something told him she didn't want her mother at this point, either. Sometimes he felt like Faith resented Grace ever so slightly, or at least was jealous of her. Everyone was excited for and supportive of Grace's pregnancy, but people looked at Faith differently.

Knocking to announce his presence, David let himself in without being invited. He walked down the stairs and knelt beside Faith's bed, rubbing her back as she cried. "Do you want to talk about it?" he asked when there was a slight lull in her tears.

She shocked him by flinging herself off the bed and into his arms, her whole body shaking as she cried on his shoulder. He was in a terribly uncomfortable position on the floor with his legs pinned beneath him, but he tried not to think about it as he patted her back and hugged her. Eventually she pulled away and stood to get a tissue, and he seized the opportunity to peel himself off the floor and sit on her bed. She came back to plop down next to him, her eyes downcast.

Putting his arm around her, David pulled her into a hug from the side. Faith leaned into him before saying in a small and forlorn voice, "He broke up with me."

His eyes widened. "Do you mean Aaron?"

Faith nodded and burrowed her face into his shoulder.

Trying to digest this information, David frowned. "I didn't know the two of you were dating," he said.

"We weren't."

David sighed. He'd long since given up trying to understand women. He and Grace had experienced a similar "break up" before they were officially dating, something Grace still teased him about to this day. Apparently a woman's definition of "breaking up" was much looser than his own narrow interpretation of the term.

"Well...?" he prompted gently.

"Aaron told me that I was using him. That the only reason I was spending time with him was because no one else wanted to hang out with me. He said I was exploiting his crush on me, and that if I wasn't pregnant I probably wouldn't even give him the time of day."

David experienced a rush of emotions. He silently fumed at Aaron for being so insensitive and callous. Aaron had been the one who told David in the first place that Faith needed support. Where was that support from *him*? Didn't he know how emotionally fragile she was right now? Didn't he realize she needed his friendship?

But at the same time, he had to concede that there was some truth to his words. Aaron wasn't the kind of guy with whom Faith would usually choose to keep company. And anyone with eyes could see the poor guy had a major crush on her. Maybe subconsciously, Faith was playing it safe by turning to him, knowing he wouldn't refuse her. Only now he had.

"The thing is, David, I'm really mad at him right now. *Really* mad. But it's partly because he's kind of right, and hurt pride always stings. He asked me to the Valentine's Dance way back at the beginning of February, and that's when I told him I was pregnant. So today he asked if I would have even considered his request if I hadn't been able to use the pregnancy card as an out. I… I wouldn't have gone with him. He's right." She sniffled and wiped her eyes before going on.

"But I'm not the same person I was then, either," she insisted, looking into David's face. "A lot has changed, and I see things from a different perspective now. Looking back, I have no idea what I ever saw in Spencer. He's stuck up and arrogant and a real jerk. I'm embarrassed I fell for him in the first place. Aaron, on the other hand, isn't cute or handsome or anything, but what makes him attractive is how nice he is. He's sweet and thoughtful and loyal." Her voice cracked. "Well, *most* of the time, he's loyal," she amended.

Faith cleared her throat and continued. "Getting pregnant in high school was a dumb thing to do. But it really opened my eyes to a lot of things. It showed me who my true friends are and how shallow most of my relationships were. And Aaron was a true friend all along, even when I couldn't see that. The world would be a better place if more people were like him. I don't want to lose his friendship. I… I actually like him now. I mean, like, *like* him," she confessed bashfully.

A tear trickled slowly down her cheek, and David hugged her again, resting his chin on the top of her head. He let her cry for a few moments, then spoke gently. "I'm very proud of you, Faith, for realizing what's important in a person. Our society is terribly fickle, placing great value on outer beauty and body image. But what truly matters is what a person is like on the inside. It's a lesson many people don't figure out until well into adulthood. I'm proud of you for learning it already."

"Thanks, I guess. Not the way I would have picked to learn the lesson, but what can you do?" She attempted a sad laugh before looking at him again. "So what should I do now?"

David was at a loss. "Ah, well... What do you think you should do?" He was terribly proud of himself for deflecting the question back to her.

"I don't know," she admitted. "He seemed really mad at me. Or offended. Or hurt. Maybe all three. I don't know if I should just give him time or if I should try to patch things up between us. Maybe I should do both. I mean, like, wait a week or so before I talk to him about it?"

She looked at David imploringly, as if asking for advice. He said, "I think that sounds like a good plan, honey. He probably does need some space right now, but I think you should eventually bring up the subject with him. For your sake and for his, I think you should work to repair the relationship."

Faith nodded and blew her nose. "Thanks for coming down to talk to me. That's a good dad thing to do."

She said this in all sincerity without a trace of sarcasm or resentment under her words. David kissed the top of her head as he swallowed over the lump in his throat. It was the closest she'd ever come to calling him *Dad*. He'd take it.

CHAPTER

39

The ringing of his phone startled Aaron out of a sound sleep, and he sat up, disoriented, to glance at his clock. Three thirty-four. This wasn't good. He fumbled for his phone and knocked it off the nightstand. Groaning, he leaned over and grabbed it, checking the caller ID.

Faith.

Aaron's heart skipped a beat as he answered at the very end of his ringtone.

"Faith? What's wrong?"

She was crying on the other end. "Aaron, I'm sorry. I don't know who else to call. I need your help. My water just broke, and I need you to take me to the hospital."

A surge of anger coursed through Aaron's body. What kind of cruel prank was this? Did she think he was an idiot? For one thing, she wasn't due for at least another month. And with all her family nearby, why would she ever call *him* to take her to the hospital? Was this just her way of getting back at him?

"Oh, come on, Faith. Give me a break," he sighed. He nearly hung up, but the tone of her voice stopped him. She truly did sound like she was panicking.

"Aaron, I'm serious! I'm all alone in the house, and I can't find anyone else to take me. Mom and David are on Mackinac Island for an early anniversary trip. Katie and the boys are staying with David's parents in Detroit. Grandma and Grandpa are with Aunt Olivia and Uncle Andy at the McNeals' cabin. Chelsea and her family are on vacation. Bree didn't answer her phone. Neither did Madison or Julie. I even tried calling Pastor but he didn't pick up, either. And even if I wanted to, I can't call Spencer because he and his parents flew out to visit his brother. I don't know what to do. Please, will you help me? Even if you're still mad at me, please come anyway. At least for the sake of the baby. I... I need you."

Aaron felt his anger melting away. He'd long since gotten over his hard feelings toward her and deeply regretted confronting her the way he had. Last week they'd had exams, and the two had avoided each other the entire week. He'd picked up the phone a dozen times to call or text her, but feared she was mad at him. She had every right to be. But the truth was, he really missed the way things used to be. He missed *her*.

"I thought you weren't due until July."

"I'm not! July 24! Aaron, I am *freaking out!*" She was hiccuping her words out between sobs. "This isn't supposed to be happening! I called my doctor, and she told me to get to the hospital. Once the water breaks they have to deliver. I'm six weeks early."

Terror gripped Aaron's heart. He was already out of bed, reaching for a pair of jeans. "I'll be right there," he promised. "Give me ten minutes."

"Okay. Please hurry."

"I will. See you soon."

He hung up and stuffed his feet into his shoes and grabbed his glasses from the dresser. He didn't dare waste time putting his contacts in. He jogged down the hall to his parents' room and shook his mom's shoulder to wake her up. Alarmed, she jolted awake and instinctively smacked her husband to rouse him as well. Both sat up in confusion and tried to focus on the intruder.

"It's just me," Aaron assured them. "Something bad happened to Faith. Her water broke already. She needs to get to the hospital, but no one in her family is in town. Her other friends are either out of town or didn't answer when she called them. She sounded really scared when she called me and asked if I could come get her. I need to go."

His mom was already swinging her legs out of bed. "I'll take you," she said decisively. "That poor girl needs a mother figure there at a time like this. Where are her parents?"

"She said they were on Mackinac Island for an early anniversary trip."

His parents exchanged glances in the dim light shining in from the moon. Aaron guessed what they were thinking. There were no ferries running at this time of day. And once the Neunabers were able to get across to the mainland, it was a good four-hour drive back home. Assuming the ferries started at eight o'clock, they wouldn't be able to make it back for eight or nine hours. If it came to it, Faith may well have to deliver this baby without her own mother there.

"They left Faith home alone?" Mark asked.

"Dad, she's seventeen," Aaron reminded him. "She probably didn't want to go stay with Mr. Neunaber's parents like her siblings."

His mother yanked a pair of pants and a shirt out of the closet. "I'll be right out," she told Aaron. "Go out to the car. I'll drive."

He nodded and numbly walked through the dark house to the garage, where he got in the car to wait. After what seemed like an eternity, his mom hurried out with her purse and a tote bag, started the car, and silently drove to Faith's house. When they pulled into the driveway, Amy reached to unbuckle her seatbelt, but Aaron stopped her. "Hang on," he urged his mother. "Let me go in alone. I'll come get you if she needs you, okay?"

Amy hesitated briefly, then nodded her assent as Aaron hopped out of the car and ran to the door. He knocked lightly, but there was no answer from inside. The house was completely dark. He knocked harder. Still no answer. He had the horrible thought that maybe she was playing a prank to get even with him. But he'd heard the panic in her voice. This was for real. He tried the doorknob and was surprised to find it unlocked.

Aaron stepped into the dark house and called, "Faith?"

She didn't answer, but he could hear her crying, so he switched on the hall light and followed the sounds to the living room. There he found her curled up in fetal position on the couch, looking very small and pitiful indeed.

"Faith," he breathed, rushing over to her. He pulled her into a hug and let her cry. "Shhh, shhh. There, there now. My mom is out in the car. She'll know what to do. We'll get you to the hospital and everything will work out. It's okay. I'm here."

She clung to his shirt, her face pressed against his chest. "This is all my fault!" she wailed. "Back when I first found out I was pregnant, I didn't want to face that. I actually prayed to have a miscarriage so no one would have to know and I wouldn't have to make a decision about abortion. I didn't want the baby. But now, after hearing his heartbeat and feeling him move and get the hiccups inside me, I *do* want this baby! He's part of me now, and I don't want to lose him! If something happens to him, it'll be all my fault. It would be God's way of punishing me."

"God doesn't work that way, Faith," Aaron reminded her gently. "You know that. God isn't punishing you. Things just... happen sometimes. It's part of life in this sinful world."

She merely shook her head, but he knew they didn't have time to waste on a discussion at this exact moment. Carefully pulling her up, he said, "Come on. We need to get you to the hospital."

"Aaron, wait," she pleaded, grabbing his hand. "I... I want you to know... Look, I know we didn't part on the best terms last time. You really hurt my feelings, accusing me of using you. I needed your friendship, and I felt like you abandoned me. I was crushed and really, really mad at you.

"Faith—"

"No, wait! Let me finish. But part of the reason I was so mad is that you were kind of right about me." She drew a shuddering breath and looked him in the eye. "It's true. If I hadn't gotten pregnant, I probably never would have gotten to know you, at least not outside of church. I wouldn't have gone to the dance with you. And maybe in a way, I was hanging out with you because I knew you wouldn't turn on me the way a lot of my other 'friends' did. So I'm sorry if you felt like I was taking advantage of you. I didn't mean to."

"Faith—"

"I'm not done! Maybe I wouldn't have gone to that dance with you, but I've changed. I've come to realize what really matters in a friend, and you were a friend to me the whole time. Maybe at first, yeah, I was hanging out with you because it was safe. But not anymore. Now I'm hanging out with you because I *want* to. When you confronted me in the car last week, at first I thought you were gonna ask me out again. And if you had, I would have said yes."

The statement hung between them and took Aaron's breath away, and he fought the urge to kiss her right then and there. He knew it was neither the time nor the place for that, but he was sorely tempted nonetheless. As he looked into her face still stained with tears, her rumpled hair, and her sweatpants and baggy shirt, he knew she'd be appalled to be seen like this by anyone else. But her vulnerability and raw honesty made her all the more beautiful to him.

Eventually he let out his breath to respond. "I... I hardly know what to say. I'm sorry. That was stupid and mean of me. I've been regretting it ever since it happened. Thanks for being honest with me now. It means a lot to me."

"So, friends?" she asked hopefully.

"Friends."

"Good. Then let's get out to the car. We need to get to the hospital."

Aaron took Faith by the hand and led her out of the house and into the car. He climbed into the backseat with her and put his arm around her protectively.

"Do you have your ID and insurance card, honey?" Amy asked before they backed out.

"Mm-hmm. Mom made me put the card in my wallet in case I ever needed it."

"Good. Are you already pre-registered?"

"Yes, ma'am. Mom made sure we both did that right away. I teased her about it, because she did it back in March, but now I'm glad she did."

Amy nodded and backed out of the driveway.

"They have a good neonatal unit at the hospital, according

to my doctor," Faith continued. "It looks like I'll need it too," she said, her voice breaking.

Amy glanced in the rearview mirror in concern. "Are you having contractions?"

"No, not yet. I don't know if that's a good thing or a bad thing."

"It's perfectly fine. Probably better that way. Are you bleeding?"

"Mom!" protested Aaron. "You don't need to ask such personal questions! I'm back here too, you know."

"I'm just concerned, sweetie, that's all. I do have some experience in childbirth."

Aaron rolled his eyes, but Faith answered. "It's okay. I don't mind. No, other than my water breaking, everything is fine."

"Is the baby still moving?"

"I felt him just before we left the house."

"Good." Amy breathed a sigh of relief. "Aaron, open my tote bag back there, will you? I brought some granola bars and peanut butter crackers. Let Faith pick something to eat."

"Mother, good grief! It's four in the morning. No one is hungry!"

"Maybe not now, but who knows what the next number of hours will bring?"

"Mom, she's about to have a baby!"

"Exactly. And that can take hours, especially for the first one. Believe me, son, I was in labor with you for twenty-one hours. By the time I finally pushed you out, I was famished."

Faith looked deflated at that information, and Aaron put his head in his hand in embarrassment.

Amy continued, oblivious to their discomfort. "Faith needs her energy. She probably hasn't eaten since dinner, which was hours ago. Give her a snack. I have some water bottles in there too."

With a weary sigh, Aaron pulled out the granola bars and water, and Faith opened one and nibbled on it.

"Did you call your mother, sweetie?" Amy asked.

"Yeah. I called her first. She was the one who told me to call Dr. Langston."

"And does she know that we're taking you to the hospital?"

"Mm-hmm."

"Good. That will set her mind at ease a bit. I'm sure she's anxious to get back."

"I'm kind of anxious for her to get back too," confessed Faith, her voice cracking.

Aaron gave her shoulder a sympathetic squeeze, and they settled into silence as they continued toward the hospital. The movement of the car seemed to lull Faith into a trance, and presently she leaned her head against his shoulder and fell asleep.

Ten minutes later, Aaron shook her gently to wake her up. "We're here," he informed her. "Come on, we have to go in through emergency." Faith looked disoriented and somewhat chagrined to have been caught sleeping on his shoulder, but Aaron certainly didn't mind. He helped her out of the car and held her hand as they went in the emergency entrance. Amy and Faith went to the registration desk and got everything settled before a nurse came to lead Faith down the hallway.

"Wait!" pleaded Faith, looking scared. "Can someone come with me? Please? I don't want to go alone."

"It's up to you, hon," the nurse said. "If you want your mom to come back, that's fine."

"She's not my mom, but I do want her to come back with me. My mom is on Mackinac Island. I don't know if she'll get back in time." The nurse's eyes widened at this, and she motioned toward Amy to come along.

Before they walked away, Aaron gave Faith a quick hug and whispered, "I'll be praying for you. You can do this." Her eyes held a look of sheer terror, and he wished there was something more he could do. Instead, he squeezed her hand encouragingly before the nurse offered Faith a wheelchair to push her down the hallway. Aaron sank down on a hard plastic couch and put his head in his hands, oblivious to the other few people who were in the waiting room with him. He was worried sick about Faith, and figured the best thing he could do was to pray. Actually, it was the *only* thing he could do.

CHAPTER

40

Grace was beside herself with worry, to the point that David thought she might hyperventilate.

"This is all my fault!" she moaned. "I was the one who pushed for this trip. I wanted one last weekend alone with you before the chaos of three babies in the house, but I knew I was playing with fire. Dr. Langston strongly cautioned me against the trip, but I was so confident about it—*Oh, nothing will happen. I'll be just fine.* Sure. *Now* look what I get!"

David wrapped his arms around his wife. "Sweetheart, neither one of us ever would have dreamed that Faith would be the one to go into labor. I mean, what are the chances? She was staying with your parents until yesterday afternoon. We planned to be back tomorrow. What are the odds that her water would break this early on the one day no one is around? It's just bad timing, that's all. No one could have foreseen it."

"I know, but David, we are *stuck* here on this island while our daughter is in labor! She must be terrified right now! She's only seventeen, and I should be there with her! Instead, Amy Sullivan is the one stepping in for me. What kind of a mother am I?"

"You're a wonderful mother, Grace. This is completely unexpected. Rather than beat ourselves up over it, let's figure out what to do now. I checked the schedule. The earliest ferry leaves at seven thirty from Mackinaw City, but it has to get here and unload passengers. It won't leave until eight from the island."

"That's still four hours away! And then it's another four-hour drive to Forest Springs! We don't have time to wait!"

"We may not have a choice."

"We have to at least try! There's got to be another way off this island. Other boats? I saw a marina. Someone could give us a ride?" She looked hopeful.

"Why don't we go ask the desk clerk?" he suggested. "At the very least, he might know someone who could help."

They quickly changed out of their pajamas, then walked hand in hand down to the opulent front desk of Mackinac Island's magnificent Grand Hotel. The normally-bustling lobby was eerily silent and deserted at this hour of the morning.

Grace turned to David in dismay. "There's no one here!" she pointed out needlessly. He could already see that. The front desk was unmanned.

"Then let's call the operator," he said as he gestured toward the phone sitting on the end of the white marble counter. Near it was a sign that read "Dial 0 for assistance."

He started toward the phone, but the sound of approaching footsteps stopped him. He and Grace whirled around in unison.

"Oh! I thought I heard voices down here. Can I help you?" the stranger asked.

"Yes, you can, Trent," replied David, reading his name tag. "Are you the manager?"

"No, I'm with security," Trent answered. "I can call the night manager if you need me to, but is there anything I can do for you?"

"Possibly," David said. "I know this sounds strange, but is there any way we could get a ride off the island? I mean right now? We have a medical emergency."

"There is a medical center on the island, sir. It's fully equipped to handle any traumas or situations that arise. I can even call an ambulance if you need one. The only motorized vehicles allowed on the island are emergency vehicles. Shall I call? I'm assuming your wife is in labor?" He eyed Grace's considerable belly warily, as if afraid she would have a baby right there in the lobby.

"No, you don't understand. It's not my wife who's in labor. It's our daughter."

Trent's eyes widened with this juicy tidbit, and Grace cut in. "Please, sir, we need to get home to her. I'm perfectly fine. I'm humongous because I'm pregnant with twins, but our daughter back home just called to tell us her water broke early. She's not due for six more weeks, and she's only seventeen! We need to get off this island *now* so we can get back to her!" Grace's voice was a near shout by now, and she jabbed her finger in the air to punctuate her words. Trent's eyes had gotten wider and wider as the strange story unfolded.

"Okay, I tell you what. Let me call the medical center. I know at least one of the doctors is an island resident and owns his own boat. I'll call to see if he's working now, and if not, maybe they can get in touch with him. Or maybe someone else there owns a boat. Excuse me for a moment, please."

Trent pulled his phone out of his pocket as he walked toward the front doors. He was already dialing when he stepped outside. David and Grace paced back and forth in the lobby, trying to catch snatches of his conversation through the doors. After a fairly short amount of time, Trent stepped back in. The Neunabers both pounced toward him, causing Trent to jump back subconsciously as they demanded in unison, "Well?"

"How about a helicopter?" he asked. "The medical center can arrange one to fly you over to the mainland."

David felt a surge of adrenaline. "A helicopter would be great! I've always wanted—"

"No. Way," Grace cut in. "David! Are you serious? Dr. Langston would have a cow if I took a helicopter ride *in the dark* while I'm in my third trimester!"

"It's very safe," Trent assured. "The—"

"No." Grace's tone left no room for further discussion.

The men exchanged glances, and David shrugged. "I guess we'd better stick with a boat."

Trent nodded and put his phone back to his ear. Apparently whoever was on the other end had just overheard the entire exchange. "The couple wishes to decline the offer of a helicopter…" His voice faded away as he walked back outside to continue his conversation.

Grace gave David a dark stare and muttered, "A *helicopter*. Seriously!" She turned her back on him and stalked away, resuming her pacing. After five minutes that seemed like five hours, Trent stepped back in, his face wreathed in smiles.

"We found someone!" he announced grandly. "One of the docs on staff has a boat. He's going down to the marina to get it ready, and they offered to bring the ambulance over here to take you down there with your luggage. I told them you were pregnant with twins, and they insisted on the ambulance. It's pretty slow this time of morning anyhow." Trent looked downright excited at this turn of events, and David was sure the whole thing would be all over social media within the hour.

Grace grabbed Trent's hands and squeezed them. "Thank you, thank you. Oh, thank you! You don't know how much this means to me. Thank you so much!" She had tears of relief running down her face, and she was bouncing up and down as she pumped his hands.

Poor Trent had a deer-in-the-headlights look, and probably thought Grace was crazy. Goodness, he probably thought their entire family was batty—part of a bizarre cult living together in some commune somewhere, popping out as many babies as they possibly could.

David firmly grabbed Grace's shoulders and turned her toward their room. "Come on, honey," he insisted. "We need to pack up our stuff before the ambulance gets here." He was well aware of how ludicrous his words sounded as he called over his shoulder to Trent, "Maybe you could tell the manager to cancel our reservation for tonight. We won't be needing the room after all."

Fifteen minutes later, they were on their way with ebullient well-wishes from Trent, who clearly felt he had played an important part in this drama. "Hey, you two take care, huh? What a story you'll have to tell! You're one of the few tourists to get to ride in a motorized vehicle on the island. Best of luck to you. I hope you make it in time. Call back to let me know what happens if you think of it. And wish your daughter the best for me!"

As they drove away into the inky darkness, David's thoughts turned from the chaos of the last half hour to what still lay ahead. He didn't know how long it would take to cross over to the mainland, and once they did, even exceeding the speed limit the whole way wouldn't get them there quickly. He wondered how poor Faith was feeling. Was she scared? Mad at them for not being there? Would she really have to give birth without her own mother there to help? David shut his eyes, praying that they wouldn't be too late.

CHAPTER

41

The next couple hours passed tediously in the hospital, Aaron on pins and needles awaiting word. He alternately paced, sat down, checked his phone, prayed, and started the whole routine over again. When the sun started peeking over the horizon, he wondered when the cafeteria opened. He wasn't hungry, by any means, but he needed a change.

He had no idea what was going on with Faith. What would they have to do to deliver the baby? A C-section? He hadn't the faintest idea how labor and delivery worked, but he guessed if they were going to do a C-section, that would probably take less time than a long labor like his mom mentioned. Should he chance going to the cafeteria, or would he miss someone coming to give him news? He sighed and plopped down again.

"First one?" an older lady asked from a few chairs away. She was dressed shabbily and had one missing tooth. She'd been in the waiting room when they'd gotten there, although Aaron hadn't paid much attention to her.

"Huh?" he replied stupidly, trying to process the question.

"Is this your first baby?" she repeated patiently.

Aaron blushed deep red. "It's not even my baby," he answered, wondering at the question. He and Faith were both clearly teenagers. If this lady had seen Faith when she'd arrived it should be pretty obvious that it was Faith's first child. "She's a really good friend, that's all. And she's not due for six more weeks. Her water broke early. I'm really worried about her."

"Ah." The lady heaved her heavy frame out of the chair and came over to sit across from him so they didn't have to speak as loudly. "I've had four kiddos myself, and each one has a different labor and delivery story. My water broke three weeks early for my second baby, and they had to induce me. Unless the baby is in distress, they'll probably give your friend pitocin to start contractions. Inducing usually takes longer than going into labor naturally, because your body isn't ready. And if this is her first baby, that usually makes it go longer too. You'll be here awhile."

Aaron was both encouraged and dismayed by her statement. On the one hand, maybe Faith's mom and stepdad would make it in time after all. But on the other hand, he just wanted it to be over for Faith's sake. And his own.

"But the baby will most likely be okay," the stranger continued. "It's amazing what they can do for preemies these days." Aaron nodded mutely, relieved at this fact.

The two sat in silence a few moments before the lady spoke again. "I'm waiting on my husband," she offered. "He got out of bed to use the bathroom in the middle of the night and collapsed on the floor. I think he had a heart attack." She said this calmly, as if stating the date.

Looking at her incredulously, Aaron asked, "Aren't you worried about him?"

"Yes and no, dearie. I hope he'll be alright, certainly, but I know the good Lord has His eye on my Larry. He's got everything under control. And if it's his time to go, well, he'll be in a better place." Her calm assurance bolstered Aaron even as he realized with shame that he should have that same confidence. God wasn't going to abandon Faith now.

"Thank you for the reminder," he said. "You're right."

She smiled at him and said, "In case you're wondering, the cafeteria opens at seven. I've already checked. You can go get some coffee if you want. It's two minutes after." She smiled conspiratorially at him, and he returned her smile.

"I'm more of a Diet Coke kind of guy," he joked.

"Just make sure it's not the caffeine-free kind," she advised, wrinkling her nose. "You'll need something to keep you awake."

Aaron chuckled. He was certain he didn't need caffeine to keep him awake. His nerves would never let him relax until he was sure Faith and her baby were safe. Standing, he asked, "Would you like to come with me?" Even as he spoke, he wondered why he was making the offer.

"Oh, no, dearie. I have a feeling they're about done with Larry. I'll stay, but thanks."

"Want me to bring something back for you just in case?" he pressed.

"Your momma sure brought you up right, young man," she smiled. "That's okay. You go on down there and have yourself a nice breakfast to get your mind off things."

"I'll do that," he promised, glad his wallet had been in his jeans pocket so he could indeed buy something at the cafeteria. "And I'm Aaron, by the way." He held out his hand, and she shook it.

"Donna," the woman informed him. "Pleased to meet you."

"You too," Aaron said. "Thanks again for the encouragement. I hope and pray your husband is okay."

Donna smiled. "Thank you. And I hope your friend and her baby get through this in good time. God bless you, young man."

"God bless you too," he replied, then followed the signs for the cafeteria. He got a Diet Coke and an omelet, which was a strange combination to be sure, but he barely tasted any of it.

When he returned to the waiting room twenty minutes later, there was no sign of Donna, but his dad had arrived, and had fortunately thought to bring his contacts for him. He knew how much Aaron hated his thick glasses. Aaron excused himself to put his contacts in, grateful for something else to do. He took much longer than usual, trying to keep himself occupied, but when he came back to the waiting room, there was nothing more to do but wait. Aaron welcomed the company of his dad next to him, even if neither of them had spoken much since his arrival.

They both jumped when their phones chimed simultaneously. Amy had texted them together. *Faith is doing fine. They have her on IVs and are monitoring her and the baby. The doc is giving her an antibiotic through the IV before they start pitocin. She's sleeping now. She'll need her rest before labor starts. Her parents should be here between 9:30 and 10:00. Looks like they'll make it.*

Mark and Aaron looked at one another as they finished reading the update. Aaron was glad Faith was able to rest, and it was good that the Neunabers would make it. But now what? He felt utterly useless sitting here, and he was sure his dad felt even more so. They had no reason whatsoever to be there, especially if they couldn't offer moral support. But neither did he want to leave without some closure. He at least wanted to stay until the Neunabers arrived, and maybe even until the baby was born. And he really wanted to see Faith afterward to make sure she was okay, but he didn't know if they'd allow him to or not.

Sighing deeply, he sank back in his chair, and his dad placed a hand on his shoulder. "You're a good friend to her," he told him. "I'm proud of you."

"Thanks, Dad. I really like her." He felt heat rise to his cheeks at the admission, but his dad took the comment in stride.

"I know," he said simply. "I've known for quite a while." After a few moments he asked, "Do you think she likes you?"

"Actually, yeah. I'm pretty sure she does." A warm feeling spread over Aaron as he recalled Faith's words to him a few hours ago. *I thought you were going to ask me out again. And if you had, I would have said yes.*

"Well, good," his father replied, a smile twitching at his lips. A few moments later, he asked cautiously, "Would you be okay with dating someone who has a baby? Knowing she's already been with someone else?"

Aaron colored at his father's directness. "Yeah, that is kinda weird. And at first I was really upset about it. But she's not like that overall. I mean, you know… like… easy or whatever. It was more or less a one-time deal." His face was burning at this point. It was incredibly embarrassing to be having this discussion with his father.

"But I've gotten used to the situation by now," he continued. "And it's not like she's trying to hide it from anyone. She's been upfront all along. She even told the Youth Group about it before everyone else started finding out. Faith is still a pretty new Christian, and she's growing a lot through all of this. She's actually much more mature than most of the girls our age. She accepts responsibility and knows what she did was wrong, but she also knows she's forgiven. And if God can forgive her, I can too. So to answer your question, yeah, I'm okay with it."

Mark nodded and stroked his beard thoughtfully, falling into silence. Aaron wondered what his dad was thinking. Did he approve of Faith or not? Would he be supportive if Aaron pursued a relationship with her? Aaron found it hard to believe he could even consider it possible that he might date Faith. Although he'd had a crush on her since the previous year, he'd never dreamed she could feel the same way about him. Yet things had changed drastically in the past few months, and he couldn't deny it was because of her pregnancy. Who ever would have thought an unplanned teen pregnancy would be the thing to bring them together?

By the time David and Grace arrived at the hospital at nine forty-three, David could tell his wife was desperate to get to Faith. Amy Sullivan had been texting them updates, and they knew Faith had started pitocin around eight thirty to induce labor. Her contractions were starting to kick in, but she wasn't about to give birth any time soon. They'd made it in plenty of time. *Thank You, Lord,* David prayed as he accompanied Grace into the hospital and down to the maternity ward as Amy had instructed.

"Are you pre-registered?" asked the attendant behind the information desk as they approached.

"No, I'm not the one in labor," Grace insisted. "My daughter is here right now having a baby. I need to get to her." With a tight smile, the attendant called the nurse's station and explained the situation, listened, thanked the nurse, and hung up.

"They're expecting you," she said. "You can go back there and a nurse will meet you in the hallway to take you to your daughter." She instructed Grace how to get there, and Grace ran off as fast as she could, although with her large belly, *waddling* was perhaps a more appropriate term.

David turned toward the waiting room, feeling completely disoriented and uncertain of what to do now. While he'd been driving, he knew his purpose: get to the hospital as quickly as possible. But now what? He was still reeling from a short night's sleep and the adrenaline rush of the last few hours, and he realized that his head was beginning to pound as well.

As he scanned the waiting room, he saw Mark and Aaron Sullivan walking toward him, and David breathed a sigh of relief. At least he wouldn't have to wait alone. Mark met him with a firm handshake and said, "Let's get you some coffee."

Mark led the way to the cafeteria and bought David the largest size available. They sat down at a table in the corner, and David took a long swallow, hoping the caffeine would ease his headache.

"So how in the world did you make it off the island?" Mark asked. "Amy and I figured you'd be pushing it to make it here by one."

With a short chuckle, David related the bizarre story as Mark and Aaron listened in amazement. Presently, Mark's phone rang, and all three of them jumped, on edge. Quickly, he glanced at the caller ID and answered, "Hi, hon!... We're in the cafeteria... Okay, see you soon." He hung up and excused himself to buy another cup of coffee for his wife.

A few minutes later, Amy entered, looking drawn. She wearily approached their table and accepted a hug from her husband.

"Well?" David and Aaron asked in unison.

She breathed out a laugh. "Not much to report. Faith is doing great in there. But I've never seen a girl so relieved as she was when Grace walked in that door. They both started crying. It was really sweet." Amy took a gulp of coffee and sank down into the plastic cafeteria chair. "Ahh, caffeine," she said. "Thanks, sweetheart." She gave her husband a grateful smile.

"So how far along is she?" inquired David.

"Well, it took awhile for the pitocin to kick in," Amy informed them. "She's having contractions now, but they're still pretty minor. The kind you wake up with in the morning and time them to see if they're the real thing or not. She doesn't want an epidural yet."

David exchanged a glance with Aaron and shrugged. Clearly Aaron didn't have a clue what she was talking about either.

"So what does that mean?" Aaron asked. "If she's at least starting contractions, does that mean the baby will be born soon?"

"Who knows?" replied Amy. "Some women have faster labors than others, but if I had to guess, I'd say Faith still has at least four or five hours to go. Maybe more."

All three men stared at her in disbelief. "That long?" David asked.

"Gracious, yes. A lot has to happen yet before she can start pushing." David wasn't at all sure he wanted to know exactly *what* had to happen first.

There was silence as the adults sipped their coffee until David spoke. "Hey, I owe you guys a huge thank you. I don't know what we would have done if you hadn't been here to help Faith. Grace was about to panic, but knowing you were here to step up set her mind partially at ease. She was still frantic to get here, but she knew Faith was in good hands in the meantime. So thanks for everything. We really appreciate it."

"I'm just glad Aaron's phone was turned on," Amy smiled.

"I always turn my volume off before I go to bed, but I'm glad in this case Aaron doesn't do the same. And you're quite welcome. I'm glad we were able to help. She's a remarkable young lady."

"Yes, she is," David replied, tears springing to his eyes. "I'm really proud of her." He cleared his throat and looked at Aaron with a small smile. "So does this mean you two aren't breaking up after all?"

Aaron's face turned deep red as his parents stared at him, astonished. They hadn't been privy to any of the drama of the previous week. "Oh, man, she told you about that?" he asked in dismay.

"What?" Amy asked incredulously. "I had no idea you were even going out with her in the first place!"

"Um, well… we, uh… Actually, we weren't," he stammered. "It was just a… you know… We had a disagreement about something, and I guess she… I don't know… thought…"

David realized he'd put him in a bad spot and stepped in. "I'm sorry, I shouldn't have said anything. And I know you weren't dating. It was more like a disagreement between friends. But Faith was really upset about it. She actually talked to *me* about it rather than her mother, so that proves how much it affected her. I'm just glad to see you guys worked through it, that's all."

"Me too," said Aaron, avoiding eye contact with anyone.

The chiming of Aaron's phone saved the day, and he quickly picked it up to see what message he'd gotten. A goofy grin spread across his face as he read the text and responded. When he looked up and realized the adults were all watching him, he flushed once again. *Poor kid,* thought David. *This has to be so awkward for him.*

"Faith?" asked Mark.

"Oh, um, yeah. She's doing fine."

Amy arched an eyebrow. She obviously didn't believe he was smiling so broadly for such a mundane message, but she was wise enough not to press the issue. "So, Mark, you took a personal day, huh?" she asked, deflecting the attention away from Aaron.

"Yes, I did. I never use them all anyway. I couldn't get back to sleep after you guys left, and I figured I wouldn't be able to concentrate at all, knowing you guys were here waiting with Faith. I'd be a nervous wreck."

David laughed. "That makes at least two of us. We make a fine club here."

"Indeed!" Amy seconded. "But, David, listen. While we're more than happy to wait here with you, if you want us out of your hair, don't be afraid to say so. We can leave if you prefer." Her husband nodded his agreement.

"I appreciate that," he answered. "But I don't mind the company. I think I'd be worse off alone with nobody to talk to."

"Understandable. Just let us know if you change your mind."

"Will do," he promised.

"So how did you get back so quickly?" she asked. She hadn't been there when he'd explained it to Mark and Aaron. The three men laughed together as David launched into the story again, embellishing the details a bit more this time around. He was starting to enjoy the retelling of the unique experience. If he wasn't careful, before long it would evolve into one of those "uphill both ways in three feet of snow" stories.

Over the course of the next few hours, updates came sporadically from Grace and Faith. At noon Grace texted David, *Contractions getting stronger and closer together. She's waiting on the anesthesiologist for an epidural.*

Half an hour later, David read, *Epidural kicking in. She's much happier now. Almost 7 cm dilated.*

Although he didn't know what the last part meant, Amy assured him Faith was making progress. "The magic number is ten," she informed him. "When she gets to ten centimeters, she can start pushing."

But it was another four hours before Faith reached the magic number. While the epidural took away the pain, it also slowed her contractions and therefore her progress. Finally at four thirty, David received the text they'd all been waiting for.

Here we go! She's ready to start pushing. I won't text or respond to your texts until the baby's born. Don't worry if you don't hear from me. It could take a while.

David felt like a jolt of electricity had just entered his body. This was for real. His pulse raced and he felt a surge of energy unlike anything he'd ever experienced before. Although he'd never been a runner, he felt like he could sprint all the way home, but he knew that was ridiculous. Instead, he had to be content to walk laps around the perimeter of the waiting room. Aaron must have felt the same nervous energy, because he paced up and down the hallway. David could only imagine how ridiculous the two of them looked to observers. Good grief, he'd never realized how hard it was simply to wait.

An hour later, Faith was getting frustrated in the labor and delivery room. It was hard work pushing, and so far she had nothing to show for it. "It's okay, sweetie," Dr. Langston soothed. "You're doing fine. Usually your first baby takes the longest to push out. Your body's never done this before. Don't worry. This is completely normal."

But twenty minutes later, as the baby was finally starting to make his way down the birth canal, a monitor started beeping, causing the medical staff in the room to look up sharply. The baby's heart rate was dropping quickly, which made Faith's own pulse skyrocket. *This is not happening,* she thought. *Please, God, don't let me lose this baby now. I'm so close.*

Dr. Langston went into emergency mode. "Call down to the OR," she barked out. "Have them prep for a C-section. We've gotta get this baby delivered *now*. Put an oxygen mask on Faith too. And give me the vacuum in the meantime."

The nurses hastened to do her bidding as Faith gripped her mother's hand in terror. "What does that mean?" she asked, panicking. "Is the baby okay?" Her voice had risen an octave.

Dr. Langston didn't answer, which did little to assuage her fears. The doctor was focused on the task of readying the vacuum to use, so Faith turned to her mother. "Mom?" Her voice was pleading, and she was fighting back tears. Grace squeezed her hand and shrugged, apparently having no answer. Instead, her mother smoothed Faith's sweaty hair away from her forehead and gave her a kiss on top of the head.

Her nurse, Susie, who had been attending her since her shift started that morning, slid next to her to put the oxygen mask on. "Shh, sweetie. We may have to do a C-section to get the baby's heart rate up. Sometimes the distress of labor is just too much for these little guys. We're doing everything we can. Keep pushing. The vacuum will help pull him out, but you need to push too. If we can get him out now, we can get to him faster, and you won't have to get a C-section."

Faith's eyes were wide with panic, but she nodded and took another deep breath as coached by Susie. When the next big contraction came, Susie commanded, "Now!" Faith pushed as hard as she could, but to no avail. She sank back, defeated, terrified that she was about to lose the baby.

"Don't give up!" Susie said. "Here comes another one! You

can do this. Deep breath… Now, go!" Faith pushed again as Susie counted to five, then paused for a deep breath and tried again. This time she felt something. She looked at Susie in alarm.

"Keep pushing!" Dr. Langston ordered. "You're almost there! Don't stop now! One more push, and he'll be out!"

Shrieking from the exertion of it, Faith pushed once more, and the baby slid out. There was a flurry of commotion as the nurses descended on the child to tend to him. "Is he okay?" she asked. "Will he be alright?"

Susie shushed her and readjusted the oxygen mask as she responded. "You did a great job, sweetie. It was better he was born this way than to have to do a C-section. He was out faster so they can regulate him right away. He's in the warmer now, and they're getting him on oxygen."

The other nurses spoke in hushed tones, and Faith had a sinking feeling it was about the baby. She also noted with alarm that Susie had not, in fact, directly answered her question about his well-being. "What's wrong?" she demanded, her voice surprisingly forceful despite it being muffled from the oxygen mask.

Dr. Langston looked over at the cluster of nurses around the baby with concern in her own eyes, and still no one answered the question. "Is he okay or not?" Faith was on the verge of hysterics.

A weak cry suddenly pierced the terse silence, and the mood of the room shifted drastically. The nurses all breathed a sigh of relief, and the worry lines around Dr. Langston's eyes turned into smile creases. Susie laughed out loud and exclaimed, "Thank heavens!" She turned to Faith, her entire face lit up with a smile. "We were waiting for that cry to make sure he was breathing on his own. He's fine, hon."

Faith started sobbing then, her emotions a jumble from the events of the past number of hours. The fact that the baby—*her* baby—might not have been okay was almost too much to process. She felt a desperate need to hold him, just to make sure he really was okay. "Ca-can I ho-hold him?" she hiccuped.

"In a few minutes, yes," answered one of the nurses by the warmer. "Let's make sure his temperature and heart rate are where they need to be and give him some time on oxygen. But you can hold him for a minute before we take him to the NICU."

Dr. Langston had delivered the placenta and was starting to stitch Faith back up when she chimed in. "Probably about the time I get done here, you'll be able to hold him for a bit," she offered, then fell into silence as she finished working on Faith. The rest of the medical staff buzzed around the room, tending to the baby and pitching in to clean up and help make Faith more comfortable. Susie removed the oxygen mask from Faith as Dr. Langston finished, and another nurse brought over the tiny newborn to hand to Faith.

Fresh tears sprang to her eyes as she accepted her son into her arms. She swallowed over a lump in her throat. "He's perfect," she said in a soft voice, stroking his tiny cheek.

"Isn't he?" Grace agreed, her own voice full of awe.

"I can't believe how tiny he is, though," Faith continued.

"He's actually a pretty good size for a baby six weeks early," Susie said. "He weighed in at four pounds, eight ounces."

"Wow. If that's pretty big for a preemie, I can't even imagine how small some of the other babies are," Faith said, never taking her eyes off her son's tiny facial features.

"Let me get a few pictures of you with the baby before they take him to NICU," Grace said, readying her phone.

Faith complied, smiling at the camera as best she could. She was exhausted and slightly overwhelmed, but her son was going to be okay. She was thankful for that.

A few minutes later, Susie approached and said, "I'm sorry, Momma, but we have to take him down to the NICU now." She carefully took the baby into her own arms and settled him back into the warmer. "I'll get you in a couple hours, and you can hold him down there, okay? The skin-to-skin contact is great for babies. I'll see you soon."

Faith nodded and watched as they wheeled him out of the room and down the hall. Dr. Langston had finished her job in the room and shook Faith's hand, promising to be back later to check on her. The rest of the staff had thinned out considerably by now, and eventually Grace and Faith found themselves alone in the room.

Grace stroked Faith's hair and said, "You did such a good job, Faith. I'm so, so proud of you."

"I know," she replied, her voice cracking. She was relieved the ordeal of childbirth was over, but her heart was breaking at not being able to hold her son anymore. She suddenly felt empty and lonely. He'd been in her womb for seven months, present with her at all times, and now quite suddenly he was gone, and she couldn't even hold him. Tears slid down her cheeks despite her best effort to stop them.

"Here, honey, wanna see the pictures I took?" Grace asked, sensing her daughter's distress. Faith nodded, and Grace pulled up the photos on her phone. She clutched at the phone desperately, as if able to hold the baby vicariously through the pictures.

"Ohh," she sighed. "Can you send those to me so I have them on my phone?" Grace complied with her wishes as Faith went on. "He's awfully wrinkly. Is that normal?"

"Oh, yes," Grace assured. "His skin will smooth out in time

when he starts gaining weight. And look at that dark hair! What a beautiful baby!"

Faith nodded in affirmation. "He sure is." At that, she teared up again and sniffled.

Grace leaned over to pull her daughter into a hug. "Oh, sweetie," she whispered. "I love you so much. And I'm so glad I made it back in time. I was terrified Mrs. Sullivan would have to be the one here to help you deliver."

"Me too," Faith confessed. "It's been kind of a crazy day."

"It has, hasn't it?" agreed Grace. The two chuckled together shakily, and then Grace stood abruptly. "I need to let David know what's going on! He's probably frantic by now."

"Go on out and tell him in person," Faith suggested. "I'm fine by myself. I'll probably fall asleep anyhow."

"Okay, honey. That's a good idea. You rest." She kissed Faith's head once more and headed for the door.

"Mom?" Faith spoke up as her mother reached the door. "If Aaron's still there, can you ask him to stay a little longer? I'm gonna check if he can come see me."

"Of course, sweetheart. I'll ask him," Grace promised.

Faith adjusted her position to get more comfortable. It had been a busy day, and she still had to introduce the baby to David and hopefully Aaron. But first there was something of far more importance to tend to. She desperately needed a nap.

The moment Grace entered the waiting room, David rushed over. "Well?" he demanded. "Is the baby born? Is he okay? How's Faith?"

"Yes, they're both fine. The baby's in the NICU now, and Faith is resting. We can go peek at him through the window in a bit. I'll let Faith rest awhile longer."

The Sullivans cheered as David grinned broadly, clearly

pleased to have a grandson. Aaron, likewise, sported a happy smile, and in their relief, he and David actually hugged each other. Then suddenly both realized this fact and instantly pulled away, embarrassed at their show of emotion. Grace bit her lip to suppress the giggle bubbling in her throat.

Amy had no such inhibitions, and hugged Grace and David both in turn. "Congrats!" she exclaimed. "What's the baby's name?"

"I… I don't even know!" admitted Grace. "I didn't ask, and Faith didn't say anything. I wonder if she's even decided on a name yet. But I do at least have pictures!" She pulled them up on her phone and showed them off as the others crowded around, oohing and aahing.

"He's absolutely beautiful!" Amy exclaimed. "He's in good hands here. And now, we really have overstayed our welcome. Come on, Mark, Aaron. We need to let this family be. Who wants which car?"

"Why don't you guys take one car and I'll take the other?" suggested Aaron.

"That's fine," Amy said. "You can stop by Burger King for us on the way back."

"Ah, well, I… um… I was thinking…"

Grace rescued him. "Faith asked if he could stay a bit. I think she wants to see him before he leaves," she informed them.

"Oh! Well, why didn't you say so?" Amy asked her son, giving him a playful punch on the arm. "That's fine. We'll grab something on our own. You can fend for yourself. Take your time." She and Mark exchanged a secret smile, then said their goodbyes and left. Amy linked arms with her husband as they walked out the door. Grace watched them leave, happy things had worked out exactly the way they had.

CHAPTER

42

"Let's go meet your grandson," Faith urged as Grace and David entered the room an hour later. Susie had already helped her into a wheelchair so she could go to the nursery. David pushed the wheelchair as Grace walked beside them in comfortable silence. They reached the window, and David helped Faith into a standing position. She looked at the sleeping babies and caught sight of the one in the middle. A smile lit up her entire face as she stared at her newborn son.

"There he is!" she pointed out proudly. "That's Griffin."

She noticed the look that passed between her mother and stepfather and knew they were surprised by the name. She was pretty sure neither of them ever would have guessed it.

"It means 'strong in faith,'" she explained, gazing at Griffin's tiny face.

"It's perfect, sweetie," her mother said in a thick voice.

"Isn't it, though?" Faith looked at them to say, "Griffin David, after his grandpa."

David looked profoundly moved by this information and swallowed twice before responding. "I'm honored, Faith. Truly honored." He pulled her into a hug and planted a kiss on the top of her head. "And I'm so proud of you. I hope you know that."

"I do," she said over the lump in her own throat. David wasn't one to show a lot of emotion, at least not to her, so she knew it meant a lot to him.

They stood together a few minutes longer as Grace tried to snap a few more pictures without getting a glare from the window glass. Presently, Faith groaned. "Ugh. I need to sit back down."

David helped her back into the wheelchair and suggested, "Let's go back to the room. Your body needs to rest and recuperate. You've been through a lot today."

When they reached her room again, David helped her into the hospital bed while her mother fluffed the pillows and fussed over her to be sure she was comfortable. Then she busied herself filling the water pitcher, turning down the lights, and shutting the blinds.

Faith lay back against the pillows, and very nearly started to doze. Then suddenly she sat up and asked, "Mom, did you ask if Aaron could stay?"

"Mm-hmm," Grace responded absentmindedly, trying to adjust the blinds for maximum darkness. "He's in the waiting room."

"Can you get him?" Faith prompted. "I want to see him before he goes home."

"We'll both go," David said, apparently perceiving that she'd rather see Aaron without them in the room. "Come on, sweetie," he said to Grace. "We need to get you a bite to eat anyhow. You haven't eaten lately, and those babies need some nourishment. And hey, maybe we can even call Trent to give him the good news." He seemed oddly excited by the idea.

They laughed together as Grace kissed Faith's forehead, leaving her wondering who in the world Trent was. David took his wife's hand and led her out of the room, joking that he would invite Trent to join their cult, but only after he'd been properly initiated by riding in an ambulance on Mackinac Island. Grace laughed her belly laugh, and Faith shook her head. Her parents were so weird.

Aaron knocked softly on the door and peeked in tentatively, feeling rather uncomfortable. "Faith?"

"I'm here. Come on in!"

He felt a mixture of awe and alarm as he walked toward her. He had zero experience with babies and hospitals, and felt completely out of his element. As he reached Faith's bedside, she pulled up the pictures of the baby on her phone. "Griffin David Williams," she informed him. "Griffin means 'strong in faith,' and David is for his grandpa."

"I like it. Wow. He's so… small." Aaron kicked himself for stating the obvious. What a dumb observation.

Faith giggled. "I know! He's, like, four and a half pounds. They said he's actually a good size for thirty-four weeks. He's… He's going to be okay." That choked her up, and she looked at him with tears shining in her eyes.

"Good. I'm so glad, Faith."

She sniffled. "Thanks again for bringing me. And for everything. You were my hero today. Well, and your mom. She was really smart to come along. I appreciate it."

A brisk knock on the door announced the arrival of a nurse just starting the night shift. "Hello, hello!" she said perkily as she breezed in. "My name is Traci, and I'll be taking care of you for the night. I hear you just had a baby. Congrats! Is that a picture of him?" She bustled to the other side of Faith's bed and studied the picture. "Oh, look at him! What a darling! He's beautiful. Just beautiful!" She glanced up at Aaron and said, "You know, I think he has your nose."

Aaron and Faith both blanched at her statement, and Faith quickly jumped in before Aaron had a chance to respond. "He certainly does have his daddy's nose; that's for sure." She shot a look at Aaron and gave an almost imperceptible shake of her head. Did she actually want the nurse to believe he was the father?

The nurse continued in a businesslike tone. "I'll be back in a few minutes to grab your vitals, but how are we doing for pain? Can I grab you an ice pack before I return?"

"That would be great," Faith answered.

"I'll be back shortly," Traci promised. "Congrats again, Mommy and Daddy," she sang as she waltzed out of the room.

"Um... she thinks I'm..." Aaron couldn't even bring himself to say the words out loud. It was too embarrassing that the nurse assumed he had fathered the child. Then again, it was certainly logical. Who else but the father would come to support his girlfriend and meet his baby?

Faith squirmed uncomfortably and fiddled with the arm band she was wearing. "Yeah, well, I... um... I told them you were Griffin's father."

Aaron felt even his ears turn red as he looked at her in dismay. "Faith!"

"I didn't know if they would let you back here otherwise! I didn't want to take the chance," she defended herself. "I rather doubt Spencer will be dropping by for a visit, so I figured you could take his spot."

He was still aghast. "What will they think of me?" he protested.

"Let them think what they want. What do they think of *me*?

I'm sure it's not the first time they've seen teenage parents. They'll think you're a good father who wants to be involved in his baby's life. Besides, I'll only be here a day or two anyhow. They'll never see either of us again after that." She settled back into the hospital bed slowly, wincing a bit.

"Are you okay?" Aaron asked, jumping at the chance to change the subject. "How do you feel?"

"I've been better," she answered with a grimace. "I seriously don't think I could have done that without the epidural. But now that it's wearing off, I realize how sore I really am. Like, all over. Weird places I wouldn't think, like my neck and my legs from the position I had to be in. That was brutal. Giving birth is not for the faint of heart."

"I'll take your word for it."

They laughed together, and she lowered her bed to a more reclined position, a look of exhaustion on her face. "You must be as tired as I am," she told him. "You've been up as long as I have."

"Sure, but you just had a baby. That takes way more energy than pacing around the waiting room. I'll let you get your rest. You deserve it."

Faith smiled wearily. "Thanks, Aaron," she murmured as she closed her eyes.

She was wearing a hospital gown, her usually silky hair was snarled and matted, her face bore the strain of exertion from childbirth, and she had huge bags under her puffy eyes, but at that moment she was even more beautiful to Aaron than she had been at her mom's wedding.

"Sleep well," he whispered. Then he couldn't help himself and bent down to kiss her.

Her eyes flew open as his lips met hers, and he quickly started to retreat. But suddenly her hand was on the back of his neck, pulling him close again. He searched her eyes and found a look he hadn't seen there before. Could it be, dare he hope... desire? His heart racing, he leaned in to kiss her again, and this time she kissed him back.

CHAPTER

43

Faith's phone chimed on the table next to her. She reached across her breakfast tray to grab it and check her new text. *Morning, beautiful*, it read. *How's Mommy and baby?*

Giggling, she texted Aaron back with one hand. *Doing great. You?*

Never better, came the reply. *Can I see you today?*

Her heart skipped a beat as she typed, *Of course. Griffin wants to see his daddy. ;)*

She could almost hear his smile. *Good! Be there early PM. Give those nurses something to talk about. :) TTYL.*

Faith put her phone down and snuggled into the pillows behind her, a huge smile across her face. She would take a shower before he came so she felt halfway human again. She knew she looked terrible, but thankfully Aaron didn't seem to mind. He was so sweet. She didn't deserve him, she knew, although *he* would never agree to that. Relishing the memory of their kiss the evening before, Faith closed her eyes and promptly fell asleep.

Around lunchtime, Grace and David arrived again, bringing

clothes and toiletries for her. She jumped at the chance to do her hair the right way, put on her own clothes, and throw on a hint of makeup. Although she could have stayed an extra day, she knew she'd be more comfortable sleeping in her own bed without nurses coming in to check on her every few hours. Griffin was bottle-fed anyhow, so the NICU nurses could handle his feedings. She had to stay an obligatory twenty-four hours after delivery, which was roughly six o'clock, but after that she was free to go.

When Faith emerged from the bathroom after her shower, her mother smiled. "You certainly look more comfortable," she remarked.

"Yeah, but look at my stomach," she complained as she shuffled over to perch on the bed. "I look like I'm still pregnant!"

"You're supposed to look that way, sweetie. You gave birth just yesterday. It'll take a while for everything to shrink back down to size again. Go easy on yourself. It's completely normal."

"Besides," David added with a devious smile, "I doubt Aaron will even notice."

Faith blushed at this, and Grace hit his arm playfully. "Oh, stop," she admonished. "Faith, this being your first baby, the weight will come off faster than you think. Me, on the other hand, not so much. I feel like a whale with these babies. I've already gained forty pounds, and I still have seven weeks to go."

"And you're as beautiful as ever," her husband pronounced loyally. "Pregnancy looks good on you." Now it was Grace's turn to blush, and David leaned over to kiss her lovingly. Not so long ago, Faith would have gagged at the exchange, but today she found it endearing. She rather hoped someday her own husband would be as sweet to her as David was to Grace.

A light knock on the door announced the arrival of Aaron, who entered with a bouquet of sunflowers. For his part, he was slightly embarrassed to find her parents both there with Faith, and he didn't miss the knowing smile on her mother's face. But the smile Faith gave him made his heart soar. She positively lit up when she saw him.

"Good afternoon, Mr. and Mrs. Neunaber," he said politely. "I hope I'm not interrupting anything."

"Not at all!" David assured him. "We were just about to grab some lunch at the cafeteria before Pastor gets here to baptize Griffin. He should be coming in about an hour. You can look after Faith in our absence."

"Yes, sir, I will," he promised as the two left the room, relieved that he could talk to Faith without adults hovering around.

"You look pretty today," he told Faith. She giggled, and he flushed when he realized her parents were just outside the door. They'd probably heard his comment as well. He crossed to her bedside tentatively, suddenly afraid their kiss the previous evening had been a fluke. Shy and unsure of himself, he fumbled, "I... um... I brought you some flowers." It was an obvious statement, but Faith seemed unfazed.

"I see that! And they're beautiful. I love sunflowers. Thank you!"

He set them clumsily on the rolling bedside table, pushing aside the remains of her lunch tray to make room. Then he turned to walk to the chair, but Faith stopped him by grabbing his hand.

"Thank you," she repeated, tugging on his hand. He realized she wanted him to kiss her again, and he breathed a sigh of relief that she *had* meant that kiss last night. He bent to kiss her gently on the lips, noting how natural it felt to do so.

"Wanna go to the nursery?" she asked when he straightened. "I need to get out of this room and stretch my legs. But you'll have to help me walk. It still feels totally weird, and I'm walking like a grandma now. You'll have to go slow for my sake."

"I'm in no rush," he assured her. "Let's go see Griffin." He supported her as she stood up, grimacing with the effort. Once standing, she held onto his arms for support.

"Hold on a second," she begged. "Let me get my balance." She took a deep breath and nodded. "Okay, I'm ready."

He let her set the pace, which was admittedly much slower than normal. She walked deliberately, taking small steps as she clutched his arm. "I'm sorry," she apologized. "I can't even begin to describe how this feels. It's surreal. At this point it's hard to imagine I'll ever be back to normal. I know someday I'll be able to run and jump again, but right now just walking takes all my effort."

They had made it only as far as the door, and Faith peeked out hesitantly, as if afraid she'd be caught. The nurse's station was across the hall and down a bit, and Faith led the way there slowly. "Is it okay if we go to the nursery?" she asked. "We don't have to go in. We just want to look at Griffin."

"Of course, sweetie. He's your baby. You're free to see him whenever you want."

"I didn't know if I was allowed to leave my room," she confessed bashfully.

"As long as you're feeling up to it, that's perfectly fine. It's good for you to be up and about. You're in good hands, I see." She winked at Aaron, who squirmed slightly, knowing they believed him to be the father.

Faith thanked her, and they walked slowly toward the nursery. Aaron relished the feel of her leaning against him, not minding in the least that they took four times as long as normal to reach their destination.

"Look at him, Aaron," she whispered hoarsely when they finally reached the window and peered in. "Isn't he perfect?"

"He is," Aaron admitted, thinking that any baby who resembled Faith had to be pretty near perfect. "And he actually looks big next to the other babies."

It was true. Griffin was over four pounds, which must have put the other babies closer to three. An extra pound at that size made a huge difference.

"They told me he'll probably stay four or five weeks. His lungs need to get stronger so they can function on their own. But I can come and hold him every day. And they have volunteers who rock preemies every day too, so they get the physical contact they need. He's in good hands."

Aaron squeezed her hand in response, but suddenly she began to sniffle. Not knowing why, he asked, "What is it, Faith?"

"Aaron, I can't do this!" she said miserably. "What do I know about raising a baby? Yes, I helped Mom a lot when Katie was born, changing diapers and feeding her when she was old enough to eat baby food, and I worked at the daycare center over the summer, but this is totally different. He's completely dependent upon me for everything! Everything, Aaron! I have to take care of another human being who can't do anything for himself. I'm not up for that kind of responsibility already! He's so small and fragile I'm afraid I'll break him. This morning they had to show me how to give a baby a bath and how to feed him and even how to pick him up to support his head. I'm completely incompetent. And since Mom will have her hands full with the twins, I'll have to farm him off every day I'm in school. I'm not ready for this at all! He deserves better than me!" She sounded panicked.

"Hey, calm down," he said softly "Take it one day at a time. God gives you strength for each day. Not a huge dose all at once at the beginning, but enough to get you through the day. Remember the Israelites in the wilderness? God only gave them enough manna for one day at a time. They learned to trust that every day He would provide exactly what they needed. He'll do the same for you.

"And you already have an incredible support system. Your mom and stepdad are really supportive and encouraging, and you have your aunt and uncle and grandma and grandpa around... well, most of the time, anyhow." She smiled. "You have Chelsea and her family, Bree, Pastor and Mrs. Lixon, the Youth Group, the members of St. John—most of them—and even Mrs. McDowell on your side, rooting you on."

He paused and looked into her eyes. "And I'm here too. I always have been."

"I know," she said simply, blinking back tears. "Thank you."

She leaned against him, and he put his arm around her. They watched Griffin's chest rise and fall as he slept, and at length Faith spoke again.

"And volleyball is out of the question now, of course," she said dejectedly. "I was really looking forward to this year."

"Yeah, that's disappointing. I'll miss watching you play too. But you had a great year last year. And hey, you could always bring Griffin to some of my Robotics competitions. He'll fit in with the rest of the observers—sound asleep." She rewarded him with a laugh, and he grinned at the sound.

"I guess this is my whole summer too," she murmured, though not bitterly. "I'll have to spend most of it here with him."

"I'll come with you as often as I can," Aaron promised her.

"We can plan visits around my work schedule. I'm only part-time anyhow, so either mornings or afternoons should be free on any given day." She nodded, and he continued. "But we should plan something special to look forward to when he gets out of the hospital. A celebration. Wanna take another shot at singing a duet in church?"

Faith giggled and looked into his face. "I'd love to," she said. "We're way overdue for that. And this time I promise not to drop any bombshells on you."

"I'd appreciate that," he replied. "And since we're making plans for future events…" He paused and tucked a strand of her silky hair behind her ear. "I was wondering if maybe you'd like to go to the Homecoming Dance with me this year."

EPILOGUE

Two Months Later

The chancel area of St. John Lutheran Church was crowded. David and Grace stood side by side with Katie in front of them. She had insisted on coming up to the font so she could see better. Sally and Trevor stood next to her, their two-week-old godchild in Sally's arms. Across from them stood Faith, Olivia, and Andy. Olivia rocked their younger godchild gently back and forth as Andy held little Griffin. Although he was seven weeks older than the twins, he wasn't much bigger due to his preemie birth. But he was here so the congregation could witness the affirmation of his baptism, which had taken place in the hospital when he was a day old.

As Pastor Lixon began the baptismal liturgy, the memory of Faith's own baptism just two years ago came back to her, and she smiled as she realized they had been a crowd then too. Her mother and all four of the Williams siblings had been baptized on the same Sunday. It seemed whenever their family was involved, it was an unusually large crowd at the font.

Forcing herself to concentrate on the service, Faith tuned in as Pastor addressed the sponsors to answer the questions in lieu of the babies who could not yet answer for themselves. The

McNeals and the Barlowes answered together, renouncing the devil and all his works and ways, in addition to affirming their faith in the Triune God. These questions answered, Pastor turned first to Olivia. Faith smiled as her aunt handed her tiny bundle to Pastor Lixon, who accepted the infant reverently in his arms.

"Charlotte Grace Neunaber, I baptize you in the name of the Father and of the Son and of the Holy Spirit," he quoted, pouring water over the baby's head three times as he said the words. Charlotte startled and began to wail, the water waking her from a sound sleep. Olivia shushed her and offered Charlotte a pacifier as she took her back into her arms, and Sally handed the next child to Pastor.

"Evelyn Rose Neunaber, I baptize you in the name of the Father and of the Son and of the Holy Spirit." Little Evelyn grunted indignantly, but otherwise remained quiet.

Pastor now addressed the congregation to announce, "Today we are also here to recognize the baptism of Griffin David Williams." He reported to the congregation the date and place for Griffin's baptism. Faith, Grace, and David, as the three witnesses, affirmed the details.

George McDowell, the elder on duty for the day, handed the sponsors baptismal candles for each of the babies. Pastor reminded them that these lights pointed to Christ, the Light of the World. Next, Pastor led the congregation in prayer, thanking God for His grace in bringing the three newest members of St. John to faith, and requesting that God keep them in their baptismal grace throughout their lives.

Faith teared up at the words, thinking of Gram. Christ had strengthened Edna with His grace to everlasting life. He had atoned for the sins of all His children—young and old alike. The Holy Spirit had worked faith already in the hearts of these three tiny infants, and He had kept His aged child in her faith until her earthly life's end. Incredible.

The baptismal portion of the service done, Faith joined Aaron in the choir loft. It was fitting that their first official duet was today, and she sat with the Sullivans in their pew behind Grace and David for the duration of the service.

The baptismal lunch was nothing extravagant. The entire family, including both Grace's and David's parents, joined the Lixons, the Sullivans, and a few other friends in the fellowship hall for sub sandwiches following the church service. It wasn't gourmet, but it was easy, and that was far more important at this point. People chatted and laughed easily, passing the babies off to others whenever they got fussy.

As people started drifting away after the meal, Olivia shooed Grace and Faith out of the kitchen, insisting that she had enlisted the Sullivans to help her clean up. The new mothers needed their rest. Neither Grace nor Faith objected. Faith went to the restroom to change Griffin's diaper before driving home. The motion of the car usually lulled him to sleep, and she wanted him to have a fresh diaper so she could leave him in the infant carrier once they got home. She had a fighting chance that he'd stay sleeping that way. Faith hoped he would. She was exhausted and could really use a nap herself.

The addition of three infants within the span of two months did not make for restful nights. Nor did Freddie's birthday gift of a new puppy make for peaceful days. Faith wondered at the sanity of her mother and stepfather for granting him such a request, though she guessed her mother was surviving on zombie hormones as was she. Faith had never realized how much work a tiny baby was, and she wondered if she'd ever be able to sleep through the night again.

Emerging from the bathroom, she realized that her parents

and siblings had already left the building. Her aunt and uncle were laughing in the kitchen with the Sullivans as they wiped down counters, swept the floor, and washed out the pitchers and coffee pots they'd dirtied. Inexplicably, Faith suddenly felt very lonely. Her family hadn't even bothered to wait for her, and Aaron was too busy to notice her. Fighting tears, she stuffed Griffin's burp cloth into the diaper bag and bent to put him into his seat. Griffin fussed as she fastened the straps, which only made her feel worse. She felt completely incapable as she struggled to fasten the straps properly. If she couldn't even accomplish a simple task like that, how was she ever going to manage when school started? She'd have to arrange childcare for Griffin, get up early, and figure out how to juggle homework around his schedule. And apparently, all this without the help of her family.

Faith was on the verge of tears and feeling very sorry for herself when at last Griffin was strapped in. She stood, swung the diaper bag onto her shoulder, and reached for the infant carrier, but a hand on her shoulder stopped her. She turned to see David.

"Let me carry him," he insisted, grabbing the handle. "I sent the others ahead in the van. Jackson can help your mom get the girls inside. The three of us will drive home together in my car."

A warm feeling spread through her body. So they hadn't all forgotten about her after all. Somehow David had sensed she would like some company. He cared. He'd chosen to stay and help his stepdaughter rather than go ahead with his biological daughters. Maybe she'd underestimated her family after all.

The three walked outside, calling goodbyes to those still left in the kitchen, and David bent to secure the car seat into its base once they reached the car. "There you go, G. David!" he said, straightening up. He grinned at Faith as he opened the passenger door for her. David had taken to calling his grandson G. David in order to emphasize the middle name. Faith was glad he took it as proof that she had accepted him as part of the family.

And she had. Somehow, over the course of the past year, David had turned out to be much more of a father figure than she'd ever thought he would be. She couldn't imagine her family without him. In just over a year, she'd gained a stepfather, two younger sisters, and a son of her own. She was indeed blessed.

Faith impulsively gave David a hug and got into the car.

It was time to go home.

ACKNOWLEDGMENTS

How can I begin to list all the people who have encouraged me on this journey? This book was a far different experience than my first novel, and I thank all those who patiently helped me along the way.

To my husband Jonathan and children Benjamin, Timothy, Miriam, Sarah, and Samuel, thank you for allowing me the time to work on my writing, and also for providing me with so many wonderful stories to work into a "fictional" setting.

Thank you to my parents, William and Janis Hessler, for providing me a solid Christian upbringing, and to my brothers Marty and Anthony for all your support. Anthony, you are website designer extraordinaire as well as my most valued beta reader. Thanks for the hours of work you've put into my website and for offering feedback on my storylines.

I owe a huge thank you to Jamie, who encouraged me to publish the rest of the Sola Series in the first place. Jamie, your "Busy Mom's Guide" books were instrumental in helping me publish this, and you were so kind as to answer countless questions via email. Thank you, thank you, thank you!

While my name is on the cover, my editor, Abi, deserves much of the credit for polishing this manuscript. Abi, you are an absolute delight to work with, and I've learned so much from you already. You were absolutely the right person to edit this book, and I look forward to working together on the next manuscripts!

Thanks to Suzie at Sunset Rose Books for the amazing cover design and for your guidance along the way as well, which extended far beyond the scope of book covers.

Kellyn, thank you for your expertise in formatting, for teaching me the proper way to use a comma, and for your amazing blog tour hosting skills.

Thank you, Vanessa, for your recommendations and for patiently answering all my questions. God bless your writing.

Tina, thanks for your honesty even when you know I don't want to hear it! Your feedback was instrumental in writing a more plausible story. I treasure our friendship!

To Dr. Juno, for your willingness to read the medical scenes and offer suggestions to lend plausibility, thank you so much.

To all my friends who encouraged me along the way and volunteered to read the manuscript, thank you. Thanks especially to Jenny, Kaethe, Michelle, Anna, Meggins, Kristin, Sandy, Denise, Kristen, Kathleen, Vicki, Emily, Nikki, Faith, Monica, and Tonya.

Dear reader, thank you as well. Thank you for reading my story and for taking my characters into your heart. You are the reason I write.

Above all, I thank my Lord and Savior Jesus for granting me saving faith. I pray that my writing reflects His perfect love.

OTHER BOOKS BY RUTH MEYER

CHILDREN'S BOOK

SOLA SERIES

Read the first chapter of each of the Sola books at:
www.ruthmeyerbooks.com/books

Discussion questions for these books, including *Faith Alone*,
are available as well.

Book 5 of the Sola Series coming soon

CONNECT WITH RUTH

WEBSITES
www.ruthmeyerbooks.com
www.truthnotespress.com

BLOG
www.TruthNotes.net

FACEBOOK
www.facebook.com/TruthNotes

AMAZON AUTHOR PAGE
www.amazon.com/Ruth-Meyer/e/B00E6QC2RI